Beyond the Curve

Beyond the Curve

Kobo Abe

Translated by Juliet Winters Carpenter

KODANSHA INTERNATIONAL
Tokyo • New York • London

Interior art by Shiro Tsujimura

Published courtesy of Shincho-sha Co., Tokyo.

Art courtesy of Seito Isshiki, Yutaka Ito, Makoto Kuze,
and several private collectors.

Distributed in the United States by Kodansha America, Lnc.,
114 Fifth Avenue, New York, New York 10011.
Published by Kodansha International Ltd.,
with offices at 17–14, Otowa 1-chome, Bunkyo-ku, Tokyo 112
and Kodansha America, Inc.

Library of Congress Cataloging-in-Publication Data

Abe, Kobo.
Beyond the curve (and other stories) / by Kobo Abe; translated
from the Japanese by Juliet Winters Carpenter.
p. cm.
1. Abe, Kobo, 1924– —Translations, English. I. Title.
PL845.B4A23 1990 895'.635–dc20   90–49456 CIP
ISBN 4–7700–1465–1

Contents

An Irrelevant Death

*H*e had company. The guest was lying face down with his legs stretched out neatly toward the door. Dead.

Of course, it took awhile for this to sink in. There was the space of a few seconds before he felt any shock. Seconds filled with a quivering silence, like a sheet of blank paper wrapped in electricity.

Then the capillaries around his lips rapidly contracted, his pupils dilated, his vision blurred, and his sense of smell sharpened, detecting a whiff of something like rawhide. As if shaken awake by the odor, A—, the occupant of Apartment 7 in M— Apartments, shivered and realized for the first time the seriousness of the situation. One look at the right arm twisted grotesquely over the man's head was enough to persuade him his guest was dead.

A— peered cautiously out into the hall through the crack in the door, which he had not closed completely. Cords in his neck made noises like snapping matchsticks. The staircase banister gave off a faint white glow, but there was no sign of movement. Relieved, he quickly pushed the door shut, wondering a little at himself as he did so. Had anyone come by, he would of course have sought help. Why not? He certainly had nothing to hide. And yet he felt distinctly relieved that the opportunity had not presented itself. He needed time to think, he told himself, but even so, something about his initial reaction troubled him.

Had he seen what lay behind this seeming anomaly and taken a different course of action, everything might have turned out differently. But once he'd closed the door, the next step was inevitable: he locked it. Introspection necessarily took a back seat. Still, who could blame him for neglecting the warning signal of that brief hesitation? The situation was far too serious, too upsetting.

He turned the lock hurriedly, as if pressed for time. It was the standard brass model, rubber-padded to fasten quietly and snugly. The dead bolt slid home with a satisfying solidness. Whereupon fresh shock swept over him, momentarily taking his breath away. Wait a second . . . Yes, he definitely remembered having turned the key in the lock to open the door. Unless the corpse had locked the door by itself, which appeared hardly likely, this clearly suggested homicide—a thought that had occurred to A— vaguely from the moment he discovered the body, yet one he had tried to shut from his mind. Not only that, it meant someone had broken in to lay the body here.

Then it had all been carefully planned. Not just the murder; A— himself had been counted on from the first as a necessary pawn. The thought of such unwarranted malice gave him goosebumps. Perhaps his failure to fetch help right away had been instinctive, a form of self-defense.

The lock on his door was certainly nothing fancy. It was apparently a simple cylinder lock, but whether it actually worked like one was not clear. Some time ago he had lost his key and was making do now with a spare the building supervisor had happened to have on hand. It was a little trickier to use than the old one but he managed with it well enough. For all he knew, any key of a similar shape would work. In that case, maybe the criminal hadn't chosen this apartment because it belonged to him, but because of, say, its proximity to the stairs. Or maybe his recollection of having unlocked the door was only an illusion, caused by the ordinary resistance of his makeshift key in the lock. Just maybe, the door had been unlocked. Still, that didn't alter the basic ugliness of the situation. It only underscored how many different interpretations there could be.

With growing trepidation, he turned back toward the body. Again there was the sound of snapping matchsticks as cords cracked in his neck. Something about the corpse was vaguely irritating. Although perfectly still, it gave an impression of subtle but incessant movement, rather like the hands of a clock. Probably this was because of the way it was lying. It had an artificially posed look, like snapshots of dancers in midleap. The left arm was tucked under the body from the shoulder down, while the right arm lay twisted out at an impossible angle, as if it had no joints. The entire weight of the neck and head was concentrated in the forehead, which pressed into the floor. Yet the hips and legs lay perfectly straight, as if cast in a mold. This alone spoke unmistakably of outside intervention.

The dead man was dressed in dark blue trousers, wrinkled at the backs of the knees, creases gone. The shoes were light brown and had rubber soles, down at the heel, with large grains of sand embedded in them. There was sand in the trouser cuffs as well. A large, dark stain ran from the seat of the pants to the crotch. Maybe he'd been strangled, thought A——. Didn't hanging victims always wet themselves? The jacket was a bright blue, with a vent cut at the back. The hem was flipped back, exposing the shirt beneath. For some reason there was no belt.

A— glanced hastily around the room. Nothing appeared to be amiss. Entryway with sink, faucet dripping. Six-mat room beyond, tatami flooring covered with a thin woven mat. Plywood ceiling with cruciform beams. Table, chairs, small bookcase. Bay window that took up half the wall, bathed in the warm orange glow of the setting sun. On a shelf above the window, a leafless potted plant and a dirty face towel.

His view of the bed, which was set against the north wall, was blocked by a cheap curtain the color of dried leaves, with a design of fish. He listened intently, but all he could hear was street noises. Never before had he realized how noisy this neighborhood was. The very squeaking of springs on a motor scooter somewhere in the distance sounded so close he felt he could almost reach out and touch it. At least three dogs were howling. Passers-by laughed shrilly. Someone was washing dishes. He could hear a train and even the echo of a ship's whistle.

The curtain swayed. Now that he noticed, it had been swaying all along. But somehow he wasn't alarmed. Perhaps subconsciously he knew that whatever threatened him would not appear from that direction. Averting his eyes from the corpse, he slipped out of his shoes, stepped from the entryway into the room and advanced toward the bed. It was of course empty. The bedding was rumpled, just as he'd left it, looking somehow terribly defenseless. For good measure, he checked under the bed. The white surface of an enameled bedpan glowed dimly.

Somewhat abashed, he drew the curtain and turned around to face the body again. From here he had a clear view of the upper torso and head. Stiff hair, cut short . . . a high, white collar, looking as if it had been yanked up . . . a wrinkled neck, muddy-colored, in startling contrast to the white of the collar . . .

withered-looking ears, pale and bloodless . . . thin, bluish fingers that looked as if they'd been sprinkled with powder . . . purplish nails . . .

He couldn't see the face clearly, but it was apparently no one he knew. Quickly he checked for wounds, circling the body nervously, one eye on it and the other on the floor beneath. It seemed imperative to find out whether the floor was stained with blood. His sudden curiosity might have been misplaced, but at least it served to bring him out of his stupor. As far as he could tell, there were no bloodstains. He stood still and stared at the man's jaw, where a single unshaven whisker stood straight up.

All at once, like a dam bursting, a flood of thoughts came rushing into his mind. They were not so much clearly formed thoughts as inarticulate impulses, reeling around like a herd of faceless creatures all consumed with a single desire: escape. But their movement was confused, like the aimless milling of cattle whose escape was cut off. Was there no way out, then? Well yes, of course—the door, right behind him. All he had to do was turn around and walk out. But that would take enormous courage. There was in fact nothing he feared more. And yet if he wanted to find words for this dread, this mad swirl of impulses, there was no other choice.

Of course, he had nothing whatsoever to do with this corpse. Of that he was now certain. But no one else would be likely to see it that way. Only those with intimate knowledge of the matter could share this certainty. For his knowledge of his innocence to become certifiable truth, he needed desperately to come up with proof. His position cried out for it. Hard proof would guarantee his safe conduct, enabling him to walk safely out the door when the time came. How difficult it might be to furnish that proof, time would tell. That his innocence was self-evident to *him* guaranteed nothing. The geometric proposition that parallel lines never converge is patently true, yet impossible to prove, while its converse—that any two straight, nonparallel lines will inevitably cross—can easily be demonstrated. In any case, there would have to be a thorough investigation.

Then why not get started now, this minute? There was the door, right in front of him. Why hesitate? At least he might put off worrying about how to buttress his story until he'd heard what the watchman had to say. Besides, it would probably seem most natural just to insist loudly on his innocence. People would overlook his lack of corroborating evidence—perhaps even sympathize enough to help him in the search. Or would they?

Was this sort of thing so commonplace that ordinary rules applied? With no warning, a man finds a total stranger dead in his room. Did this conceivably happen often enough that it would be dealt with mechanically, as a routine nuisance? No, of course not. This incident was so bizarre that no amount of caution on his part could be excessive. How easy or hard it might be to furnish proof of his lack of involvement was beside the point. The very necessity of having to provide it hinted of a dangerous trap.

Out in the corridor he heard a light cough. His face twitched. Holding himself absolutely motionless, he strained his ears to hear better. Shudders coiled upward from his feet in ringlike waves, constricting him and prickling his skin. But not another sound could be heard. It struck him then that the same thing had often happened before. It had something to do with the acoustics of the building: noises originating in some other apartment would often seem to come from right outside his door. Not just any noises, either, but the sound of paper being torn, say, or a long sigh. The sort of noise that normally went unnoticed. That's what this must have been.

Somewhat relieved, he held up his head, opened his mouth and took a deep breath—but then abruptly clamped his lips shut again and turned his face away from the corpse, afraid he might accidentally inhale some toxic substance. Then he was swept away by a new worry: what would he do when the corpse began to smell? So far, no sign of that. But it was only a question of time. He had never smelled decaying flesh, but he had a fair idea of what it must be like. Unbearable, gruesome, no doubt.

He couldn't stay here indefinitely, whatever the danger of passing through that doorway. And what lay beyond the door wouldn't remain as harmless as a disembodied cough forever—nor would the corpse itself just go on quietly lying there till doomsday. A——'s colleagues from work, or someone far more unwelcome, might pay him a surprise visit. In a short while, the corpse would start filling the whole apartment with the stench of death—a form of self-expression that nothing could deter. For A——, getting cold feet now might well mean abandoning all hope of escaping this predicament. Like a man in the grip of a snake with its tail in its mouth, he had fallen into an insoluble quandary. There was nothing to do but strike out at random and chop the snake in two.

But not even that was as simple as it sounded. It might seem that where you struck the snake wouldn't matter much, but that wasn't true. It could matter a great deal. And so despite the staunchness of his resolution, he wasted precious time debating the fine points, while the snake drew its coils ever tighter.

He shivered. The temperature was dropping. In no time, it seemed, the sun which had set the bay window ablaze had vanished without a trace. How long ago was that? Evening came on fast these days. Barely any time might have passed. And yet it felt like an eon. He glanced quickly at his wristwatch. Ten after five. Why the devil hadn't he checked the time right away? Damn. He felt a wave of fierce self-reproach. Evidently his faculties were badly muddled.

Soon it would be pitch black. He'd have to turn on the lights. A vision of the lighted window, seen from outside, came fleetingly into his mind. And then a burning sensation hit him in the region of his neck. Someone might see those lights. Once anyone did, he no longer had an alibi. He'd be guilty of concealment of a body, accessory after the fact, if nothing else.

But he couldn't very well leave the lights off. In the first place, he wouldn't be able to function in the dark. However brilliant a solution he might come up with, he would be unable to carry it out. Besides, he was by no means certain that he was safer with the lights out. In this building the slightest noise, like that cough a moment ago, carried a surprising distance. His footsteps, the sound of his key in the lock, the rattle of the doorknob, the squeak of the hinges—someone might already know, having heard all these, that he had come home. There might even be an eyewitness, for all he knew. Such a person would think it strange if the lights in A—'s apartment remained off—and later, when the business about the corpse came out, let his imagination run riot!

The outlook was grim. The only way to get himself off the hook now was either to make it seem that he'd never come home at all, or else get rid of the body somehow. Barring either of those alternatives, what could he do? Nothing but resign himself to his fate, square his shoulders, and report the discovery to the police.

Out of the question. Exactly what the criminal would want him to do. Who knew what sort of trap he might be walking into? The police officer would respond with a tight-lipped smile: "Oh, really? A complete stranger? You don't say." Of course it didn't matter what the police said, in the absence of incriminating evidence. Yet there was no way for him to prove his innocence, either. Had he known the dead man, the fact would have been simple to establish, but unless they were willing to take him at his word, establishing that this was a total stranger was next to impossible.

Back to the serpent with its tail in its mouth.

Darkness was creeping into the corners of the room. The hue of the corpse's complexion had also darkened considerably. Suddenly it occurred to A— that he still hadn't had a good look at the dead man's face. If he was ever going to get one, now was the time. He was fairly certain he didn't know who this was, but then again a person might look considerably different dead than alive.

He was in no rush to touch the body, but might as well get it over with. He'd grab the hair and lift the head, pulling to the left. First he practiced on himself. So far so good. Better use both hands, and twist. The head would be heavy, so he'd need all his strength. He didn't want to touch it with his bare hands, so he took the face towel from over the window and wrapped it around his right hand. Afterwards he'd throw it away. He positioned himself on one knee next to the body, and got ready. The thing to do was get it over with fast.

The neck was incredibly stiff. He could force it to turn, just barely, but this was going to take some time. At first he miscalculated the distribution of his strength, lost his balance, and ended up falling right on top of the corpse. It was stiff all over. Rigor mortis had set in.

He had to turn the neck slowly to overcome a heavy, creaking resistance. The hair felt cold and clammy. Finally the face turned toward him. The mouth wore a funny expression, as if tasting something sour. The eyes were half open, the pupils just visible beneath the lids. The cheekbones were prominent, the facial structure rather elongated. There was something droll about the nose. Except for the strange hue of the skin, it was on the whole a likable face and expression, rather sheepish, as if the owner was embarrassed at being caught oversleeping.

A— screamed soundlessly, and jumped away. His whole body trembled, and every joint in his limbs felt as though it might start to jerk spasmodically at any moment. Clumsily, he tore the towel off his right hand and hurled it at the corpse's face, covering most of it, if not all.

This sudden fear signified nothing new. Certainly there was nothing in the face that he recognized. He simply hadn't been expecting such individual expression. He was suffering the consequences of his own lack of imagination, as it were. Intermittent groans escaped from his lips, totally independent of his will. He forced himself to walk around the corpse's head, crossed the room, and collapsed at the table. Supporting himself with his elbows, he massaged his temples with his thumbs.

For a long time he did nothing but massage his temples. Then suddenly he sprang up. He knew what he had to do. All that was necessary was to get the body out of here. No one knew it was here but himself and whoever had put it here. If anybody else knew, they would hardly keep it to themselves so long. By now, all hell would have broken loose. If he got rid of the body, the criminal was not of course going to protest, and A— would be in the clear.

So much for the snake—all it needed was a decisive blow. Deciding to move the body not only solved his immediate dilemma, but removed his obsessive fear of the door. What had he been so concerned about? He had thought he'd considered everything, when in fact he'd thought of nothing at all. Things were different now. A combination of logical inferences and realistic decisions had saved the day. Moving the body was no cockeyed idea born of desperation. It had a solid foundation, with any number of excellent justifications.

Looking at it from the other man's perspective had stood him in good stead. In moving the body, it only made sense to put himself in the shoes of whoever had first laid it here. The very simplicity of the problem—an isolated, unidentified corpse in the room—made it hard to get a handle on; but when he thought in terms of whoever had started all this, all sorts of approaches came to mind.

For one thing, the perpetrator very likely lived in this building. That seemed apparent, since the body had been hauled here in broad daylight, sometime during the ten hours or less that A— had been away; whoever was responsible could hardly have carted the body through town in the middle of the day. It made much more sense to assume that the entire operation had taken place within the confines of this building.

Of course, there was still no way of telling whether the villain had chosen this room deliberately or at random. In any case, the information that no one was usually home during the day, and that the lock on the door was all but useless, was probably known to a large number of people. But those conditions weren't unique to this apartment, by any means. Of the fifteen other apartments on the first and second floors, several others met the same prerequisites. This apartment's position at the top of the stairs made it the natural choice of someone heading up from below. The explanation probably lay somewhere along those lines.

One thing he felt sure of was that like this corpse, the killer could have no possible connection to him. In theory, it was conceivable that someone had dumped the body here just to harass him, but reviewing his entire circle of acquaintances he couldn't think of anyone who might be capable of such an outrageous act. Nor could he recollect having done anything to earn such enmity. Probably the murderer was looking for a deliberate stranger.

Someone totally uninvolved. There wasn't a reason in the world why it had to be him in particular.

He could think of no reason not to move the body. Unless the murderer had maneuvered somehow to implicate him, that is. That was always possible. If I were him, A— thought, I would certainly go to work on that angle early on. There could be any number of ways. Convince the supervisor that I had smuggled in an overnight guest last night. Or call the building and ask for me. Then when the supervisor reported that I was out, the killer could snarl that he knew I was home and that I must be holed up in my room, that he'd been double-crossed. Make himself disagreeable, like some sort of gangster. The supervisor would naturally assume that he was some crony of mine. Yes, that's what I'd do, all right. Make a strong impression, while keeping a distance.

But such tactics could work against him only if there was in fact a body in the room. If he could prevent that, he'd be in the clear, whatever traps the murderer might have laid. If there was a door-to-door search in the building, no tenant could escape suspicion; whoever was saddled with the body would be the loser. However loudly that person shouted his innocence, the hard fact would remain that the body had turned up in his (or her) room. He or she would be obliged to convince skeptical police that the body was indeed that of a total stranger. And provide an alibi. What a sure and simple way to get rid of the body! Far better than just digging a hole and burying it.

Getting down to practical matters, though, which apartment should he choose? A— stood with his back to the window, staring across the body at the door, as if he could see through it into every corner of the building. There was a surprising amount of noise, he thought. Five fifty-five p.m. Most residents were single, or working couples, so there was little daytime coming and going, but now was a busy time of day. Of course, noise and confusion could always serve as a cover. All he had to do was put that natural rhythm to good use. Things might actually proceed more smoothly because of it. At the very least he wouldn't have to worry too much about opening and closing the door.

He had a plan ready for transporting the body. A trick he'd seen and admired once in a movie. You pretended to be supporting a drunk. A— wasn't much for going arm in arm even with the living, so shouldering a corpse was the last thing he wanted to do, but this was no time to be squeamish. Besides, trying to conceal the body in a quilt would only attract more attention. He'd have to make good use of the conventional wisdom that dead bodies were something to hide. That was probably what lay behind the murderer's decision to dump the body here in the room of a perfect stranger. Whatever was hidden would eventually be found. All you could do was try to control the circumstances of the discovery to your advantage. At this hour, taking the body downstairs might be a little too risky. However successfully he might camouflage the operation, it would be best to avoid being seen. Anyway, better not reverse the direction, but keep the body moving deeper into the building, away from the entrance. He had to make it seem that he had only just returned. Anything that suggested otherwise could raise questions in people's minds. Practical considerations therefore dictated that he target one of the apartments on the second floor.

The best choice would be one of the three that lay beyond his, away from the stairs. Fortunately, all three were usually empty during the day. Whether they were so now, of course, he had no idea. He hadn't heard any footsteps, so perhaps no one was back yet. The place next door was inhabited by a big, bearded fellow, single, with a round face and a habit of clicking his tongue loud enough to hear through the wall. He was a sales-man for a company that made welding equipment, and when he came home drunk at night, the drunker he was, the more he clicked his tongue. Apart from a couple of times they'd run into each other in the public bath, A— and he had never exchanged words.

Across the hall was a stoop-shouldered fellow with long side-burns. What he did for a living wasn't clear, but whenever A— passed in front of his door, he was humming some old ballad or other. His comings and goings were completely irregular; at times he'd rush in and out in a dither, and at other times there'd be no sign of him for days on end. Sometimes he'd make an enormous racket, turning his radio on full blast as if he'd sud-denly flipped out, but when someone went to his door to com-plain, there'd be nobody home.

The third door, at the end of the corridor, belonged to a mar-ried couple. Unfortunately, A— knew next to nothing about them. Not that he really needed to know much in order to carry out his plan. As long as they were strangers, he'd be okay. In fact, the less he knew about them, the better. . . .

But when he thought about the couple's probable consterna-tion upon finding the body in their home, he couldn't help feel-ing a little sorry for them. As husband and wife, each bore some responsibility for the anxieties of the other, so their pain and con-fusion would be doubled. Unable to sit back and think calmly about the stern police interrogation awaiting them, they might rush right out the door and incriminate themselves. But that wouldn't be my fault, A— thought. I was in the same boat and I've thought of a way out. Everybody has to work out their own solution. There are lots of other doors of other strangers. Come to think of it, whoever had dumped the body here in his room might've had the same thing done to him by someone else!

Maybe the body was being passed from apartment to apartment, in a macabre sort of round robin. A teeth-clenching sense of the absurdity of it all rose in him. Nothing to get worked up about, he reassured himself. You're only doing the very same thing that everybody else is. This realization dissolved his twinges of guilt.

He worked out his plan, step by step. First, of course, he'd have to make sure the target apartment was empty and then unlock the door. From his experiences with his own lock, he was confident he'd be able to manage that one way or another. At least one of the three doors should open. He'd try them all in turn. Might as well let that determine which apartment to use. Then he'd return to his room and check outside the window. How long could he allow himself? From the time someone entered his field of vision, how long would it take that person to enter the building and reach the bottom of the stairs? Tracing the path with his eyes, a little quickly, he timed it at thirty-five seconds. In other words, if no one was in sight when he started, he had at least thirty-five seconds to do the job. He'd shoulder the corpse and step immediately out into the corridor, leaving his door open. That would not only save a few seconds, but also provide a screen. Another advantage of choosing one of the apartments at the end of the hall. Thinking of the various steps involved—throwing the corpse into the target area, relocking the door, and retracing his footsteps—he acted them out there in his room and timed himself at exactly twenty-four seconds. More than ten seconds to spare. In case the dead man's shoe fell off, or some such thing, he'd have ample time to take care of it.

The revulsion he had felt was wearing off. But the corpse was still far from pleasant company. Really, of all the disgusting, stupid boors. The guy was a damned nuisance, causing trouble for people he didn't even know, being passed around from place to place. But now all A— needed was a little more patience. Already, he thought, the corpse was beginning to look like a weightless blue shadow.

He took his room key out of his pocket. Over and over, he threw it in the air, caught it, and rubbed it between his hands. Ten more minutes, he thought. By then it would be too dark to make out newsprint. Then, no matter how lazy you were, you'd have to get up and turn on the lights. So if no light appeared in the crack over the doorsill, he could be sure there was no one home, and set to work.

He put a cigarette in his mouth and hunted for a match.

Really, when you thought about it, it was funny. Just throwing the corpse out wasn't going to change his relationship to it—or lack of any, rather. But then, what the law would reproach him for was not any connection as such, but his own clumsiness in allowing himself to be put in a position where he had to prove that there was, in fact, no connection. Call it stubborn go-by-the-book formalism, or gentlemanly restraint: either way, as long as he didn't screw up, a man was always free.

Of course, a man was always in danger of screwing up unwittingly. But that wasn't necessarily cause for complaint. This moving operation, for example, could very well turn into a farce, should the one he chose to foist the corpse on be the very one who had brought it here to begin with. That was the impartiality of the law for you. Unfortunately, somehow this thought failed to cheer him. What was the matter? Why this peculiar heaviness in his chest?

His hands groped over the tabletop, searching through the stack of old magazines and under the anodized aluminum tray loaded with dirty dishes, but no matches. Damn. He was positive he'd left them here. Or had the corpse gone and filched them, and stuck them in its pocket?

Suddenly it clicked. The ludicrous notion of the corpse pocketing his matches, combined with the realization that the corpse might end up going around in circles, set off an insistent, terrifying alarm. That's right, there was always the possibility of material evidence surfacing. Why hadn't a simple trick like that occurred to him sooner? All it would take to keep the corpse from going around in endless circles was a little ingenuity. Like taking a book of matches off the table and sticking it in the dead man's pocket. That particular matchbook was from the Three Cats, he remembered, a favorite coffee shop of his. The design was rather striking as well: three black-and-green striped cats against a gold background, skewered like sardines. There might even have been some sort of memo on the back, scribbled in his own hand. Even if not, there would be no denying his connection with those matches. How stupidly careless he'd been. The difficulty of proving his innocence was not just theoretical, after all. And matches were only one possibility. It might be a business card or a photograph or a hair of his wrapped around the dead man's finger. Almost anything in the room would do the job.

The cigarette fell from his lips. He let it fall. Never before had he realized how heavy a cigarette could be. He turned and peered out the window, but the light he sought was nowhere to be seen. There was only a faint transparency lingering at the edge of objects. In order to strip the body of whatever ersatz proof had been planted there, he had no choice but to turn on the light, thereby creating clear proof that he had been in his room at this hour.

If at all possible, he had wanted to dispose of the body before turning on the lights. Of course, he hadn't yet given up on his plan. He intended to go ahead with it, just as soon as he satisfied himself that the body was free of incriminating evidence. He had to, because even if he did rid the body of whatever had been planted on it he was still left with the problem of establishing that he had no connection to it. Once he had safely transported the body elsewhere, he could switch on the lights without fear. In fact, it would be better to have them on, to support his claim of innocence. But if searching the body was a precondition for the successful completion of his plan and if he needed light for the purpose, then it looked as if he had no choice but to trust in his eventual success and go ahead and turn the lights on now. Never mind what would happen if he remained stuck with the body, and had his lights on.

The brightness of the lights came as such a shock that he started to perspire. His nerves must be in a terrible state for every little thing to startle him so. The space around him, brought into sharp focus, seemed to press in on him, seeking a restoration of its old relationship. Above all, the corpse made a dazzling show of its existence. The familiar walls and furniture were one thing, but to have even the corpse making a claim on him was unnerving. But the lights were on. Just as an unmoving boulder in the middle of a stream emphasizes the flow of the water, so time began to move with unrelenting swiftness around the body, urging A— on, drawing him gingerly toward it.

The coat pockets, left and right, were both under the body. The trouser pockets would also be difficult to handle in this position. There was nothing for it but to turn the body over so that it was lying face up. He gauged the amount of strength he would need, calculating the optimum position, direction, and result. He wanted to keep his contact with the body to a minimum. What if he slipped a broom handle under it and used that as a lever to roll it over? Or he could go around to the other side, grab its clothes, and pull. But if the stiffness of the neck was any indication, by now that extended right arm must be hard as a rock. He might be able to flip the whole thing over just by pulling on that. But that wrist was so eloquently dead. It seemed to bear a far greater concentration of death than even the face, as if even one touch would contaminate him. He sandwiched the wrist between pages of a magazine, grabbed it from the top, and yanked. Contrary to his expectations, it was limp. Not only the wrist; the elbow sagged, too. The arm had been twisted oddly from the start, and now it was bent at a still stranger angle. The bone must have been broken. Something about a broken bone in a corpse was nauseating, far more so than the same injury in a living person. Could it be that once broken, a joint didn't harden? Or was something else going on?

In any case, he had to wrap up this unpleasant task as soon as possible. He picked up a shoe from the cement floor in the entranceway and slipped it on his right foot. It might have seemed a little disrespectful, but he planned to roll the corpse over by kicking the torso. He exerted steady pressure with his foot, and the body complied by turning over on its back with a thud—first the upper torso, followed by the hips and legs. All went well, except that now the blue jacket bore a clear, light imprint of his shoe. He felt a cold chill. For an instant his action seemed ominous and irreversible. Hastily he got a clothes brush and whisked the spot. Fortunately it came straight off, so that to the casual eye nothing could be seen.

But as it turned out, that was the least of his troubles. What he saw next was far worse. Out of the corner of his eye he spotted a brownish stain like a piece of brown wrapping paper sticking out from under the collar of the dead man's suit. Pulling back the shirt collar for a better look, he found that the shirt had been torn, and it was the torn flap that he had seen. The brown spot was a dried, faded bloodstain.

Automatically, he glanced down at his feet, where the body

had been lying. Just as he'd feared, there was a rust-colored stain about the size of a penny. It was irregular in shape, like a scab, with a luster around the periphery and a translucent spot of red embedded in the center. Blood must have trickled through the tear in the shirt and hardened on the floor.

His reaction wasn't as violent as might be imagined. It was more a deep, paralyzing stupor. After a while he bent down and picked up the towel that had fallen off when he moved the body, and automatically began rubbing at the spot with it. He spat on the floor and rubbed some more. Before long the surface of the matting was stain-free, but the blood that had soaked down in between the fibers remained. He went over to the sink to wet the towel. On the way, he glanced casually at the face of the corpse. It was mottled with dark spots on the left side, the side that was now face up, but had been down. But wait a minute—the first time he saw them, these spots had been concentrated around the nose and the lower jaw. Maybe these were what they called death spots. Did they move every time the body was shifted, according to the pull of gravity? Maybe a corpse was something like a sponge bag, soaked in colored water.

The dampened towel served only to remind him of just how hard it was to clean the mesh of the floor matting. If only he'd had lighter fluid, or alcohol, or even an eraser. Maybe soap would do the trick. That's what he used when he nicked himself shaving. Might as well try it. He put some soap shavings around the bloodstain and worked up a good lather with a wet cloth. He wrung out the cloth and mopped the spot. After repeating this twice, he found the stain was at last gone, with barely a trace. Unfortunately, the matting too had been scrubbed bright and clean.

Nobody would be fooled. Not even the most careless glance could miss the spot. If he ever did become a suspect, this would be the end of him. He had heard that there was some sort of chemical test they could perform that would pick up even the faintest trace of blood; all they had to do was sprinkle the chemical around and the blood gave off a blue fluorescent glow. So it looked as if the corpse was going to use this tiny bloodstain to drop anchor here in his room after all. Moving it wouldn't accomplish much now. Sooner or later the spot would be discovered, wherever he moved the body. Door-to-door investigations would begin when the body was uncovered and detectives would examine all the apartments in turn, whether the occupant was a suspect or not. This sign of something having been recently wiped off would have them licking their chops. He couldn't even hide it with a piece of furniture, because it was smack in front of the door.

And what, he wondered, was this bloodstain prepared to tell the detectives when they found it? No doubt the investigation would start out the usual way. They would match the bloodtypes or some such thing. Next would be the time angle. There the role of the bloodstain would be decisive. It proved that the body was here while the wound was fresh—in other words, either at, or soon after, the moment of death. Just how would that fact entangle, and finally ensnare him? It was sure to cling to him to the bitter end, and never let him go.

Still, just because it was hard to clean a sticky substance from your hands, you couldn't very well stop trying. Terror-stricken as he was at the discovery of the bloodstain, his hands went on with their business of investigating the dead man's possessions. However hopeless things might seem, he couldn't just stand by and ignore the danger of having had false evidence planted there against him. Even a suicide, after all, sets his belongings in order.

But every pocket was empty. Not only was there no business

card of A—'s and no book of matches from the Three Cats, there wasn't so much as a broken matchstick. No loose change, no handkerchief, no scrap of paper with a phone number written on it—none of the things people normally have with them. The corpse was picked so clean that either it was just back from the laundry, or someone had gone over it with a vacuum cleaner. Even the label on the jacket had been cut off, which just proved that this was premeditated. There was nothing whatever to identify the man. No clues except for the large grains of sand embedded on the soles of the shoes and lodged in the cuffs of the trousers; all he had on was ordinary, ready-made articles of clothing.

The situation hadn't improved, but it hadn't gotten any worse, either. Back to square one. He'd almost expected it. This was much smarter of the murderer, anyway. A lot more so than leaving a pile of false evidence around. If it weren't for this stupid bloodstain, everything could have gone so well. Even the murderer probably hadn't planned on this.

Someone came up the stairs with small, hesitant steps. There was the unsteady clatter of high heels. Could it be her? But today was only Wednesday. What in God's name was she doing here on a Wednesday? With an alacrity he himself could scarcely believe, he whisked the corpse under his bed. He heard the bedpan bang against the wall. The footsteps clattered past the door. He heard the faint sound of a key turning in the lock of the endmost apartment.

Breathing hard, he wet his lips, but they still felt dry. Not just dry, but cracked. With the woman home, his work would be cut out for him. But that wasn't what upset him the most. There were plenty of ways around that. If she was in the way, then all he had to do was lure her out somehow. He could call her from the public telephone on the corner. He'd already turned on the lights in his room anyway, so there was no reason to fear being seen. While the building supervisor was calling her to his phone, A— would rush back to the building, leaving the receiver dangling. While she sat in the supervisor's apartment, waiting for someone to come on the line, he could sneak upstairs and promptly dispose of the body. It would easily be more than twenty-four seconds before she gave up. He was pleased with his own ability to come up with such plans on the spur of the moment.

But now should two of the three apartments be blocked off, leaving him only one to work with, the situation would get a bit ticklish. His plan wouldn't necessarily be ruined, but the risk would be many times greater. If he was ever going to get rid of the body, now was the time. Still, there was no point in doing it unless he was sure of success. His plan might backfire all too easily. If only there was some way to escape this confounded bloodstain.

Without the corpse, the room looked amazingly spacious, emphasizing the whiteness of the tiny spot where the bloodstain had been. Suddenly he was felt tempted to expand that whiteness into the surrounding area. At first it was not so much a conscious thought as a physiological impulse, but the moment it entered his consciousness, the idea swelled with significance. Yes, yes, in order to get rid of that white spot, all he had to do was apply soap to the entire matting, and wash it all.

From there, he took the idea a step further. Why not just get rid of the whole matting, then? He couldn't very well put it out front with the trash, of course. He'd be found out for sure. He'd cut it into bits and burn it right here in the ashtray, a little at a time. The ashtray was a large one he'd bought to save himself the trouble of emptying it out often, so it would do perfectly. He could dispose of the ashes by flushing them down the toilet.

That settled everything. There'd be plenty of time to worry about the corpse later. If not tonight, then tomorrow.

The matting fibers burned well. He enjoyed pulling them apart, one at a time, and throwing them on the fire. Each one burned brought him a step closer to freedom. The smoke was terrible, though. He coughed and wiped tears from his eyes. The smoke alone he could have stood all right; this smell of burning was another matter. The supervisor was sensitive to the least odor, so how could he fail to notice this? A— looked up and saw that the room was already filled with smoke. The light bulb had a hazy, murky look. And he hadn't even finished burning the first handful of scraps. Then there was no hope. He poured water on the fire from the kettle. A pillar of steam rose in the air and the ashtray cracked in two.

However much trouble it was, it looked as if he had no choice but to scrub the whole thing. He filled the sink with water, rolled up his trousers and sleeves, and set to work applying cleanser. Innocence was certainly hard work.

After a while it occurred to him that he might have been taking a very foolish detour. Might it not be that this very bloodstain he was so determined to remove could in fact have been his salvation, the one piece of proof establishing his innocence beyond all doubt? In other words, if the corpse was examined with any care, it should be possible to pinpoint the time of death based on the degree of rigor mortis, the condition of the death spots, and so on. Knowing that, they should then be able to figure out what time the body was brought to this room. The bloodstain would serve as indisputable material evidence. Then as long as he had an alibi for the time in question—and in fact, he hadn't once left his desk at work today, right until quitting time, so there should be no difficulty there—his innocence would be assured.

But by the time he thought of that, the entire floor had been scrubbed sparkling clean. Detergents nowadays had potent bleaches in them. Looking around at the fresh and gleaming floor, he stood agape. How the devil was he going to explain this ridiculous whiteness to strangers? It would only call attention to itself and arouse further suspicion. When the bloodstain might have been his salvation . . .

Worse, after discovering the body he had said nothing and kept it hidden all this time. There was no way to defend himself now. In the process, he had all but destroyed his own alibi. And the longer he waited, the worse it would get. Perhaps the best thing to do was stop wavering and make up his mind once and for all to turn himself in. In that case, the sooner the better.

But oh, the awful whiteness of this floor! It seemed final, irreversible. Maybe he shouldn't give up after all, but carry on the struggle with the corpse. In any case, he needed courage. Whether he turned himself in or went on grappling with the corpse, he would need courage. And whichever choice required the most courage was bound to be the right one.

But it was already almost dawn, and he was a little too tired to decide what courage really was.

The Crime of S. Karma

(excerpted from a larger work)

I woke up. Waking up in the morning is a perfectly natural thing to do; nothing unusual about that. So what was different this morning? Something or other was definitely odd.

To know something is odd, and have no idea what it could be, is damned odd in itself—and as I washed my face and brushed my teeth, things got odder still.

To see what would happen (don't ask me why), I gave a cavernous yawn. Straight away the oddity converged in my chest. It felt as if somehow my chest were hollow.

Attributing this sensation to hunger, I went down to the building café (following my normal routine), where I breakfasted on two bowls of soup and six slices of bread. The numbers stick in my mind for a reason: normally, I would never eat so much.

But the sense of oddity only intensified, along with the sense of hollowness in my chest, so eventually I gave up. My stomach, at any rate, was full.

I went over to the register and the girl there handed me the account book to sign. For some reason I hesitated. The hesitation seemed to bear some relation to the peculiar mood I was in; I glanced over at the gray infinity beyond the window, searching for my reflection.

Suddenly I became aware of my predicament. Standing there gripping the pen, I was unable to sign my name. For the life of me, I couldn't remember what it was—that was why I was hesitating.

Still, I felt little surprise. I had read that lots of people—scholars absorbed in research, for example—often experience momentary difficulty in recalling their names. (This was in a respectable academic paper, too, not a smear of the scholars in question.)

So with perfect serenity, I took out my case of business cards. Unfortunately, it was empty. Flipping it over, I checked my ID card on the other side and saw to my amazement that my name had disappeared.

Swiftly I pulled out a letter from my father that I'd stuck in my appointment book. The address and salutation were gone.

I checked the label on the inside of my suit. Gone.

In growing alarm, I thrust my hands into every cranny of my pants and coat, scanning every scrap of paper I could find, without luck.

Every place my name had been recorded was now blank.

Frustrated, I asked the girl at the counter what my name was. We were casual acquaintances, so she must have known, but she only gave me a queer smile and made no effort to speak. I had no choice but to pay cash.

Back in my room, I hunted vainly in every drawer of my desk. My brand-new box of business cards was empty. My ex libris had disappeared from every book on the shelves. My name was gone from my umbrella, from the inside of my hat, from the corners of my handkerchiefs—in short, from every conceivable place where it should have been.

Catching sight of my reflection in the door pane, I saw that I wore a look of unmitigated shock.

I decided to sit down and try to make sense of things. But other than the possibility of a link between this bizarre development and the sense of hollowness in my chest, I came up dry. I quit trying.

Time always took care of things like this, I reassured myself. And once you finally did figure out what was going on, it always turned out to hinge on some triviality. There had to be an easy explanation for it all.

Just then the 7:30 A.M. siren sounded at the nearby valve factory, reminding me that it was time to go to work. I prepared to leave, only to find my briefcase missing. I was beside myself. Not only did it hold important documents, but it was genuine leather and had taken me three months to pay for on the installment plan. After hunting carefully in every corner of the room—which took only a minute or two, the room was so small—I had to conclude it was the work of a thief.

I stepped out, on my way to the police, but then stopped short. I'd been forgetting about the seeming disappearance of my name. Without a name, how was I going to file a complaint? Maybe the thief took that, too. Clever son of a bitch. Vague admiration gave way to anger, then stupefaction. In that dazed state I set off on foot for the office, empty-handed.

The rush-hour streets had a frenzied, alien look. The lack of a name left me feeling helpless. Walking nameless through the streets of town was a new experience for me; just thinking about it made me feel self-conscious and ashamed. The hollow in my chest seemed to expand.

I arrived at work slightly late. The first thing I did was check the employees' name plates in the reception area. Mine was second from the left in the third row.

S. KARMA

S. Karma. I tried saying it over to myself. Somehow it didn't much sound like my name, and then again it did. But however many times I repeated it, I felt none of the rush of satisfaction or pleasure that comes with remembering something that's been on the tip of your tongue.

In fact I began to suspect it was some kind of mistake that this name was mine. But since that really didn't seem likely, I began to suspect instead that it was some kind of mistake that I was me. I shook my head to chase away whatever was confusing me like this, but it didn't help. Every shake seemed only to increase the apparent hollowness in my chest. I decided put the whole thing out of my mind.

Automatically, I reached out to switch on the light beside my name to show I was here and realized with a jolt that it was already on. Someone must have turned it on by mistake. That sort of thing is easy enough to do.

Feeling rather relieved at not having to lay a hand on that unsettling name after all, I set off blithely for my office on the second floor.

The door to my office stood wide open, my desk clearly visible from the doorway. My mind had been traveling about ten yards ahead of the rest of me, so that mentally I was already at my desk when suddenly, overcome by an unaccountable emotion, my physical self stood rooted in the doorway. To my consternation, another me was already seated in my chair.

I couldn't be seeing my own mind. It had to be some sort of optical illusion. But then my mind cleared, and I saw it was no optical illusion after all. Overwhelmed and abashed, I pressed back into the shadows, afraid that if anyone saw me now, the consequences would be disastrous.

Fortunately, my vantage point afforded a clear view. My other self was dictating a report on the use of concrete bricks in fireproof construction to the typist, Miss Y—. The missing briefcase was right where it belonged, next to my desk. With its left hand, the other me was tracing a finger along some papers, while with his right hand he furtively caressed Miss Y—'s knee. My inward sense of shame came bursting to the surface, and I felt my eyes turn hot and moist.

It was definitely me over there. But again, as at the sight of my name downstairs, I was afraid that to accept this stranger as "me" might be tantamount to confessing that I was not "me," but someone else.

Just then a voice yelled in my ear, "Hey! What are you doing there!" It was the custodian.

Feeling like a paratrooper shot down behind enemy lines, I returned his gaze. He showed no sign of recognizing me, and came on with such arrogance that I became flustered and bowed my head obsequiously as I replied, "I was, uh, wondering if I could see Mr. Karma." It was acutely embarrassing to speak of myself so respectfully.

With a contemptuous jerk of his head the custodian said, "Who, Karma? He's right there, dictating to his secretary."

The other me apparently overheard this exchange. Stiffening, he spun around and met my gaze with a frown. In that instant, I penetrated the secret of his identity. It was my business card. As I studied him closely, it became steadily more apparent that this was indeed every inch a business card. How could I have missed it? The fellow had all the attributes of one.

Closing my right and left eyes alternately in rapid succession, I hit on the reason for the double image. With my right eye, I clearly saw a duplicate of myself, like a mirror image, but with my left eye I saw nothing but a large paper card.

N— Fire Insurance
Data Department
S. KARMA

I well remembered having had those cards printed up, not long ago. I'd ordered them from the union printers and splurged on the finest paper. When they were ready, Miss Y— had picked them up for me, and in return I'd treated her to a cup of Viennese coffee.

As I was thinking all this, my card handed Miss Y— a sheaf of papers, whispered in her ear, and stood up decisively. But he was only a piece of paper himself—my left eye saw him slide down onto the floor.

"If you want to talk, let's step outside," he said, and brushed on by me. I glanced over at Miss Y—, but she was absorbed in her typing, seemingly unaware of my presence. Two or three of my colleagues, none of whom I was on very close terms with, rested their gazes on me, but only in a random, meaningless sort of way; they didn't really see me. It was odd that they didn't see the card for what he really was, and odder still that they failed to recognize the real me.

In front of the storage closet at the end of the corridor my card turned around and growled, "What do you think you're doing here? This has always been my turf. You've got no business sticking your nose in here. If any of the bozos who know you catch sight of us, they'll figure out our connection. You'll cause no end of trouble. What did you have to come here for anyway? Hurry up and leave, would you? Frankly, I'm ashamed to be mixed up with someone like you."

The words I should have flung back at him sank to the bottom of my hollow chest and wouldn't come out. For some seconds we faced off silently. During that interval my confused thoughts took off quite on their own, totally apart from my emotions; they even gave a cheerful sort of jump, like a Cossack dance—it's hard to explain. Finally—just as I was thinking how hilarious it was to see things so differently through my right and left eyes, and wondering what Marxian influence this might be—my card suddenly yelled "Asshole!" and I lunged for him. I had a vivid mental picture of how he would look disfigured by a pitiless tear. And that wasn't all: mentally I underlined the tear, and scrawled "Value: one yen, twenty sen" on his face.

But my foe proved unexpectedly wily. In a flash he became one hundred percent card, the same in both my eyes, and slipped through my fingers. I reached out for him and cornered him against the wall, but with a malicious sneer, he slid right through the crack in the closet door. The door was locked, I knew, and the custodian had the key. And yet in my frustration I couldn't help jerking the doorknob and rattling the door.

The commotion attracted the custodian. Once again he loomed up beside me.

"All right, what's going on here?" he said with a cough. "What's the matter?"

I barely managed to squeak, "Mr. Karma is inside here."

"The hell he is. This is a storage closet."

In the face of his overt hostility my anger reverted to shame, then humiliation. Without a word I excused myself and fled the building. I placed a hand on my chest. The sense of hollowness had intensified.

I still hadn't given up hope. When he left the office, my card would have to come home. Even if he was just my business card, he was still "me" in a sense, so where was he going to go at night, if not my room?

What would I say when he got here? I wondered. I'd have to stand up to him. Knuckling under would only increase the humiliation. I'd have to get to the bottom of all this. Yes, that had a good ring to it, I told myself smugly. If I hadn't happened to startle myself just then with a thump on the chest, I would undoubtedly have gone on imagining all sorts of eventualities and preparing all sorts of clever comebacks, carried away with the anticipation of a good argument. (I can't help it, that's the way I am.)

But instead, I got so wound up that I thumped myself on the chest, producing a sound so bizarre that it brought me swiftly to my senses. The sound was hollow, like the echo of an empty barrel—nothing like any sort of noise that could issue from a human body—and so parched that my lips all but dried and cracked on the spot.

I opened my shirt and tapped on my chest here and there, in the manner of a doctor. Damned if the sound didn't echo. Unnerved, I sat down on the edge of the bed with my head hanging, hands pressed against my chest. This was no mere sensation of hollowness; my chest really was hollow.

I was badly shaken. Even my conviction that the card would come home began to waver. Insecure as I was, if he did come back might I not end up being thrown out of my own room? If it came to blows, I could easily handle a piece of paper, however fine the quality, but my lack of a name was a serious disadvantage. The law might very well take the card's side. Especially considering that my name had not been stolen, but had gotten up and left of its own volition. . . .

Dendrocacalia

*T*his is the story of how Common became a dendrocacalia. One day, Common absently kicked a stone by the side of the road. It was early spring and the street was black and moist. The stone was an inconspicuous one, dry as a cinder and about the size of a man's fist, and for some reason he felt like kicking it. And then, that apparently ordinary action came to take on very peculiar overtones in his mind.

You know how it is. It happens to us all. You glance cautiously around to see whether anyone is watching. Even if they are, you say to yourself, what the heck, people do it all the time without giving it a second thought.

After some such fatuous rationalization, Common aimed a second kick at the stone with his other foot. And instantly felt an emptiness, a sensation of being swept away. Was my mind always so blank? he wondered, and then it happened: something plantlike began to take hold in his mind. There was no other way to describe it. He had a distressing sense of physically falling—unpleasant, yet strangely agreeable. The earth rumbled.

It shook . . . and then things grew stranger still. Common suddenly felt the firm tug of gravity. He felt glued to the spot, as if attached there. He *was* attached. Looking down, he was dismayed to find his feet lodged firmly in the ground—and himself a plant! Transformed into something soft and thin, greenish brown, neither tree nor grass.

After that everything went dark. Within the darkness he saw his own face staring back at him, as if reflected in the window of a night train. A hallucination, of course. His face was on inside out. Frantically, he tore it off and put it back correctly. The moment he did so, everything reverted to normal.

He set off at a fast pace, glancing around nonchalantly to see if anybody had been watching. Was it his imagination, or was that man staring at him? Flustered, he took a few more steps and then deliberately stumbled, looking down as if to say it was all the fault of his shoes, hoping this would lay the man's suspicions to rest. Surely the man would think his eyes had been playing tricks on him, Common thought, trying to dismiss the matter from his mind.

A year went by and nothing happened. At first Common was uneasy, but gradually he began to forget. He began to think he'd imagined the whole episode. But then the next spring, suddenly he suffered a recurrence of the same disease.

It happened like this. One day he received a note.

> I need you. I am your destiny. Tomorrow
> at three, at Kanran Café.
>> Sincerely,
>> K—

The writing was clearly feminine. Suppressing a rising excitement, Common thought, K— . . . now, who could that be? The name struck him as familiar and then again it didn't. He had no idea who it might be, yet he had a feeling it was someone he knew quite well. As he pondered, he began responding to suggestion. He was almost positive he had once had a girlfriend named K—. He carefully refolded the letter, put it back in the envelope, and stood perfectly still, holding it tightly between his palms, feeling them become eyes, ears, nose, and mouth, melting, finally, into the letter. With great care he folded it in half and stuck it in his breast pocket. His eyes took in nothing before or beyond the text of the letter. He was utterly content with its message.

Morning dawned. All night long a savage rain had lashed at the windows, but now skies were clear and promising. It was still a few hours early, but Common left his apartment. Glancing back, he stopped for a moment and fixed in his memory the fish-shaped crack in the window and the half-rotten rope dangling from the eaves, hung there for a purpose long forgotten. Then he turned and went on down the black, rain-slicked road, hopping from one island of dry asphalt to another. He couldn't contain his excitement. Who could blame him? A soft breeze crept by him. His breathing shook his shoulders.

Kanran Café—there it was, his destination. He ordered a cup of coffee, and, to suit the extravagance of his mood, a bag of peanuts. He took a corner seat by the window where he could keep an eye on the street. The moment he sat down, his mind was flooded with a torrent of thoughts. How sudden this was! He might have been secretly hoping for this to happen all along, but never to have realized so was nothing short of appalling. For all he knew he might have sat at this very table with K—, deaf to her declarations of love. Without his ever knowing, all had been building toward this day. Yes, yes, he repeated to himself contentedly. It all seemed so natural, so right! This is what I've been waiting for, he could tell himself with no impropriety. This was how it had to be. He laughed out loud to himself.

At such times things have a way of looking bigger than life, as if seen through a magnifying glass. Glancing around at the faces of others in the room, he was able to distinguish moles alongside noses, warts under ears, gold teeth, and long nose hairs—all with heightened clarity. The ring of that man in the jacket was gold plate, starting to wear off. A small spot stained the front of the schoolgirl's uniform. Carved on the table, partially hidden by the elbows of a middle-aged man whose jowls pressed against his collar, was a heart pierced with an arrow. In front of the sharp-chinned student jabbering excitedly, a plump girl with slits for eyes was diligently mopping his spittle off her face. At her feet, in an out-of-the-way corner where doubtless no one's eyes but Common's had ever traveled, there was a small hole where a mouse peered cautiously his way. The floor was sprinkled with water, and dust floated in the air like white dandruff.

Thoroughly satisfied with all he saw, Common turned his attention to the street, as if the room, sated with his gaze, were driving it away. Outside, the road leading to the railway station had dried to a pale hue; even the mingled shadows of passers-by seemed to float above it, faint and parched. Bicycles raced by, smashing the dessicated shadows to pieces and blowing them away.

Ten after two.

In the doorway, unmoving, stood a large man, twisted like a stick of licorice . . . staring hard at Common. Common felt his neck come unhinged, his head flop down on his chest, his eyeballs draw level with his heart.

No! It had been an illusion, a trick of light; this was no large man, though neither, of course, was it a young girl. It was a short little man with thick glasses and a black starched collar. His face was broad, the features twisted and uneven. Beside a flat, shiny nose, the whole right side of the face seemed to slant upward. The right eye in particular was like a vast cavern behind those thick glasses. It was as if he sucked things in with his narrow left eye and swallowed them with the right. A prominent vein bulged at his temple; no doubt when he was agitated it started twitching like a caterpillar.

Could this be K—? God forbid. And yet, after a quick survey of the room, the man came striding purposefully over to Common's table and sat down opposite him. Nonplussed, Common sat bolt upright, and was on the point of speaking, when he encountered such a glare that he quickly pretended merely to be adjusting his chair. What to do? This can't be K—, thought Common. This turd could never write a graceful, girlish hand like that. Hell no. K—'s got to be an old flame, a beautiful young thing. Damn it all, what does he think he's doing sitting there. Or maybe . . . Common became uneasy. Maybe this turd knows K— and came here to make trouble. The thought began to drive him mad. How could he communicate with her before she entered the café? Maybe he should go right now and wait for her in front of the train station. But what if she came by bus? He could keep a lookout in front of the cigarette stand on the corner. But then what if she came in the back way? In tandem with the loss of his composure, the workings of the wall clock over his head seemed to quicken visibly. Time felt like sand, spilling through his fingers.

To drive away the growing sense of oppression bearing down on him from all sides like a sudden increase in atmospheric pressure, Common looked up. With his one cavernous eye, the man was peering into Common's eyes as if to penetrate all the way to his bowels. His face announced that he knew all . . . and

Common was inclined to believe it. But that can't be, he can't even know who I am!

Try as he might to deny it with one part of his mind, immediately another corner of his mind would be overtaken by the strange and growing conviction that in some way he didn't understand (yet surely would acquiesce to if he ever could understand) this man did indeed know everything. He'd had the same sort of feeling once before. But when? Suddenly a poster on the telephone pole outside the window fixed him with a meaningful look.

Tree-planting Week.

Yes, that was it, plants.

Filled with an ominous presentiment, Common lowered his gaze, wretchedly conscious of a gradual tightening in his chest. Destiny. *Destiny is something each man must wrest for himself,* he remembered; the maxim struck him as peculiarly appropriate to his situation. Something was bound to happen. Now for the first time, Common urgently felt the preciousness of the life which K— was to make possible.

All right, whatever happened, he must protect K— from this man.

Two-fifty. Almost time. Carefully Common studied the people coming and going along the street. He counted out the money he owed and laid it on the table, preparing to dash out as soon as he saw her. Yet he had to appear calm, as if nothing was up. Mentally he had to work ceaselessly at building a stone wall between himself and this man in front of him. The thought of those eyes made him feel that the wall crumbled as fast as he put it up. He tried not to look at the man, but found himself haunted by that face. Even with his back turned, Common sensed the man's triumphant half-smile. Avoiding his gaze afforded little relief.

Gradually the activity outside seemed to quicken, growing more intense, surpassing his ability to take it in. Were his consciousness able to keep pace with the constant stream of motion, he should be able to grasp it in static terms as a series of still scenes, but something was the matter. In his lagging consciousness, every movement left a dim trail. Was this what it meant to have your head swim? It was as if an intricate piece of cut glass were spinning around and around, creating a dazzling display of light. The vast assortment of cars and bicycle-drawn carts, and of pedestrians with their different clothes and styles of walking, faded gradually to gray shadow, dissolving and merging in the layers of brilliance. In this dizzy score of symphonic light, picking out her approaching figure would be next to impossible. The harder he tried to recall some distinguishing trait by which to identify her, the less sure he became, and the more likely it seemed that he would miss her. All of a sudden I'll just look up and see her standing here, he thought in panic. What discouraged him even more was the realization that he'd been staring intently at that confounded poster for Tree-planting Week.

What was going on? He must be tired. He looked up at the sky. Yes, the sky! Its heaviness filled his whole body, pouring in smoothly through his eyes, displacing his internal organs. Someone stood bent over him, staring down at him, wavering unsteadily as if unsure which way to go. Instantly he knew it was his own face, framed in darkness, looking back at him. The muddy earth rumbled. The intoxication of a pleasant satiety—here it came, another of those seizures.

Before long, just as had happened once before, his face inverted itself, and virtually his entire body became a plant. A strange sort of vegetation, neither grass nor tree; his fingers became leaves, shaped rather like those of chrysanthemums. Not a terribly attractive plant and not a kind he had ever seen before, either. Desperately forcing movement into his stiff, unresponsive limbs, he seized his face, tore it off, and put it on right side out. In that instant, everything reverted to normal.

No, not everything. How could so much time have gone by? It was already three-thirty. The man was no longer around. The appointed time had come and gone. She must have come in just as Common was changing into a plant, and been spirited away by that man. Or—much as he hated to admit it—perhaps there never had been any girl. Perhaps K— was indeed that man. Like it or not, assuming so made things far easier to understand. But nothing would soften the stares of all the people in the room, pressing in on him like a wall of thorns. He didn't have the courage to look up. His head bent in shame and despair, Common fled the café.

He felt equally out of place on the crowded street, among the throng. That no one stopped him or insulted him or placed any restraint on him at all seemed remarkable. But he could hardly think that this freedom would last long. When would this interval end? It never occurred to him to put an end to it himself. He just kept on walking, carried along in the stream of pedestrians, following the green lights. His surroundings were quiet and bustling by turns. Somewhere, a poster on another telephone pole was talking.

"This week is Tree-planting Week. Ladies and gentlemen, let's show more love for trees. Green things restore harmony to our dissipated hearts and bring cleanliness and beauty to our streets. . . ."

Where was he? Must have gotten lost. Weird place. The charred remains of a building at the top of a hill, with nothing standing but blackened walls. From the position of the sun, it must be after five. No sign of people. Common was suddenly tired. He came on an empty lot with no walls. From recent events he well knew what danger he was in, what would happen if he paused here, yet somehow he couldn't resist the temptation to sit down on a block of stone and rest. When he sat down, he felt his face coming loose, and sensed keenly that the least thing would set it going again—but again, the process was beyond his control. It appeared that his face wanted to reverse itself. Apparently it felt more natural that way. Trembling all over, he pressed both hands to his face, trying to steady it. It twisted and squirmed like a live fish, doing its best to slip out of his grasp. He was tempted to rip the damn thing off and throw it away once and for all. But wait—if he did that, what would remain? All at once he went limp, exhausted, and his hands loosened their grip.

This time he was acutely conscious of the process of transformation. Only it seemed to him rather that the entire outer world became him and that the tubular thing which had been, but no longer was, him was what turned into a plant. But he no longer resisted. That poster was right. "Our dissipated hearts . . . ," Might as well let himself be reduced to a vegetable, here and now. Having decided that, he found there was even a kind of pleasure in the process. Why not be a vegetable, indeed!

Were it but to tide over this life of woe
Why not become a laurel tree
With repand leaves
Amid the shady green?

Some such fragment of poetry might have crossed his mind. The rusty brown of the charred ruins seemed to have seeped inside him. The fireplace had escaped the flames and the chimney rose tall as a pillar, covered with stains like the outline of a map. Between broken, scattered pieces of slate and tile there now grew weeds.

None of these could stave off the swelling ruins on the far side of his consciousness. Common made up his mind to go ahead and allow his transformation to take place. Had not an unexpected voice then taken him by surprise, undoubtedly the process would have been irrevocably completed on the spot.

"Just as I thought, a dendrocacalia!"

The voice seemed to echo within his ears. The explanation was simple: his face was again turned inside out.

Beside the miserable, squat shrub next to the stone block stood the stocky man in thick glasses and black starched collar. He kept pushing up his glasses each time they slid down, on his lips a thin smile of unconcealed depravity as with large, square hands he covetously fingered the plant.

Needless to say, it was the same fellow who had appeared in the Kanran Café. But what was he doing here? Had he followed Common, then?

"It really is a dendrocacalia!" the man chortled. And then for some reason he took a shiny seaman's knife from his pocket.

Common blanched and jerked involuntarily, but his transformation was now almost complete, so he was unable to get away.

"What a piece of luck, to find a specimen here of all places!" As he spoke, the man raised the knife high and plunged it down into the earth at his feet. Then by sheer chance his shoulder bumped against what remained of Common's face. Pushed from below, the face began to tear off like a scab. It was a brief but intense moment—a slight but precipitate reversal in which a measure of movement was restored to Common's arms. He reached up and straightened out his face.

With a strange, guttural cry of alarm, the man jumped back, pressing himself against the stone wall across the street. Where the shrub had been, Common now stood, having reappeared in human form.

Common himself couldn't fathom everything that had happened. The train of events had taken place in a realm outside his awareness. On its own, his face seemed to want nothing more than to turn itself inside out, while his hands, at any rate, seemed intent on preventing such a reversal.

Nor was that all his hands intended to do. As he stood gazing down at the knife stuck in the ground at his feet, suddenly, despite a sharp cry of protest from the man, his hands darted out of their own accord, swiftly grabbed the knife, and stuck it in a breast pocket. Common himself was a mere observer, detached, uninvolved. Then, as if they too had a will of their own, his legs began to move and before he knew it he had run past the man, who had recovered somewhat and was now peering cautiously and searchingly his way. Common—still a detached observer, uninvolved in this decision to flee—ran farther up the street.

Presently he realized he could hear a second pair of footsteps. The sound was an echo, yet not an echo. The other set of footsteps beat out a rhythm totally unrelated to his own. But when he paused, the sound stopped. The ditch at his feet, all but buried in rubbish, overflowed with dirty water. Just as some dead leaves came floating by, he started off again—and there!—he heard the footsteps once more. Turning abruptly to look behind him, some thirty yards back he saw a short black figure leap like a fish into the shadow of a wall.

Hearing the clatter of a streetcar, he quickened his steps in that direction.

That evening, when darkness had nearly settled in, he returned to his apartment. For a long, long time he stood motionless in the center of the room with his head bowed as if trying hard to re-member something. Finally a troubled frown crossed his face and he clucked his tongue in resignation. Collapsing into a chair, he closed his eyes and fell fast asleep, without any covers.

He finally woke up some time after noon. The wind had died down and it was raining. Branches of a luxurious evergreen were plastered against the windowpane, dripping wet. Peering out between them at the street, Common jumped and shrank back. Below, the rain-soaked figure of the short man in the black suit passed slowly by. Common fell back in the shadows of the room, terrified, and swallowed a lump in his throat.

After a while he roused himself from the table he'd been ab-sently leaning on and went out.

He didn't know where he was headed. He knew only that he felt a strong impulse to track something down, to do something.

Carrying a full load of passengers, their outlines dim through the rising steam, a streetcar pulled in to the stop with a painful shudder, its green skin pouring sweat. People who'd been hud-dled under the eaves now stepped out into the rain, while others closed their umbrellas. Common took one look around and climbed on board, as if evading pursuit.

The window was wet so he couldn't see clearly, but it seemed to Common that the black figure which had so terrified him be-fore now glided smoothly by. He tried to get a better look, but the streetcar was already swinging around a sharp curve.

"Next stop, public library . . ."

At the sound of the conductor's voice, Common had a sud-den flash of inspiration and decided to get off. Had any human being ever turned into a plant before, and if so, why? He would look it up.

The first source that occurred to him was Dante's *Divine Comedy*. Hadn't there been one place in Hell where human beings turned to plants? As a way of understanding what was happening to him, it was a start. It might be a trifle unscientific, but in the hope of coming across some sort of clue, he filled out a card and presented it to the librarian. And then, for all the world as if he'd been waiting for Common to check out that particular book, the librarian handed it to him immediately and said, "Read page 82."

Looking up in surprise, Common saw that the librarian was none other than the dark-suited man. Flustered, he fell into the nearest seat, feeling cornered. A bookmark was inserted in the book, so that it fell open naturally at page 82.

Canto XIII of the Inferno, the story of Pier Delle Vigne.

> . . . and, all along the mournful forest,
> each body shall hang forever more,
> each on a thorn of its own alien shade.

According to Dante, this was the second round of the seventh circle of Hell, the punishment reserved for suicides. But what harm had Common ever done to himself? Even if there was no comparison with the sin of Pier Delle Vigne, who had "held both of the keys that fitted Frederick's heart," he might have been convinced if he could have thought of anything, however trifling, that he had done to deserve the wrath of Minos, judge of sinners in Hell. Why he should be accused of the sin of suicide, he could not imagine. But as he read on, he began to understand. Sinners in Hell had no awareness of their sin. In Hell there was no sin, only punishment. This presented Common with but one possible conclusion: it must be that he had already committed suicide, without knowing.

Through the library, where everybody's head was downturned, Common ran with his own head bowed lower still. His feet seemed to sink into the heavily-waxed floor. All the people he passed seemed fearful of the light. And the machinelike librarians kept a stern eye out for those indomitable few who lifted their faces to the light. It was not only that the windows had atrophied, like the eyes of an earthworm; the eyelids of Common's own mind were heavy and drooping. Nor was the chill solely the result of his soaking in the rain; it was as if this place had been left behind by the seasons, and spring had yet to come.

There was a peculiar moment: a tranquility as if time had stopped, and then everyone around him changed into a plant, all at once. Of course it might have been an illusion. The moment was fleeting. But to Common, it was Hell.

At the doorway he was grabbed firmly by a male receptionist. Raising his head to protest, he saw that it was the familiar black figure yet again. "What is it!" he shouted. The face was that of a Harpy, one of the bird-monsters that feast on the trees of the living dead.

Common flung off the man's restraining hand and pressed his hands to his face, which had started to slip off. And then, without looking back, he ran.

Even outside, he couldn't relax. The rain had become a fine mist, creating a shortage of air. He felt like a fish suffocating at the bottom of an old pond. He quickened his pace, seeking to escape, but Hell clung to his heels, spreading through the streets.

Since there was nowhere else to go, he went back to his room—and then suddenly recalling the letter, he pulled it out of his breast pocket. Here and there the edges were worn, but it was still in good shape. Slowly he tore it up. He held a lighted match to one of the scraps, and before it burned out he transferred the flame to another, watching steadily until all the scraps were consumed. Little by little, his attention shifted from the letter to the fire.

Girlfriend? How ridiculous. He'd really fallen for it. Look, she's burning, your lover is burning to a crisp, sang a contrabass below the texture of the fiery music. Might it be the song of the sons of Iapetus? Might this fire be the fire of Prometheus? Fire sent to purge the tribe of Zeus—patricide, oppressor of mankind—from the sacred mountaintop?

There was a final puff of white smoke, and among the ashes there shone the reflection of far-off streetlights. Common rose suddenly, burying his face in his hands. He was going into seizure, about to be transformed. Someone had stolen the fire. Suddenly it was clear: his metamorphosis into a plant was undoubtedly the doing of the tribe of Zeus.

Common set off for town again, and after a long search finally found a volume on Greek mythology. He had to learn all he could about everyone transformed by the gods into plants.

First there was Daphne, saved from the embraces of Apollo when her father Peneus, the river-god, changed her into a laurel tree. But to Common it did not seem at all that she had really been saved. Was not this too a province of Dante's Hell? Of course it was. Daphne had been about to throw herself into the Peneus River. Still, maybe it was a kind of salvation, at that. Maybe laurels were more deserving of redemption than human beings. He tried to tell himself this but remained unconvinced. She was not saved. She was only transformed in punishment for eluding the advances of a god! The same was true of the nymph Syrinx, who fled from Pan and was changed into reeds.

Hyacinthus, who became a hyacinth, and Adonis, who became an anemone, were nothing but mementoes for the gods mourning their deaths—Apollo and Aphrodite.

Heriades became a larch in sorrow at the death of Phaethon by Zeus' hand, and who could say that Clytie, who was changed into a sunflower, was not the victim of Apollo?

Finally, while the transformation of Narcissus into a flower may have been an expression of the gods' sympathy, all it accomplished in the end was to give him the freedom to die. In his transformation lay nothing but the freedom of despair itself.

Transformation into a plant meant avoiding unhappiness, at the cost of future happiness; salvation from sin meant being thrown into the midst of Sin. These were not the laws of human beings but the laws of the slaves of Zeus. Oh, for a newer and stronger Promethean fire!

One day, another letter was slipped under his door.

Dear Mr. Dendrocacalia Crepidifolia:
It was a great surprise to find that you exist north of the Hahajima archipelago. It is really most peculiar.
I would love to meet you. I'll call at six this evening.

Yours,
K—
Director, Botanical Gardens

Ah, it's from the Harpy, thought Common, remembering that familiar black figure. He was indignant. And really it was an audacious letter.

The Harpy came at six on the dot.

He seemed less like a bird of Hell than a messenger from Zeus. The thought made Common, still angry, leave his guest unattended and rush back to his book on Greek mythology. He'd been right. Harpies . . . daughters of water, descended from Neptune . . . come to put out the fire!

Without waiting for the other to speak, Common burst out, "I was just reading all about you!"

"Aha, good for you!" A surprisingly screechy voice. "What

do we have here? Greek mythology. Well, well. What does it say?"

"That the Harpies are bird-shaped monsters, daughters of Neptune—"

"That's very interesting, but you know, Mr. Dendrocacalia—"

"The name's Common."

"Really, Mr. Dendrocacalia, Greek mythology is a bit unscientific, don't you think? That will do more harm than good. Shall I tell you something more interesting? Have you read Timiryasev's *Life of Plants*? Here's what it says: the difference between plants and animals is not qualitative but quantitative. Scientifically speaking, in other words, plants and animals are basically the same. Isn't that a good way of looking at it? An approach devoid of value judgments. In my own opinion, plants are the answer to schizophrenia. They are the hope of our age. The gods of modern times. Large numbers of hysterical people will become believers and emulate them. But that approach is slanted. I myself am satisfied just to accept Timiryasev's definition of terms. And so—"

"You are a messenger from Zeus, come to put out the fire!"

"Nothing of the kind. I simply came to pay my respects. You seem awfully on edge. Please just listen to what I have to say. I've been wanting to tell you this for some time. It is very simple: I'd like to offer you a room in the Botanical Gardens. We've fixed it so that the climate is exactly like that of Hahajima. It's a paradise, in fact. And it's fully supported by the government. You'll run no risk whatever. Many people who have become plants find they are happiest living at my place."

"Many?"

Hastily the Harpy put a finger to his lips.

"Ssh! You mustn't tell anyone. There are others who are after you people—dealers. But my place is different. It's safe.

Government protected, don't forget. The people I've singled out are all happy."

"Happy!"

"Well, basically. But what difference do happiness and unhappiness make, anyway? They don't matter in the least. The point is whether you can live more purely, more richly. Isn't that so? At any rate, when you make up your mind, please drop by at the Botanical Gardens. I'm sure you'll like it. I'll be expecting you. Do give it some thought. What would happen if you had one of your seizures right in the middle of the street? Some little boy, or some ignoramus, would take you for an ordinary weed and lop off your head, that's what would happen. Heaven forbid. I know it's no concern of mine, but the thought gives me shivers. Please come. If not for your sake, then for mine . . . I just couldn't bear to see such a tragedy happen."

"You Harpy . . ."

"Oh, Mr. Dendrocacalia, you're wrong, wrong, wrong. Please, let's try to be more scientific about this. 'Harpy' has such a disturbing ring to it. What exactly do you make of the transformation of humans into plants, anyway?"

"It's a sign of Zeus' pity on his slaves. The Harpies put out the fire and drive humans into this barren punishment! I suppose you're going to tell me it's a beautiful sacrifice."

"Certainly not! You're under a delusion! Plants are the very roots of Logos. What you are talking about is only myth. And a very ancient one at that. In the new mythology, plants are the gods. They are absolute purity; the very word, banned, alas, from our everyday speech, is the high beating of their hearts."

"Hearts of plants? Plants are sacrifices to the heart, you mean!"

"No, no."

"What do you mean, no? The innards are changed into

leaves, made into surface features so that you can feed on them with greater ease, isn't that right?"

"Oh, Mr. Dendrocacalia, I'll say no more. But do take a look at Timiryasev. You'll feel better. And then think it over carefully. I'm sure you'll decide to come to the Botanical Gardens. We have a wonderful hothouse. And state supported, too, don't forget. Good-bye, then. I'll be looking forward to seeing you. I'm sure you'll come. I would even bet on it."

"I'll be damned if I do!"

"Oh, you'll come! But never mind. Oh, and listen, just because I follow you around, I don't want you to take it amiss. It would just be such a pity for you to be uprooted somewhere at the side of the road by some mischievous little boy. And so unnecessary. I'd feel responsible. Good-bye then, for now . . ."

Poor Common. In his excitement, he couldn't stop shaking. It went on for three days. He thought and thought, with scarcely a wink of sleep.

Something hidden from virtually everyone had been revealed to Common. Or perhaps it was not so extraordinary. It might simply be that Chance, which had been out making a pilgrimage within Necessity in the guise of a beggar, had happened to knock at his door.

Early one morning Common quietly left his room in the darkness before sunrise. In his pocket was the seaman's knife he had stolen from the Harpy. The first streetcar came wheezing along. He had made up his mind: I can't avoid becoming a plant forever. I'm already a suicide victim, in life. Having been chased once by Death, there is nothing left for me to fear. I'll kill the Harpy. The Harpy who steals fire from humans. And if I could, I'd like to save all the people imprisoned in the hothouse.

He'd planned to attack the man in his sleep, but to his surprise everyone in the Botanical Gardens was already hard at work.

"Well, if it isn't Mr. Dendrocacalia! Perfect timing. Today is Potted Plant Day, the highlight of Tree-planting Week. I had a feeling you might be along. Come along, please, this way. I want you to have a look at our hothouse. A big celebrity is scheduled to arrive today, with his family, and in honor of the occasion we've dressed up all the plants. Each leaf has been carefully polished, and the plants decorated with flags and streamers, as you see. It's a real celebration!" He lowered his voice. "You see, you won't be a bit lonely. It's wonderful. Don't you think we have a nice place here?" Then he laughed. "Looks like I win the bet, after all."

It was a spacious hothouse, steam-heated to just the right temperature, the glass windows perspiring. Common began perspiring heavily himself. He gripped the knife tightly, trembling. Plants bent backward, plants growing crooked, plants drooping as if starting to melt, plants bent over double, plants that were shiny or fuzzy or shooting tendrils straight into the air like so many jets of a fountain . . . all of them plunged Common into a dark sadness.

Just then, two men who had been spraying the plants with an atomizer went out, leaving only three people in the hothouse: the director, Common, and an assistant curled up in a far corner with a book. Slowly, keeping a wary eye on his surroundings, Common thrust forward the knife.

"Harpy, this is the end!"

With a look of wonder, the director plucked the knife easily from his grasp, lifted it, and said, "Hey, this is my knife! Oh, that's right, you ran off with it the other day."

Common must have been dead tired. He had never expected things to come to such a lame conclusion; taken by surprise, he lacked the strength to recover from his astonishment. He stood there dazed, with his hands still uplifted.

Oh Common, you were wrong, pal. You were not the only one to have those seizures; you didn't know it, but people everywhere are subject to that disease, enough to make a world! You can never destroy the Harpies that way. We can't protect the fire unless we all join together.

"Harpy, I lose."

"What do you mean, lose? And I'm no Harpy. No one wins or loses."

"I was going to kill you."

"Good heavens, no. Now, Mr. Dendrocacalia, now that things have come this far, why make such a fuss? Don't forget, today is a special day for all the plants. This is absolutely for your own good. And it's government protected!" He called to his assistant in the corner. "Hey, M—! Get things ready for Mr. Dendrocacalia, will you? Show him to his spot."

Common was led over to a corner where some of the steam pipes that crawled around the hothouse formed a sort of partition. The director and his assistant grabbed him on both sides and forced him into a large pot. Even if they hadn't acted with such force, by this time Common had lost all power to resist.

It was almost dawn. Still heavier drops formed on the windowpanes, dripping down like wax. Right behind Common loomed a nondescript tropical plant, and if he moved even a little there was a soft swish like that of a fan.

"All right, Mr. Dendrocacalia?"

Common nodded weakly.

He closed his eyes and quietly held out his arms in the direction of the unrisen sun.

Immediately Common disappeared, and in his place stood a poor-looking tree with chrysanthemum-like leaves.

The assistant, new on the job, thought, Huh! He's nothing special. Big deal.

But for some reason the director began to laugh, and couldn't stop. Try as he might to recover his dignity, his mirth seeped out from between his compressed lips. In the end he burst into loud guffaws. The assistant laughed too, not knowing what the joke was. As he laughed, the director wrote in elegant calligraphy on a card.

Dendrocacalia crepidifolia

And then he fastened the card securely to Common's trunk with a big thumbtack.

The Life of a Poet

*W*hir click clatter. *Whir click clatter.* From early morning until late at night, the thirty-nine-year-old crone went on pumping the shiny, oil-blackened spinning wheel, cutting back on her already scanty sleep and toiling like a machine in human guise. All so that twice a day she might fill her stomach-shaped oilpan with noodle-shaped oil, and keep the machinery inside her from ever stopping.

On and on and on she worked, until eventually, it came to her. She realized that the machine made of parched flesh and yellow bone was overflowing with the dust of her weariness. And she was seized with doubt.

"What have my innards got to do with me?" she wondered. "Why have I got to go on working this spinning wheel for their sake, when they're a mystery to me? If it's only to feed the weariness inside me, there's no point in going on, for Weariness, you've grown too large for me to hold." *Whir click clatter.* "Ah me, I'm as tired as if I'd turned to cotton."

Just as she was thinking this under the yellow, thirty-watt bulb in her tenement workroom, the crone ran out of fiber. She issued a command to the machinery inside her to stop. But strange to tell, the spinning wheel kept right on moving of its own accord, showing no sign of slowing.

Implacably, the wheel spun round and round, grasping with the last bit of thread for a loose fiber with which to continue its work. Realizing there was no such fiber to be found, the loose end stuck fast to the young crone's skin, winding around her fingers. And so from the fingertips on, her body, so limp and bone-weary it resembled nothing so much as a wad of cotton, began to elongate, unravel, and wind onto the wheel. Only after she was completely turned to thread, and the thread was wrapped entirely around the bobbin, did the machine finally slow to a stop with a light, moist *rattle rattle rattle*.

"First you fired fifty workers and made us do their work in addition to our own. Then, with those people gone—the ones who had the courage and the conviction to speak out against your injustice—you forced us to work even harder, and earned a profit of fifty million yen! We demand a raise!"

The son of the thirty-nine-year-old crone had been fired for distributing handbills printed with such inflammatory words. For the sake of his unfortunate comrades left behind, he had spent one entire day stenciling words of purest oxygen with which to rekindle the dying flames in the furnaces of their hearts, and another turning them out on the mimeograph machine. Then, exhausted, he had lain down and fallen fast asleep at his mother's feet, his bare midriff covered with old newspaper, as she pumped the foot-treadle of the spinning wheel with a *whir click clatter*.

With the final *rattle rattle rattle* he opened his eyes, just in time to see the tips of her toes slipping away, through her black, dirt-encrusted work clothes. He watched, horrified, as her toes stretched out longer and thinner, only to disappear through the narrow hole on the spinning wheel.

"Mother!" The old son of the young crone sat cross-legged with his arms around his knees and his fingers laced, tightening his grip until the nails turned purple. Whenever he encountered something too taxing for his mind to contemplate, or too overwhelming for his heart to feel, he unconsciously assumed this position. After a time, he cast aside the newspapers, laid his mother's empty clothes across his midriff, and stretched out again, succumbing to the wave of exhaustion that swept over him—an inescapable law of physical existence. When this man who owned nothing but his cast-off bonds once gave himself over to sleep, nothing could deter him.

The next morning brought the footsteps of the woman next door, who was as poor as he was. She had come to collect the thread that her neighbor had spun the night before. She used it to weave jackets in order to stimulate the metabolism of her family of five, which tended to grow sluggish on her husband's meager salary.

—Where's your mother, out? Now where could she have got off to so early in the morning? Oh no, just look at all this thread not rewound. What'll I do? I'm in a hurry, so I'll take it as is. But tell her I've got to add on a little service charge, will you?

The aged youth stifled a yawn, sat cross-legged, and laced his fingers over his knees again.

—I have a feeling it's not such a good idea for you to take that away.

—Oh, you do, do you? Well, that's all very fine. Tell me, have you invented a magic formula so we can fill our bellies on air? When you do that, don't look so mopy, will you?

—That's my trouble, ma'am, I don't know how I should look.

—Of course not. If you did, I'd give you the back of my hand! Oh, go on. What a boy you are to tease me like this, so early in the morning!

In three days, the crone was woven into a jacket.

The woman who had woven it went out on the street carrying it over her arm.

On the corner by the factory, she called out to a passer-by.

—Mister, how about a nice jacket? It's good and warm. You won't catch any colds with this on.

—Why, maybe you're right. It's even warm to the touch.

—Of course it is. This is one hundred percent wool, I'll have you know! Clipped from live sheep.

—It almost seems as if someone was wearing it until this moment.

—Nonsense. This is no second-hand item. I just finished weaving it myself.

—Are you sure something else isn't mixed in with it?

—Come closer and feel it again. The wool is from a live ewe.

—Maybe so. Hey, did you hear that funny noise? When I pinched it, it yelped. Is that because the wool is from a live ewe, too?

—Don't be silly. All you heard was the growling of your own belly. You must have eaten some rotten beans.

Inside the jacket, the young crone fought back her tears. Seeking to become the jacket completely, she thought with a brain of cloth and felt with a heart of cloth.

The crone's son came by.

—Ma'am, are you going to sell that jacket? I have a feeling it's not such a good idea.

—Oh, you do, do you? Well, I have a feeling you'd better not stick your nose in my business! That's all I need, to be teased by a pauper like you.

—Jackets are made to be sold, aren't they, he mused.

—And don't forget it. Anyone who thinks they're made to be worn has got another think coming. Say, mister, come take a look! This would look terrific on you. All the girls'll give you the eye. And you'll never catch cold.

But try as she would, she found no takers. It wasn't that the jacket was poorly made. The knitting needles she'd been using for the last thirty years were by now extensions of her fingers, and with them she had woven a sturdy, practical garment. Nor was it the season, for soon it would be winter.

The problem was simply that everyone was too poor.

The people who needed her jacket were too poor to buy it. Those who could afford it were members of the class that wore expensive, imported jackets. So the jacket ended up in a pawnbroker's storehouse, in exchange for thirty yen.

All the pawnshops were already full of jackets. And all of the houses in town were full of people who owned no jackets. Why didn't they complain? Had they forgotten that there even were such things as jackets?

Crushed by poverty like so many pickles at the bottom of life's barrel, the bags of skin surrounding their flesh had been drained of dreams, souls, and desires. Ownerless and unprotected, these dreams and souls and desires hung now in the air like invisible ether. They were what had needed jackets. Yes, that was it. The same poverty that kept people from buying jackets had robbed them of anything inside requiring the protection of one.

The sun stooped, shadows lengthened and paled, winter arrived. Traces of the escaped dreams, souls, and desires of the poor gathered in the sky as clouds, cutting off the sunlight and making the winter bitterly cold.

Trees shed their leaves, birds molted, and the air became as smooth and slippery as glass. People walked hunched over, ends of noses turned red, and words and coughs froze in the air like clouds of cigarette smoke, causing suspicious teachers to whip their students, and foremen their laborers, out of misplaced zeal. The poor feared the coming of night and mourned the coming of dawn. Men in foreign jackets spent all their time cleaning and polishing their hunting rifles, and women in foreign jackets pirouetted before their mirrors thirty times a day, adjusting expensive furs around their necks. Skiers melted wax for their skis, and skaters oiled grindstones to sharpen their skates. The last swallow flew away, and the first coal-seller stood on the streetcorner, rubbing his hands to keep warm.

All of this, along with the normal changes attendant on the coming of winter, chilled the cloud of dreams and souls and desires within and without until each dream, each soul, each desire froze and crystallized. And one day, they began falling to earth as snow.

In such orderly fashion did the snow fall, filling all crevices, that when you stared hard it seemed rather as if space itself was flowing heavenward. The snow soaked up all sounds of ordinary life in the streets. In the strange quiet, late at night, you could hear the soft jingle of snowflake brushing snowflake, like the chiming of tiny silver bells in a great, soundproofed room.

Naturally, this snow of crystalline dreams, souls, and desires was no ordinary snow. The crystals were wonderfully large, complex, and beautiful. Some had the frigid whiteness of fine, thin porcelain, and others the faint off-white glow of ivory shavings made with a microtome; still others bore the seductive gleam of thin, polished fragments of white coral. Some looked like an elaborate arrangement of thirty swords, others like seven varieties of plankton in layers, and still others like the most beautiful crystals of ordinary snow, seen through a kaleidoscope and magnified eightfold.

And this snow was colder than liquid air, for someone witnessed a flake of it fall into liquid air and vaporize with a puff of steam. It was also unusually hard. Those sword-shaped crystals could have shaved whiskers.

When automobiles passed over it, far from melting in accordance with the law of regelation, the snow jingled underneath and its sharp edges slashed the tires to ribbons. Nearly every substance known to science would either be cut to pieces before it could grind down one of those snowflakes, or freeze before it could melt one away.

What examples should one give to illustrate such coldness? In imitation of Verlaine, should one speak of the snow that fell on the brows of lovers sitting cheek-to-cheek in a wintry park—and left them hard and unmoving as a painted Dali sculpture? Or of the snow that fell on the brow of a man with a temperature of 106, as he lay groaning on his deathbed—freezing him midway between life and death, unable to stir in either direction? Or of the snow that fell on a beggar's oilcan stove as it burned feebly by a tumbledown wall, freezing the flames motionless as glasswork?

Hour after hour, day after day, night after night . . . on and on fell the snow, ceaseless as the conveyor belt in a Ford factory. Endlessly, softly it fell, with a jingle as of tin on wood floors, falling

on branches of roadside trees,
on mailboxes,
on empty swallows' nests,
on roofs,
on roads,
on sewers,

down manholes,

on streams,

on railway bridges,

on tunnel entrances,

on fields,

on birdhouses,

on charcoal burners' lodges,

and on the pawnshop storehouse where the jacket lay. . . .

And then fresh snow fell on the old, covering and softening the hard edges and turning the whole town into soft slopes and gentle curves until, in a matter of days or perhaps hours, as if the gears of a movie projector had suddenly ground to a halt, the entire town stopped cold. The axis of time disappeared from Minkowski's theory of space-time, and only space, as represented by a single plane, moved against the direction of the falling snow.

A worker carrying his lunch sack leaned partway out the door to gaze up at the sky, and froze that way. A ball thrown by children playing in an empty lot froze in midair, as if caught in an invisible spider's web. A pedestrian about to light a cigarette froze with his head tilted to one side, holding in his hand a match lit with a still, glasslike flame. A clump of smoke came crawling out of a large factory smokestack like a mischievous imp with a black cloth over its head, and froze motionless, like gelatin that had hardened in cold water. And—before it had a chance to hold fast in midair like the ball—a sparrow fell to earth, shattering like a light bulb into a thousand pieces.

The snow continued to fall.

The mercury column plunged lower and lower until there were no calibrations left, and the thermometer itself began to shrink.

From time to time, cracks raced across the surface of the

town, raising great swirls of snow as they went. But these, too, were soon buried under falling snow.

Even so, in the beginning a few families managed to keep from freezing. They were the families wearing imported jackets. The imported jackets themselves had no great warmth, mind you, but their owners, being wealthy, all had roofs impervious to snow, and blazing stoves. In time, however, even these people noticed the growing emptiness of their larders. Gathered around their hot, glowing stoves, family members began to keep sharp watch on the size of one another's portions at mealtimes. Fuel ran short and sofas gave way to wooden chairs, then orange crates; then people sat on the floor, and then one by one the floorboards were carefully ripped out. Electric lights gave way to oil lamps, then to candles, and finally to darkness. The ladies who had worn sleek furs shriveled into dried-out foxes, and the gentlemen who had polished their hunting rifles while thinking of their bank stocks turned into hairless, rheumatic dogs. Their college-aged sons, once absorbed in detective stories, armed themselves with pistols and raided their mothers' hoards of canned goods stored carefully away in bedrooms.

From out of the darkened windows, in place of dignified voices scolding the maid, or the gentle, refined laughter of victorious gamblers, there began to issue curses, screams, the thud of heavy objects falling, sounds of ripping cloth, and loud, heartbreaking moans.

Heads of families consulted hysterically with one another over independently-powered, cordless telephones, and finally decided to appeal for foreign aid. This was the response to their inquiry over the wireless:

—Buy another five thousand jackets. New design. Ideological tiger-crest, mottled black and white. Or would you prefer fifty or so atom bombs?

It became apparent to them all that the only solution was to get the poor in motion again, get the factories operating again, and start a war.

One resourceful fellow made a bundle of sticks, fastened bent wire on the end, stuck it out through a crack in the window, and tried to hook one of the frozen pedestrians outside. For an instant, all the families in imported jackets stopped fighting and held their breaths, glued to their binoculars and cordless telephones. But the pedestrian only crumbled silently to pieces.

Then came the final, self-destructive burst of hysteria. People were undone, like toys with broken springs. Despairing, they sought the quickest route to becoming meaningless matter. Open a window, stick an arm out into the snow, and freeze yourself—this, it seemed, was the last remaining option of a rational being.

Strangely enough, just when it seemed that every imaginable creature was frozen solid, there was still one mouse whose life went on as before. She lived in the storehouse of the pawnshop where the crone's jacket was stored. She was looking for material to make a warm nest for her five babies, soon to be born.

Unlike humans, the mouse knew nothing of poverty that could bar the fulfillment of one's deepest desires; when she found the wonderful jacket, she didn't hesitate a moment. Taking it in her mouth, she gnawed off a piece. All at once, blood flowed from the severed place. The mouse's teeth had sunk in just over the crone's cloth heart. Uncomprehending, the mouse fled back to her nest in astonishment, and promptly miscarried.

The crone's blood spilled out quietly and spread into every corner of the jacket, staining it bright red.

The snow suddenly stopped. It is likely that the limits of cold had been reached, freezing the very falling of the snow and so making further precipitation impossible.

Then the red jacket, still glossy with blood, rose lightly into the air as if it had been donned by some invisible creature, and glided outside. Through the unmoving snow-space, where day was indistinguishable from night, it glided and swam.

Before long the crone-jacket located a young man in the snow. It was her son, frozen by the factory gate with a wad of handbills stuffed under one arm, caught in the act of handing one to a worker, who stood frozen with a hand outstretched to receive it.

The jacket stopped in front of the youth and wrapped itself around his aged body. He blinked. Then he moved his head gingerly from side to side, and shook his body little by little. He looked around in wonder, then down at his red jacket. All at once it came to him that he was a poet, and he nodded, smiling.

He gathered the melodious snow in his hands and gazed at it. Now he could touch it without freezing. Had it become even colder than the snow, then, that gleam in his eye? He scooped up snow like sand at the seashore and poured it from palm to palm, without injury. Had it become harder than steel, then, the skin of his hands? He was confused. He had to remember. How had this transformation come about?

Frowning, he tried hard to focus his thoughts. Yes, there was something that he must remember. Something that every pauper knew, if memory were not suspended, frozen. Where had this snow fallen from?

Even if he didn't know the answer, perhaps he could feel it. Look at these crystals of snow, he told himself, so marvelously large, complex, and beautiful. What are they if not the forgotten words of the poor? Words of their dreams . . . souls . . . desires. Hexagonal, octagonal, duodecadonal, flowers lovelier than flowers, the very structure of matter . . . the molecular arrangements of souls of the poor.

The words of the poor are not only large, intricate, and beautiful, but succinct as mineral, and rational as geometry. It stands to reason that none but souls of the poor can become crystalline.

The youth in the red jacket listened to the snow-words with his eyes. He decided to write them down on the backs of the handbills under his arm.

He grabbed a handful of snow and threw it in the air. It flew up with a jingle jingle, but when it fell back down the sound changed to "jacket, jacket." The youth laughed. His happiness escaped through his barely parted lips as a quiet, cheerful melody, and disappeared into the distant sky. As if in answer, the snow all around him began to hum "jacket, jacket."

After that he began a precise, detailed investigation of each separate crystal. He wrote everything down, decided on his notation, compiled and analyzed statistics, made graphs, and listened again, even more carefully. He could hear it—the words of the snow, the voices of the dreams, souls, and desires of the poor. With tireless, amazing energy, he went on working.

Gradually, the snow started to melt. Having finished speaking to him, evidently it had no further reason to exist. In the order that they finished speaking, those crystals of snow so cold they had frozen flames now melted away without a trace, like the snows of early spring that vanish the moment they light on the black, moist earth.

In fact, it was almost spring. With every word that he wrote in his notebooks, as if the pages were calendar leaves, spring crept ever closer.

One day, through a crack in the clouds, the sun thrust out a ray of light like the arm of a mischievous little girl. And then, as if groping for a golden ring let fall by mistake into the bottom of a water pitcher filled with old, foaming brew, slowly it shook the town from its slumber.

One could sense creatures stirring. A man came reeling forward, half-paralyzed, saw the young man and laughed, holding out a hand in greeting. Touching the arm of the youth, he muttered "Jacket," and ran away. Before long the youth was surrounded by a large group of people, new ones joining all the time; "Jacket," each one would whisper, laying a hand on his arm, and then go off, smiling. These people spread throughout the town.

All around, the unattended storehouses were opened, and countless jackets were carted off. "Jacket!" The joyful, powerful paean was sung out ringingly to all the messengers of spring: to the heavy, moist black earth; to the babbling stream, tumbling and racing along like a three-year-old just learning to run; and to the pale green jewels poking out from between the lingering islands of snow. Though it was spring, there was still a chill in the air, so how beautiful, how wonderful it was to see those poor people clothing themselves in jackets!

The last flake of snow gone, the youth's work was done. The factory whistle sounded, and all around him, crowds of people wearing jackets set off to work, smiling. Returning their greetings, he closed the last page of his poetry collection, now complete.

And vanished into that page.

Record of a Transformation

On August 14, I came down with cholera, and my unit left me behind in a barn. Toward evening, another unit came along from the north, likewise in full retreat. I crawled out of the barn and waved, but no one stopped or looked my way.

I lay down on the gentle, stone-strewn slope, looking up at the too-wide sky. Heavy, leaden clouds edged along the bottom in bright red leaned precariously over, threatening to topple down on me at any moment. Closing my eyes, I heard the distant rustle of wind eddies scraping along the ground and colliding. From the south, sand rose up in the air. Suddenly my throat burned, and the thought of water made my senses reel. But my canteen was dry.

From the waist down I was soaking wet from chronic diarrhea, yet from the waist up I was drier than stale bread. Consumed by thirst, I put a sour pickled plum on my tongue and greedily swallowed the trickle of saliva it drew forth. I clawed the ground in the desperate hope of at least breathing in the smell of moist earth, but beneath the sand was a layer of clay as hard as tile.

I decided to go down the slope, lie in the middle of the road, and wait for water to come along. The ground was burning hot. I tried not to breathe, afraid I might dry up and blow away. Before long a truck approached from the north at full speed, a machine gun mounted in front. It pulled up just short of where I lay and was consumed briefly in a cloud of dust. When the dust settled and the truck reappeared, the driver waved an arm out the window and yelled, "Move! Or I'll run you over!"

Prostrate, I scraped my head on the ground, able to say only one word: "Water . . . water . . . water."

The truck was carrying officers. They all rose at once and looked at me suspiciously.

Again I said, "Water . . . water . . . water," scraping my head on the ground.

A small, swarthy second lieutenant jumped down and threw me a cider bottle. I missed it and the water spilled out. A dark stain spread across the ground. I grabbed the bottle and bit at its mouth. Something broke, either the glass or a tooth, with a grinding noise. The water had a heaviness like that of mercury. My entire body became a throat.

As I was thus absorbed, suddenly before my vacant eyes there appeared the muzzle of a pistol. For an instant I had the illusion that I was peering up a water faucet. Before I could grasp what was happening, my nose seemed to tear off in the direction of the back of my head, and a lump of steel shot through me. And then I died.

I regarded my corpse from a short distance. In the past twelve hours my body had become a mass of wrinkles, a dried-out and withered-up carcass, like a wooden carving of a wizard. Perhaps for that reason, only a small amount of blood was trickling from the gunshot wound. It looked as if I'd grown a third eye beneath the other two.

Full of tenderness for my own body, I grew sad. I had been killed by the second lieutenant. He now gave my body a kick to clear the road.

"Don't touch him, you'll get cholera!" someone shouted.

He returned quickly to the truck. I followed him, crawled up, and took an empty seat. Naturally, no one noticed me.

The truck rolled over my body, crushing it, and went on, leaving my left arm torn half off and my left leg standing up backward, broken, like a signpost marking the boundary between past and future. The past receded swiftly, growing steadily smaller until it disappeared and was swallowed by a rise in the ground. Yet it lingered on, in me. Watching the incessant eddies of sand swirling up from beneath the wheels of the truck, I knew that the memory of that erect leg, a signpost in the middle of nowhere, would follow me wherever I went. I suffered, swept by a yearning to jump off the truck, run back, and embrace my leg.

There were four officers in all: one lieutenant general, one lieutenant colonel, and two second lieutenants, the smaller of whom was my killer. In the front seat sat the driver and a non-commissioned officer. It was a small truck, but with only four riders there was plenty of room. The remaining space was crammed with luggage. Crates of rations, ammunition, and gasoline were lined up neatly. As on any moving day, odds and ends had been thrown in pell-mell: a heater, folding chairs, a photograph of the emperor, slippers, a tent, a teakettle, a large water-filled drum that could double as bathtub, a large bottle of saké . . . oh, and yes, a small bronze statue of Emperor Jimmu. There was also a hot-water bottle.

"Not a damn thing we can do about it," one of the second lieutenants was saying. He sat next to the colonel and wore glasses; his arms and legs were so long as to seem out of joint.

The colonel looked up questioningly, studied the other's face a moment, then nodded without interest and resumed his scrutiny of a map. The map had red and blue markings. One broad red line running north to south divided it vertically in half. He took out another map and lined it up with the bottom edge of the first, and the red line continued due south.

The general, who'd been leaning back against the heater applying moxibustion to his shins, now leaned forward and asked, "What were you two discussing?"

A drop of sweat fell from the colonel's white eyebrow onto the map. He wiped it away with a finger and glanced up as he answered expressionlessly, "Nothing, sir."

"Oh, yes, you were," replied the general suspiciously, his big Adam's apple bobbing up and down just below his face, the skin of which was covered with a web of fine wrinkles. The colonel returned the general's gaze wonderingly. His face, which resembled that of a plucked bird, shook with the vibrations of the truck. The general's Adam's apple fell still, and his dry, powdery cheeks reddened.

"Oh, that," the colonel said, smiling faintly as if he had just remembered. He turned to the second lieutenant beside him. "Lt. Minami," he said, "you just made some remark or other, didn't you? The general wants to know what it was about."

Minami, deep in thought, jerked upright and answered quickly, "It was about cholera, sir."

"Cholera?" Suddenly the colonel's eyelids narrowed to slits. "What do you mean, 'cholera,' Lt. Minami? You were thinking of the soldier, weren't you? You're forgetting, Lieutenant, that on the battlefield a soldier isn't a man, he's a trigger finger. And that soldier back there wasn't even a soldier any more. A soldier with cholera is only cholera masquerading as a soldier. He killed the cholera, Lieutenant, for the soldier's own sake."

"I was just afraid cholera might get on the tires, sir."

"No, you were thinking about the soldier. But the value of a soldier isn't in his life. As long as our Imperial Army survives, every soldier lives, even if dead. We must fight to survive, for all of their sakes."

"Sir, I—"

"Yes, you're right, cholera may have gotten aboard this truck, just as you fear. If that happened, what would you do?"

"Shoot to kill, sir."

"Good." The colonel patted the maps with a hairy hand and glanced sideways at the dark, parted lips of the general, who'd been listening intently to this exchange. Then he buried his head again in the map. But the sunlight had taken on a purplish cast, making fine lines difficult to see. The colonel picked up the map and held it up to the last bit of sunlight glowing red along the horizon. The map flapped noisily in the wind, like a captive bird struggling to escape.

Suddenly the truck jerked to a stop, and the noncommissioned officer turned around and rapped on the window. The colonel picked up his voice tube and put it to his ear. The NCO said, "The rear of the unit is in sight, sir."

"Good," said the colonel. He climbed up on top of the truck, binoculars to his eyes. Simultaneously, the small second lieutenant who'd shot me stood up and rested his hand on the machine gun. The colonel wheeled around, checking the horizon on all sides, and issued a command into the voice tube without lowering his binoculars. "Wait here for orders to start." Then he added, "Take ten minutes to eat."

Minami passed rations for two through the window to the

NCO in the front seat, who gave half to the driver. No one in the back of the truck made any movement toward their own food. Only the general, after adjusting his dentures with his fingers, opened a can of jam.

"At this rate, when do you think the unit will pass Y— Junction?" the colonel asked Lt. Minami.

Minami took the map, set it on his lap, and looked at it with a flashlight, glancing from it to the sinuous gray horizon. "I think it's about half a mile from here. The front of the unit is probably there already. There's an old willow tree there that was struck by lightning, and a small dirty pond. After that it's open terrain again until the next town."

When the general shoved the can opener in, red jam burst out with an audible pop. Trying to press it back in with his fingers, he said uneasily, "And will we make it there by eight o'clock?"

"Don't worry, sir." The colonel swung his head around as he said this and stared at Minami's hands, whispering something into his ear in a voice so low that not even I, sitting directly behind them, could hear.

"What's that? What are you talking about?" the general asked, leaning forward hastily. The colonel smiled faintly, the corners of his thin lips twitching. Minami stiffened as if to deny his own existence and buried his face in the map. Two drops of sweat fell in succession from his bared elbow.

The general swiftly stuck his jam-covered fingers in his mouth, his Adam's apple bobbing as he fixed dusty eyes on the region of the colonel's chin. The chin was cleft and red, as if chafed. The colonel rubbed his jaw on the collar of his shirt, stood up, and glanced up at the profile of the smaller second lieutenant, who was staring straight ahead, his hand still on the machine gun. The second lieutenant's head inclined suspiciously and his lips trembled. Turning around, his eyes met those of the colonel and he exclaimed sharply, with a voice that could have split firewood, "Look, sir! The unit's halted!"

The colonel snapped the binoculars to his eyes. Consternation showed plainly in the shaking of his elbows. "They're on to us." Lower lip thrust out, he removed one eye from the binoculars and stared for a while at Minami's frightened face. Then, closing his eyes, he sighed, his shoulders slumping, and slowly asked, "Lt. Minami, can you guide us beyond the railway bridge over K— River, without using the highway?"

Minami stole a look at the general, who had grabbed the hem of the colonel's shirt and was shaking his head wildly, as if unable to believe his ears.

"Lt. Minami," continued the colonel, "according to our intelligence, the Red Army will reach that bridge no later than ten o'clock tomorrow morning. We have to get there first, before dawn if possible."

"Why?" asked the general, clutching at the colonel. "The last military train passes the town of P— at eight o'clock. So tell me why we've got to go to K— River!"

"Don't worry, sir."

"Then are we leaving right away?" asked Minami.

"Yes . . . let's." The colonel looked up at the darkened sky, stretched his fingers, and stamped his feet. Above the grayness of the sky floated wispy leaden clouds. Off in the distance echoed the soft moan of the steppe.

"I don't know if I can do it, sir," Minami blurted out. "The steppe is like the sea—awfully easy to get lost in. And tonight there are no stars. Anyone would get lost tonight if they left the highway, even a native."

"Even so, we have to go. Lt. Minami, our mission doesn't permit us to get lost."

"I don't know anything about a mission."

"You want to know? Then listen. Our mission is to cross into the mountains, hole up there, and fight to the last. Ten thousand soldiers hand-picked from every unit will rendezvous there. Even if the mainland falls, we are to go on fighting; the Empire is always with us, wherever our feet tread the earth! His Highness Omotoshi is also heading there, in an airplane. This truck is carrying a war chest, and it's our job to make sure that it gets to the mountains safely. All right, Lieutenant, now you know the mission. Will you lead the way?"

"Why can't we take the road, sir?"

"They"—this with a nod at the road ahead—"have found us out. That's why they stopped at the junction. They're after our war chest."

"Everyone thinks the war is over, sir."

"That's why I said we've got to kill the cholera."

"Sir, we do have to stamp out the cholera. But that's to save soldiers' lives."

"You meant to say human lives, didn't you? That's a coward's way of thinking. Cholera grows where there are people. To eradicate cholera, you eradicate people."

"We're going to P—, Colonel Tsumura, P—!" bawled the general, rapping on the heel of the colonel's shoe with the scabbard of his sword.

"Don't worry, sir."

"I do worry. How can I help worrying when I listen to you? I've got to go back home. I've my goldfish to tend to."

"Let's get going."

"Sir, I cannot be your guide," Minami said flatly. "All I know is that from here you have to head south-southeast. If all goes well, you should be at the edge of K— River by morning. I'll get off here, find the unit, and travel with them."

"Lt. Minami, get back here!"

The colonel called after him, but Minami was already halfway out of the truck. A shot rang out. The smaller second lieutenant stood with smoking pistol in hand, his eyes downturned like those of a mischievous urchin after a scolding. Minami collapsed forward, his body quietly folding in on itself, blood staining his neck red as he fell.

But Minami's soul was frozen in the act of dismounting from the truck, one leg on the runner and the other extended to the ground, both hands gripping the edge of the vehicle. He looked around wonderingly, caught sight of me, and made a startled gesture, as if about to speak; then he jumped off the truck, knelt protectively over his body, and burst into sobs.

"What the . . . of all the colossal . . . ," the general said in a frail, trembling voice. He squeezed the can hard, oblivious to the fact that his fingers were being driven deeply into the jam.

"Please don't worry yourself, sir," said the colonel impatiently, without turning around, and issued a series of commands into his voice tube. "Let's go! Off the road. Head south-southeast at 60 miles an hour."

"What about P——!" screamed the general. No one answered. The engine started.

"General!" shouted the second lieutenant in a fierce voice. He leaped on the general and pinned his arm, which was stretched out, trembling, toward the case of hand grenades beside him. The colonel stood in front of the general, looked down on him coldly, and pushed a crate of candy over between the general and the crate of grenades. The truck jolted and swayed.

"Sir, we're leaving," I called to Minami. He looked up at me with tear-filled eyes, hesitating, but when I held out a hand to him he grabbed it and climbed aboard.

The truck zoomed forward, plunging into the steppe. Thousands of grassy leaves and stalks stroked the belly and flanks of the truck, and in that noisy silence, like a ringing in the ears, all other sounds vanished.

Minami stood in the back of the track, watching his body recede into the distance. It was dark now, so the body quickly turned into a fuzzy black spot, and finally was lost behind the waves of grass. He buried his face in his arms and murmured a brokenhearted farewell.

The truck lurched violently up and down and side to side. An hour of this and the luggage would be entirely reorganized, or lost overboard, I couldn't help thinking. The truck sometimes leaped a foot or more in the air. Every time that happened, something broke or fell out.

The general had curled up tightly in blankets, clutching the emperor's photograph. Next to him the colonel was letting whiskey fall on his tongue, drop by drop.

The second lieutenant was cleaning his pistol in the last remaining light, but before long he fell asleep, seated as he was, his head bumping against a projection on the partition separating the cab section from the rear of the truck, hard enough to stain his ear blood-red.

Minami sat with his face buried in his arms, motionless as a stone.

"Sir, would you like something to eat?" I called to him, and he looked up, surprised.

"Can we?" he asked doubtfully.

"I don't know," I admitted, and sat down beside him, thinking the idea a little strange myself. I hadn't suggested it out of any particular conviction, or really given it any thought; I'd just said the first thing that came into my head, trying to restore a little sense of everyday normality. "I sort of feel hungry, like I could

eat, but it's only a feeling, and it probably wouldn't work out. Still, we could always pretend, sir."

"You can drop the sir," he said irritably, lowering his eyes. "Who needs to imitate the living?"

"Well, okay." I began to feel a strange, frightening sensation. "I'm glad to hear you say that. Shall we call each other by name, then? My name's K——. I guess rank doesn't mean much now, does it?"

He snorted. After a moment he said slowly, "But you know, I do feel like pretending I'm alive."

"You want me to go back to calling you sir?"

"Would you just shut up?" He shook his shoulders angrily, and buried his face in his arms again.

The truck zoomed ahead at breakneck speed, vibrating so violently that it seemed in danger of falling apart. It wasn't so much running as it was being knocked around with terrible force on all sides. The colonel sucked on his whiskey bottle, rasping his teeth, and searched the black sky for stars. The general, sandwiched between the stove and the crate of candy, let out an exaggerated moan every time the truck shook. The second lieutenant slept on heedlessly, bumping against the projection and now and then punctuating his dream with something that sounded like a chicken squawk.

Suddenly I thought of myself. What was I going to do? Now that I was dead, I didn't have to do anything, if I didn't want to. If I felt like sitting and doing nothing, I could do it for as long as I wanted. No one could say otherwise. How about that. Not bad. Get up any old time I felt like it. Lie in bed snug as could be and have myself a smoke. Assuming, that is, that smoking was still possible. Anything that was possible to do, I could do—including doing nothing at all, if I felt like it.

Minami cut me off harshly. "Cut the crap."

Had I been thinking aloud? Oops. I hadn't even noticed. But then I got mad.

"What if it is crap?" I said. "Right now I don't want to think about anything that isn't crap. Nothing hurts more than dwelling on things you have no control over. You know that? All my life, I suffered on account of that. But if I hated them now, the only one to suffer would be me, not them. It would be different if I were alive. And you know, Minami, you would be one of them, too."

He groaned. "My heart feels ready to burst."

"Don't be melodramatic. How is the heart of a dead man going to burst?"

"I *want* to exaggerate. Why shouldn't I? Tell me that. It's no worse than that crap of yours."

Again he burst into tears. It was all I could do to suppress great spasms of sadness. I had never imagined that it would be like this. Had I known, I might have lived differently. I didn't intend to try to console him. If he stopped weeping, I was afraid I'd start. I had tried to be cynical, but the effort was doomed, like trying to build a tower of blocks to the sky.

Then I made a strange discovery.

"Minami, look!"

He stopped crying, raised his face a little, and glanced up at me.

"See there? I'm shaking with the vibrations of the truck! Just as if I had a body!"

"Fathead," he said derisively. "Didn't you notice? Look at me. I'm shaking, too. But only because I'm imagining it. The proof is that my movements don't match the vibrations of the truck at all. That's partly what I meant about imitating life. Actually I want to imitate it too, but the truck's vibrations are too irregular and unpredictable. I realized this the moment you held out your hand to me before. I only pretended to grab it, you know. And just because I thought I could pretend to grab your hand, I went off and abandoned my own body."

Again he began to sob. I was overcome with a wave of remorse so intense that I could have bitten off my lips. He was right. I too was only imagining that the truck was shaking me. Once I realized this, I could think of nothing but vibrations—just as before I died, I could think of nothing but water. Desperately, I tried to match the vibrations of the truck.

Unable to bear it any longer, I buried my face in my hands and began to cry. I knew that stopping wouldn't be easy. Probably dead people never wore themselves out crying. They probably never wore themselves out, whatever they did. But there was a certain comfort in the feeling that nothing worse could happen while I was crying. Someone once said that the more civilized a man is, the more he laughs, and the more primitive he is, the more he weeps. But never mind.

Some three hours had gone by since we left the road. Suddenly the brakes squealed and we came to an abrupt, crunching stop. The steppe broke off, and directly in front of us the gate of a small Chinese village was lit up in the red glare of anti-airraid lights. An old woman stood before it with arms outstretched, barring the way. She turned toward the village and began shouting a warning.

"Fire!" growled the colonel at the second lieutenant. Into the voice tube he said sharply, "Pay no mind. Run her down!"

Split by machine-gun fire, the smooth blackness of the night air emitted a scream. The old woman stumbled a few steps toward us, clawing the air, then fell forward and lay still, face down. The truck rolled right on, crushing her arms. But off to one side, the soul of the old woman pointed scrawny arms straight at us, fixing us with an angry, accusing look.

The truck charged straight into the village, which sat like a lump of clay, soundless and inert. It seemed as if the only possible inhabitants could be clay dolls. But I was wrong. Catching sight of a clay wall and thatched roofs, I looked up and shuddered as if every pore in my body had expanded to the size of the eye of a needle.

Dozens of dead, young and old, were staring down at us. At virtually the same moment, they all began to shout vitriolic curses at the truck. They stamped their feet and shook their fists, and some even tried to grab things and throw them. But, of course, nothing came flying through the air.

It was all over in a moment. Once we were through the village, a road opened up; we crossed it and were soon floating again on the steppe.

I sank into thought. The emotions I felt were new. What to call them, I had no idea. I grew melancholy at the thought that some things were still unnameable.

Suddenly Minami began to laugh. It was not a pleasant laugh, but one that made me feel like grinding my teeth. Stop, stop . . . it's ghastly. . . .

"You can say that again," he said. "A ghastly mistake." Teeth chattering, Minami grabbed my arm and went on in a shrill voice, "Where do you think this truck is going? I've been doing some calculations. This driver is drifting one degree to the right every minute. In three hours, that makes 180° . . . so that village we just went by is the little village by the highway, not half a mile from P—. In six hours, 360°, we'll be back where my body is. After nine hours, at daybreak, we'll hit that village again, and they'll finally figure out what's happened, but by then it'll be too late. The Red Army will have occupied P—. Might as well issue an invitation, Here, give me a bellyful of bullets! For cryin' out loud."

Directly overhead, the clouds seemed to part as a fire tore through them, illuminating the truck for a brief instant in a burst of white light. Then there was a great noise, as if a locomotive had run into a mountain of gravel at full throttle. The general leaped up, startled, and landed on his back in front of me. The kettle fell on top of him and shattered the glass over the photograph of the emperor that he clutched to his chest. He might have been hurt, because he lay there motionless, not even groaning.

"Looks like the general dropped his dentures," Minami said sarcastically. I looked in the direction he indicated with his finger and could indeed see the dentures, broken in two and looking somehow rotten, with one half trapped under the drum. "Even if I could, I'd be damned if I'd tell him where they were."

Something struck me odd. "Minami, how come we can see so clearly? Shouldn't everything be pitch dark?" The words were barely out of my mouth before we were wrapped in blackness, unable to see a thing.

"Ah!" Minami let out a faint cry. "We'd forgotten. I guess we should've gone on forgetting, too. You remember that night is dark and just like that, everything turns dark."

"You're right. Every time we remember something, we pay for it."

"You can't see, either?"

"Not a thing. I can hardly even tell where I'm sitting. But I don't really mind. Don't you think it was stranger being able to see?"

"Let's just drop it," said Minami uneasily. After a moment he added irritably, in a hoarse voice, "The reason we can't stop imitating our bodies is not that we love them so much, but that we're trying to forget them."

"But whatever we do to try to forget only calls up new memories."

"Yeah, like the heat of an August night."

"Mosquitoes."

"Thirst."

"I feel like a smoke."

"Not only that, it's high time we were getting sleepy."

"There's something even more important we ought to be thinking about. Revenge."

The word overwhelmed us and set off a new round of tears. In my mind's eye I turned cautiously and looked backward. I saw my broken leg, jutting straight up and . . . damn, sand flies boring holes in it, and now flies would be sure to lay their eggs inside . . . my dead leg, swollen twice its size with maggots, like a waxwork . . . beautiful, oh how beautiful it had been . . . and then, swept by unbearable jealousy of my former self, I wailed even louder than before. Nothing fleshly could ever weep like this, I knew . . . and I didn't care.

We stopped once to fill the gas tank. The driver took five benzedrines and a swig of whiskey. And then we moved on, at a steady speed of about twenty-five miles per hour, across the dark steppe. We were each a jumble of excitement and exhaustion, wakefulness and sleep, unable to utter a word. The officers were dark shapes, and so was the sky. But morning came steadily nearer. And the truck moved steadily around the perimeter of a circle 155 miles in diameter.

Morning came just as the truck had finished one and a half laps. The night was slow to leave, but morning's arrival was swift. When sky and earth parted, night was sucked quietly into the roots of the steppe, while morning flew up with a flock of hundreds of crows, covering the sky in a moment. Above the red, rippling surface of the steppe there flowed a white mist.

"This is it!" Minami stood up, looking at me with laughter in his eyes. At the same moment the truck emitted a stifled screech as it hurtled out of the steppe. Before us stood the gate of the village. Behind us the steppe was still moaning with the voice of night.

Beside the dry, white gate of clay, a spattering of black bloodstains remained, but the old woman's body had been removed. In its place, five armed youths in T-shirts stood close together. Behind them, the souls of hundreds of dead, including the old woman, glared at us. It was easy to tell they were dead because of the way they swayed back and forth without moving their feet.

Before the youths could scatter or take any sort of action, the second lieutenant's machine gun opened fire, and the colonel yelled into the voice tube. "Idiot! Have you gone out of your mind?" There was doubtless much more he wanted to say, but unable to articulate it he simply groaned, saliva running from the corner of his mouth. His brows were knotted into hard lumps, and every vein in his face was swollen in anger. His eyes popped out, making him look more and more like a bird. But he didn't wait for a reply. "Hurry! Back up! Run for it!" he shouted.

With the last words, the colonel's face drained of color. He hurriedly set the box of grenades down next to the machine gun and hurled two of them into the village, one after another. The truck veered widely to the right, shuddered, and plunged back into the steppe. By the time bullets began to land with accuracy on the flank of the truck, the engine was smoking with an all-out effort.

But we did not make a clean getaway. The next thing we knew, a dumpy, black little airplane was circling slowly overhead, watching. The colonel grabbed the machine gun and fired at it. But the airplane paid no attention.

Suddenly the general tore the voice tube out of the colonel's hand and shouted, "Cease fire!"

The colonel put a hand over the tube, saying derisively, "Please don't alarm yourself, General."

The truck stopped. "Out of the way!" said the general. He was clutching a hand grenade.

The second lieutenant called "General!" in a hoarse voice. The colonel made way for his commander, stepping back without expression.

Trembling, the general put his foot on the runner, looked back, and said in a voice of considerable dignity, "You see, I must get back to the mainland and see to my goldfish!"

He crawled clumsily down, adjusted the belt on his pants, and after ascertaining where his sword was, set off wordlessly in the direction of the village. The colonel turned to the second lieutenant, muttered, "Salute!" and, after waiting for him to touch his fingers to his cap, pulled the trigger on the machine gun. At first his aim was off and clouds of smoke rose up around the general's feet. Jumping about in a droll way, the general cried out sadly. And then he spun around on his heels and collapsed, face up.

The face of the second lieutenant was stiff with terror and he stared at the colonel with tears in his eyes. The colonel averted his eyes and spoke into the voice tube, ordering the driver to move on. The engine roared.

Minami whispered to me, "Let's go. This truck is as good as captured. It's been taken by the steppe."

We jumped down from the moving truck. The doomed truck drove off, leaving behind only an amber track in the deep grass. Listening carefully, we could hear the roar of the airplane, rolling with the wind. The sky was startlingly blue.

We dead can walk anywhere with equal ease. Only love for our lost selves makes us go to the trouble of pretending to struggle through tall grass. It wasn't hard to find the general. All we had to do was follow the tire tracks. The general, or rather the general's soul, was lying next to his body, staring vacantly at the sky. "Well, General, we meet again," Minami called out to him, and the general started and leaped to his feet.

"We were there the whole time," I said, and the general's temples twitched with displeasure. But I was not to be deterred. "And we'll stay with you now, too. Lt. Minami is familiar with the local terrain, which is a big help."

"Oh, it doesn't take much," Minami said. "After all, P— is less than a mile down the road."

"That's what strikes me as so funny," I said. "Damn, this grass has sharp spikes, doesn't it. Say, Minami, do you have any idea what this stuff is called?"

"Sorry, I'm a city boy. Ask the general. He probably knows."

"That's right, what with him being such a nature lover, and all—you know, goldfish and that."

The general grabbed the hilt of his sword and shouted, "You bastards!"

We had been laughing loudly, in a rollicking mood. We were showing off our greater experience as dead men, trying to sound witty and superior. We waited expectantly for the general to burst into tears. But he did no such thing. Far from crying, he turned on his heel and marched confidently off in the opposite direction. Pushing aside the waves of grasses with his scabbard, he marched on in masterful simulation of his former stride and speed—a feat I could not hope to match. Minami and I looked at each other in dismay. This was impossible. Unbelievable. It was as if in death the man knew everything. We were the ones who felt like crying now. All we could do was follow humbly along behind him, hoping for a reconciliation. We called out to him in turn, but he never glanced back.

But soon, the secret was explained. We were back on the road, in sight of the water tank that supplied P—. On top of the tank we could see a red flag fluttering. The general looked up at it and shuddered. Ah yes . . . we were filled with admiration. Naturally he was doing this for our benefit, but it was not the sort of performance you could easily see through. What an extraordinary man. Disgusted by our own childishness, we couldn't help nodding to one another, on the verge of tears. Then it happened. The general ran over to the side of the road and threw himself down on the ground. For the record, there was no sign of anyone around. Not even anyone dead.

Puzzled, we followed quickly, and it was then, while we were approaching, that it happened. There was a dark lump. At first it looked like a large tree root, but then we saw that it was really a human figure lying on the ground. The general pounced on it. He was drawn inside it and seemed to disappear.

By the time we got there, the general was gone. There was only the body of a dying Japanese child, evidently an abandoned waif, and alongside the body, its soul. But the child wasn't dead. The general's soul had apparently entered the waif's body, displacing the original soul.

The general staggered to his feet and scowled at the waif's soul in contempt. With evident joy he clapped his new hands, stroked his new face, and stuck his fingers into his new nostrils; then, after leering in our general direction, he set off briskly down the road.

Hastily the displaced soul took off in pursuit. "Hey, mister, wait, you can't do that! That's not fair, come on, mister. . . ." And so, weeping and pleading, he followed after the general. Of course, it was of no use. The general could neither see nor hear his pursuer.

Minami and I walked along with the waif between us, listening to his story and trying to comfort him. He had fled with his family from a settlement, and at P— his parents had succumbed to cholera. The boy had been starving, so he decided to leave the town and go out in the country, but things were worse there and he headed back for town without finding any food. Before he could reach town he had lain down and lost consciousness.

Minami and I talked it over and we came to the conclusion that the general was no doubt a repeat offender. In other words, before becoming a general, he'd been some other dead person. He knew too much. He even knew how to steal a body. Why, it was amazing! We became thoroughly excited, moved no longer by sympathy for the boy but by self-interest. The three of us would follow behind him to the end, observing, and ferret out his secret. Even if we failed to do that, we decided to keep our eyes on him till the day he died. Because there was no doubt that one day he would die and rejoin the ranks of the dead.

And so it happened that Minami, the waif, and I set out with the fake general in the waif's body, on a most strange journey.

Intruders

*J*ust as I was drifting off to sleep, I was awakened by a mass of soft, padding footsteps. A crowd of people were apparently trying to tiptoe down the hall without disturbing anyone, but doing it so clumsily that the effect was peculiarly grating. I pulled the covers over my head and rolled over.

With a rustle like that of a centipede, the footsteps mounted the stairs and passed by the lavatory, heading my way. Damn, I thought, that thieving insurance agent must have dragged home a bunch of his cronies—pickpockets and bums, every one. But the footsteps kept straight on; now they were in front of Room 8. Oh, crap, I thought, what did that bowlegged whore go and do, take on five customers at once? But the footsteps went past her room as well. All right, then, it's number 9. Now what—that zombie cab driver gets done in by car thieves?

But the footsteps went on by Room 9. Unless they were going to plunge straight into the wall at the end of the hall, they could only be heading for the last room, Room 10—mine. The moment I realized this, I sprang up like a mousetrap, nearly leaving my head behind on the pillow. Who would come here, and why, at this hour of the night? I was clean. I didn't know anything. What the hell was going on?

The luminous dial of the clock by my pillow registered 3:20. I straightened myself up, pulling down my undershirt and groping for my trousers, which lay where I'd thrown them before getting into bed. The footsteps came to a stop before my door. There was a moment's silence, as profound as the silence at the bottom of a ravine. I held my breath and pricked up my ears. The whine of insects was maddeningly loud, the air sluggish as before a typhoon, making my eardrums seem to thicken and swell.

At first there was a light scratching. Then I heard a distinct rap, quiet but powerful. My heart began to pound loudly, as if in reply. Low murmurs, a short pause, then another rap, louder than before.

"Who is it?" I tried to call out, my voice welling up from somewhere in the region of my stomach and liver but getting no farther. The back of my tongue felt sticky.

The knocking grew louder; there was a commotion.

"Who is it?" I tried again, my voice distinct this time, but having a far-off quality as if it had issued from my ears instead of my mouth.

The courteous voice of a middle-aged man called out my name, adding, "Terribly sorry to arrive in the middle of the night like this."

A youthful female voice chimed in, "You must forgive us for disturbing you at such an hour."

The ordinary domesticity of their voices pulled me back to reality, dispelling my fears like mist in sunlight. There was the sound of many feet scraping on the floor, in evident abashment.

Smiling to myself at the eerie psychological effect of midnight hours, I pulled on my trousers and switched on the light. For some reason I couldn't find my belt, so I hoisted up my trousers with both hands and unhesitatingly, even willingly, opened the door to greet my unknown visitors. The light gave me courage, and curiosity filled me with benevolence.

In front of me stood a gentleman in black formal attire complete with bowtie, accompanied by a matron in a fluttering dress, who was evidently his wife; they were both beaming. To one side, leaning on a cane was a wrinkled old lady—how many hundreds of years old was anybody's guess—tottering and baring her gums in a grin. Behind her was a clutch of children, too many to register immediately, ranging from a strapping youth of about twenty down to a little girl holding a baby. They filled the hall, swaying left and right and smiling.

"Well, shall we?" said the gentleman over his shoulder, and though I hadn't uttered a word they all nodded and came trooping in. Altogether there were nine of them. My room was immediately full.

"A bit cramped, isn't it?" the gentleman said.

"Yes, it is a bit cramped, dear," his wife agreed.

"I'll put this away," I said hurriedly, starting to fold up my bedding.

"No, leave it there," said the old lady, laying the end of her cane across my arm. "I'm so tired, I think I'll just lie down and go right to sleep, if you don't mind."

Who does she think she is, I thought, exasperated, and turned to the gentleman only to find he had pulled open my desk drawer and was rummaging through it. Surprised, I restrained his arm and said sharply, "Hey, what are you doing!"

"Looking for cigarettes," came the matter-of-fact reply.

"What do you people want, anyway?"

"What kind of a thing is that to say?" It was the gentleman's turn to look exasperated. Frowning, he demanded boldly, "What do you mean by asking a question like that when we've just gotten home! Young fellow, you certainly have a strange way of expressing yourself!"

"Now wait just a goddamn minute. This is my room!" I said defiantly. "You people can't all be drunk. This is absurd! A bunch of people I never even saw before come along in the middle of the night and tell me this is where they live. It's not even funny!"

The gentleman stuck out his chest, thrust out his lower lip, narrowed his eyes, and stared down at me. "What have we got here, a hardhead? At this time of night, why should we get into a longwinded debate about something so simple? You're just a troublemaker. Here, let's put it to a test. You'll see whether this room is ours or not." He looked around the room and announced, "Listen, everyone! We have someone here who's attempting to encroach on our home. I suggest we call a meeting to discuss the issue, even if it is late. If someone will nominate me as chairman, I'll preside."

"I nominate you!" the children all shouted at once.

I shuddered, afraid the noise would wake the neighbors.

"Very well," said the gentleman, "I will preside. The topic for discussion is whether or not this room belongs to us. What do you say?"

"Of course it does," shrugged the oldest, a solid fellow who weighed a good 175 pounds.

"It's so obvious, it's crazy to even talk about it," said the second oldest child sullenly. He and his brother both looked like hooligans.

"Hear! Hear!" shouted everyone else in unison, except for the old woman and the infant, who were both asleep.

"Well, there you are," said the gentleman to me.

"What's that supposed to prove?" I fumed. "Horseshit!"

At that the gentleman drew himself up imperiously and said, "Horseshit, is it? Are you calling majority rule, the basis of democracy, horseshit? Why, you're a damn fascist!"

"Call me anything you want," I retorted. "This is still my room, and you have no business being here. So will you please clear out? Go on, get out, on the double. This is what I get for letting in a bunch of lunatics!"

"You dirty fascist," said the gentleman with a malevolent sneer. "When things don't go the way you want them to, you resort to violence, trampling on the will of the majority. You're a monster to turn this old woman, these innocent children, out onto the street in the middle of the night. The only way for us to protect our freedom is—"

The eldest son completed the sentence for him: "—to arm the camp of humanism!"

The second son chimed in, "Fight violence with the power of justice!"

Suddenly the trio surrounded me. "I have a fifth-degree black belt in judo, and I used to teach at a police academy," said the gentleman.

"I was on my college wrestling team," said the eldest son.

"I went in for boxing," said the second son.

The two youths each took one of my arms, and the gentleman rammed his massive fist into my solar plexus. My pants dropped to the floor, and in that humiliating state I lost consciousness.

2

When I came to, it was morning. I was lying bunched into the kneehole under the desk. None of the intruders was yet awake. All of my bedding and clothing had been scattered around on the floor, and the family was lying piled on top of it, peacefully asleep. Morning light came streaming through the window, filtering between tree leaves, and from the street below I heard the musical call of the tofu-maker. Linked to these commonplace events of my everyday existence, the figures of the brazen intruders took on a horrifying reality.

The gentleman was sleeping in the middle, on his side with his head pillowed on one arm. His jacket, which he had thrown across his stomach, rose and fell with the rhythm of his gentle snoring. On his left lay the old lady who had taken over my bedding, her jaw wagging with pendulum-like regularity as she slept. Beside her lay the wife, spread-eagled, one arm and leg so positioned that she seemed about to climb inside the old woman's bedding. Seen in this light, her costume was truly bizarre. It looked like the sort of get-up used in operatic productions to indicate foreigners of no discernible nationality. It was green, pleated, trailing pink scraps of ribbon that made the wearer look something like a poorly-scaled fish. The skirt had crept up her thighs in a way that struck me as deliberate. An upsetting thought. On the gentleman's other side lay his two eldest sons, sleeping at right angles to him with their heads burrowed into his side, face to face. Every time one of them breathed out, the hair of the other moved. Curled at his feet lay a sweet-faced girl of about seventeen, her long hair plaited, the baby in her arms. At the gentleman's head, directly in front of the desk, slept a mischievous-looking boy-girl pair, head to head, on their stomachs, in incredibly twisted poses. The boy seemed to be dreaming about running; every so often his ankles shook as if juiced with electricity. The little girl's mouth moved in a fishlike way. They looked like a pair of vulgar brats.

Taking one more look around to confirm beyond a doubt that this was no dream, I crawled bleakly out from under the desk, the joints in my body making cracking noises like splitting bamboo. The sound caused the wife to kick out reflexively. She hit the old lady in the kidneys, causing her to roll over, but fortunately no one woke up.

Pulling up my beltless pants, I stood forlornly in a corner of the room like half a pair of disposable chopsticks, until the thought came to me: This is my room, damn it. Why should I listen to them? I've got a perfect right to wake them all up and tell them to get the hell out of here.

Having arrived at this reasonable conclusion, I still hesitated, fearfully recalling the violence of the previous night. No, better leave it to the authorities, I decided. Nobody could sanction behavior this patently unjust, this absurd! Why, it was an offense against the social contract!

Quietly I prepared to go out. Silently, I removed my jacket from its hook and found my missing belt hanging underneath. I put on the belt and jacket, and checked my pockets. My wallet was gone. So were my lighter, pipe, and tobacco case. My train pass was there, but the booklet of meal tickets and photo of S— (my girlfriend) I kept with it were both missing. The only things untouched were a broken mechanical pencil and my appointment book.

I was appalled, and yet not in the least surprised. Determined to get outside, breathe in the air of reason, and make plans for a counterattack, I picked my way along the wall, tiptoeing with intense concentration as far as the door.

My relief at getting there undetected was short-lived, however, for someone laid a hand on my shoulder. It was the girl with the sweet face.

She drew close to me, as if to avoid being overheard, and murmured with breath smelling of milk, "I thought I'd better warn you. It's a good idea to boil up the tea-water and get breakfast ready before everyone wakes up. My brothers are always in a terrible mood in the morning. If they're unhappy, they'll only call another meeting and put you on the spot."

How was I supposed to answer that? Silently I picked up my shoes, meaning to put them on, but then thought better of it, stealthily opened the door, and stepped out into the hall with them still in my hand.

She whispered after me, "After you went to bed they held a meeting and agreed to give you the use of your clothes and shoes."

I tried to push the door closed, but she pressed against it from within and added, "Don't tell anyone I talked to you. If they found out, they'd be furious. But I sympathize with you. I want to be your friend." She smiled, and quickly retreated inside.

Once out of the room, the first thing I thought of was who to turn to for help. I couldn't help regretting the way I'd treated my neighbors in the past. If only I'd tried harder to get along with the other residents! Now who would take my side? I'd end up a laughingstock.

I stole down the hall to the lavatory, where I finally put on my shoes before going in; then I urinated and washed my hands and face, using my shirtsleeve for a towel. Feeling refreshed, I felt my courage returning and decided to go talk to the manager. That took some courage, all right. She had a dull-witted look, like an ancient chimpanzee, yet she was the soul of rapacity. I had never thought of her except in terms of how I could avoid running into her; her ruthless dunning for the rent had me terrorized. Yet now here I was, going to see her in her room of my own accord, to enlist her aid with a personal problem.

I found her sitting at the window facing the street, elbow on the sill, puffing on a thin, old-fashioned metal pipe in rhythm to the early-morning exercise music just starting up over the radio.

She was staring sidewise, through narrow, disapproving eyes, at the housewives lined up at the communal sink. Without moving her head she rolled her eyes in my direction and glared coldly at me. The pipe left her mouth, and the corners of her thin, purplish, wrinkled lips began to quiver, as if limbering up in preparation to spit out the word "Rent!"

Not wanting to lose the initiative, I moved quickly forward and bowed, making what I sensed was a poor attempt at a smile. "Good morning, ma'am," I said. "There's something I'd very much like to have your help with." At this, the quivering of her lips only increased, so I rushed on. "Last night, in the middle of the night, this strange bunch of people came along, and . . . ," I blurted out the whole story and when I finished, she gave her pipe a tap and looked away.

"Well, I haven't got the faintest idea what you're talking about," she said flatly.

"Surely it's not all that difficult. Basically, I'd just like to have you certify that Room 10 belongs to me."

"I don't give a hoot in hell who uses the room. I let it out to whoever'll pay the rent, and whoever that happens to be, it's fine with me."

"But paying rent means leasing not only the room but the right to live there, doesn't it? I'm the one paying rent, so how could people I've never laid eyes on before, who have no connection to me, have any right to come barging in?"

"What do you mean, right? You tenants can all do as you damn well please, as far as I'm concerned. If you really want to know, I don't let out my rooms to people, I let them out to money. Speaking of which," she went on, her eyebrows shooting up dramatically, "you're behind in your rent, aren't you? You want me to start looking for some other way to get the money for your room?"

The next thing I knew, I was standing outside, crestfallen. I hadn't expected her to jump to my rescue but neither had I expected so curt a dismissal. I stood motionless on the steps of the courtyard, forgetful of time.

"Morning!" Someone clapped my shoulder and grasped me by the arm. "Hey, I can almost see the wheels spinning. What's up?" It was the second oldest son with my brand-new toothbrush in his mouth, his teeth gleaming white.

Just then along came the sexy widow from Room 3, fan in hand. "Good morning, ma'am," the youth called out, taking my toothbrush out of his mouth and waving it at her as if he'd known her for years. As she passed, she gave us an arch look. He went after her and grabbed her by the arm. "Oops, sorry," he said, "guess some of my tooth powder spilled on you by mistake." With that he began stroking her hip, as if brushing off powder. Turning back to me, he said, "Dad's calling a meeting. I'd hurry if I were you."

Even though the widow was always flirting with me, sometimes stopping in the hall when no one else was around and deliberately sliding up her skirt or smoothing out wrinkles in her stockings, I'd never given her the slightest encouragement—or felt any interest, for that matter; but for that loathsome teenager to put on such a show in front of me filled me with a grim foreboding. What I felt was not jealousy, certainly, but rather a painful conviction that I was being treated to a preview of the power of this enemy to gradually destroy my life.

As I started out the door, he called to me again, "The meeting's starting. Better be there if you know what's good for you. Hurry up."

I walked on out defiantly, without any destination in mind. Swept along by inertia, however, I decided to pay a visit to the corner police box, despite my habitual distrust of the place.

It might be more accurate to say that because I couldn't think of any other place to go, I was left with no alternative but to visit the one place I was less eager to set foot in than any other.

Two policemen, one young and one old, were leaning back in their chairs, smoking cigarettes with an air of boredom. When I began to explain my problem, the younger one turned away and began flipping through the pages of a notebook, scribbling now and then as if he'd just remembered some work he had to do. The old one listened with a glum expression, nodding periodically to reassure me that he was still paying attention.

"Well," he said finally, "you know, we're sick to death of stories like these. As you can see, we're very busy. Well, maybe it wouldn't be apparent to you, but we are, so how about if you come back some other time, when we're free?"

"But can't you see, I can't afford to wait? I mean, they've taken my wallet, they've made a complete mess of my room—"

"You've still got your train pass, don't you? Then there's no reason why you can't go to work. And when you get right down to it, there's not much we can do in these domestic disputes. Our hands are tied. To begin with, you say they're total strangers, but we have to listen to both sides of the story. What will they say? If they say they know you well—as they're bound to do, if I know anything—have you got concrete evidence?"

"Nothing but reason, common sense."

"You won't get anywhere with those. We've got to have solid proof or nothing. See how hard to handle these cases are? Personally, I think they're impossible to settle to all parties' satisfaction. Tell you what. Try a little harder to get along with everyone, and stay calm. These things have a way of settling themselves."

When I opened my mouth to protest, the young policeman said impatiently, "Look, you. If you don't watch out, it's your ass we'll be after." Tossing aside his cigarette, he twisted around as if to pick up the phone and shoved me outside.

It was still a bit too early, but I set off straight for the office, without going back to my room.

3

On my lunch hour, I invited S— out to eat. Too late, I remembered I didn't have my wallet. I turned red, but she comforted me by saying lightly, "Oh, well. Today's payday!" Ordinarily I would have been overjoyed, but today somehow the thought only added to my depression. The apparent shakiness of my proprietary rights had left me distrustful.

Saying she had a new picture of herself to replace the old one, S— handed me a snapshot much more attractive than the one stolen, together with my meal tickets, by the intruders. I was about to swear never to part with it, or some such nonsense guaranteed to please her, when I paused, unable to go on. I felt a strong urge to tell her everything, but then I wasn't sure I understood everything myself yet, and there seemed no point in plunging her into needless worry and confusion. In the end I said nothing.

After lunch I felt a loneliness so intense it was like being sucked up into a void, while the flow of time seemed to move forward in jerks suggesting a debility like urethritis. In my mind things lost all coherency. My work made no progress. Finally, I felt a consuming anger. By quitting time, my face was dark and swollen with a reckless, visceral determination to fight. I vowed to go home and give them all a run for their money.

Before I left work, I turned to S—, who was expecting me to invite her out as usual and even seemed eager to go; without any explanation, I pressed my pay envelope on her and said, "Here.

I want you to take this home and keep it for me. Tomorrow's Sunday, so we can go see a movie. I'll stop by for you." Still talking, I started to run off, then paused and looked back. I saw her standing there with a dazed look on her face, like a Picasso statue—indescribable, inorganic, fragmented.

I tore through the courtyard of the apartment building. Just as I was about to set foot on the stairs, a woman's voice called out to me in a coy simper. "Oh, Mr. K—! Your guests are such *interesting* people!" It was the widow. I tried to come up with a nasty comeback, one that would convey my opinion of both her and them, but nothing came to me in time. I let it pass.

In my room, the family was seated in a circle, in the middle of dinner. The gentleman wiped his mouth with the back of his hand, smiled magnanimously, and said "Well, back, are we? This morning you left without breakfast. Not only that," he went on, his face now darkly accusing, "you left without fixing us so much as a cup of tea, which was a terrible inconvenience. If that's the way you're going to behave—"

His wife took her lips away from her teacup, evidently startled. "If that's the way you're going to behave," she repeated vacantly.

"—you put us in a difficult position," finished the gentleman. "We had to go out and buy a set of dishes, light the fire, and do all the work, dividing the chores among ourselves. Hard, unaccustomed chores, in an unfamiliar neighborhood, mind you. Please be more considerate in the future, would you? It's a good thing today is payday. We had to pay for everything with what little there was in your wallet. Not a penny left, I'm afraid. I'm telling you this for your own good, because we don't want to pose an unnecessary financial burden. From now on try to do things more systematically. Talk everything over with us first, won't you?"

After marching home so ready to vent my anger, I felt like a dog stroked lightly on the muzzle. The flood of words I had prepared drained suddenly away.

"Well, don't just stand there, come on in!" he said heartily.

As he spoke, his teenaged daughter moved over to make room for me, turning toward me with a smile. Sheepishly I sat down cross-legged in the space she had vacated.

Before I could even take a breath, the eldest son, Taro, spoke up. "First, I really think you ought to clear away the dishes and put on some tea, don't you, K—?"

At that I leaped up, with a perilous sense of tumbling down a steep slope, and shouted at him, "What the hell is that supposed to mean? I have no obligation to wait on you! What I have got is the right to tell you to go park your butt some place else. I'll never give in, so just resign yourselves. Go on, all of you, start packing your bags."

"Bags? Were we going somewhere?" Jiro, the second oldest son, said this in a mocking way, looking around the circle. Everyone burst into laughter; even the baby joined in.

I trembled, beset by such strange confusion that sharp pain shot through my tear glands. Had the girl not spoken up just then, I have no doubt I would have flown into a hysterical rage.

"He still isn't used to our modern way of life. It's cruel to laugh at him like that," she protested gently, her words calming my turbulent emotions.

"All right," said the gentleman. "It looks as if we'd better take a democratic approach here. Our friend K— still doesn't think he has to pull his own weight, even though it is the democratic way. Troublesome as it may be, I suppose we'll have to go on having meetings and voting on everything until he gets acclimated. All right, let's choose someone to preside. We've got to decide whether K— does or does not have any obligation to clear away the dishes and serve tea. Who's going to preside?"

With one voice, the children all cried, "You! I nominate you!"

"So be it," said the gentleman. "Let us begin. Ladies and gentleman, I ask you: does K— have such an obligation or not? All those who say he does, raise your right hands."

The words were barely out of his mouth before everyone's hands shot up. They all glared at me as if to say, How could anyone be so stupid as to think otherwise! To my astonishment, even the baby, who could barely talk, stuck his chubby little arm straight in the air without hesitation.

"That settles it," the gentleman announced. "An overwhelming majority. In the old days, minorities ruled by sheer force, and the only possible recourse was through individual violence. The human race has come a long way. Now, through the most rational of processes, the voice of the majority carries. What could be more reasonable and humane?" As he looked at me gloatingly, rubbing his hands, Jiro spoke up from one side.

"Hey Dad, give me a smoke."

"What? You know very well I don't run a tobacco shop."

"Give me a break. It's been three hours already since my last smoke. You know what happens when I run out and start to lose my temper!"

"Yes, Jiro, we know," said his brother, "but why don't we forget about threats, and see what we can work out? You know, even if Dad shared his pack with you, that would only be a temporary solution. And Dad, I know you can't help it, but aren't you being too emotional? Look, why don't we take this chance to settle all our finances once and for all? As you just mentioned, Dad, today is, fortunately, K—'s payday. Why don't we have him bring out his pay, so we can work out a budget?" He paused briefly, then turned to me. "K—, let's have your pay envelope."

My premonition had been painfully on target. A wave of heat consumed me, so fierce that every bone felt sheathed in electricity. "I can't imagine what makes you think I got paid today," I said. "I only wish I had. But even if I did have any money on me, I sure as hell wouldn't hand it over to any of you."

"Listen to the awkwardness of that delivery," commented the gentleman. "It's true what they say—honest people can't tell lies. And intelligent people can't be fooled, either. It would take a fool not to see that only that last statement came from the heart. Come on, K—! The dirty dishes are waiting, Jiro's getting antsy from lack of nicotine, and we've got an important budget meeting on the agenda, so hand it over and be done with it." In a menacing tone he added, "Time is money, so if you don't make it snappy, I'll charge you interest."

"Can't hand over what I haven't got," I retorted.

"All right, if that's the way you want to be, we'll have to change tactics." Signaling to his sons with his eyes, he went on, "You insist you haven't got something that you *have* got. Such irresponsible use of language is nothing but a form of violence. Language is a precious tool we all share, one that's indispensable if people are to live together in a civilized manner. How dare you use it in such a self-centered, pernicious way! It's a fascist outrage. Faced with an attitude like yours, what can we do?"

The two youths rose swiftly and came over to stand one on either side of me. "We have no choice but to demonstrate scientifically whether or not he's got it," said Taro.

Jiro added, "And if he tries to stop us, we'll have no choice but to use force."

Simultaneously, they each grabbed one of my elbows. I tried to shake them off, but their strength was amazing, far beyond mine. Seeing I had no money on me anyway, I remained still, letting them do as they wanted. I couldn't wait to see their faces.

With surprisingly practiced hands, the gentleman frisked me, took out my train pass and handed it to the girl, who was standing beside him. "That's funny," he said, exchanging puzzled glances with his sons.

Take that, you bastards, I thought.

Meanwhile the wife had snatched the pass away from her daughter, and now she shrieked in consternation, "The filthy man, the filthy man, it's another picture of that woman! Oh, you filthy man, shame on you!" It was the picture of S—.

"What do you think you're doing!" I shouted.

"Mother, give it back to him," said the girl.

"Anyway, don't tear it up yet," suggested Taro, on my right. "It might come in handy, you never know. Look, it's signed on the back. This is the same chick as in the picture you tore up last night, isn't it?" He turned to the others. "If this is the fascist's girl, she must have a good idea of what he did with his pay."

"Yes, of course!" said the gentleman. "Well, K—, knowing you, I'd assumed your feelings for this girl were unrequited, but I see now you may have something going with her after all."

"Have something going!" exclaimed his wife. "Oh, how filthy. How disgusting."

"Now, now," said her husband, "you've got to hand it to K—, he used his head."

"Well, I have a suggestion," said Taro, releasing his grip on my arm and tearing the snapshot from his mother's hands. "I've got a talent for digging things out, so why not let me handle this?"

Jiro stood in front of him as if to bar the way. "Now just a minute," he said. "It's not that I don't trust you, but as long as there's money involved, wouldn't it be better for us to work as a team? I'd better go with you."

"I appreciate the offer, Jiro, but let's be realistic. It's not as if

I was setting off for some place either of us knows, with a clear destination in mind. I've got to do some snooping around. That takes a special kind of skill. And I've got to do it alone."

Jiro indicated me with a motion of his chin. "Why not just make him tell us?"

"What, using Dad's hypnotism?" He smiled sardonically. "No reflection on Dad's technique, but really . . ."

"Taro! What are you saying!" their father put in sternly.

"Nothing, nothing. It's just not necessary to go to all that trouble. Besides, let's be realistic. We're dead broke. The only way we can get around now is by using this pass. If only one of us can go, it should be me." He turned to his brother. "Just think for a minute. This is a naive chick. Once I figure out where she lives, I've still got to convince her to tell me where the money is. It's gotta be one on one, believe me."

"Now you're talking about *my* specialty," Jiro said heatedly. "I'm telling you, you'd better let me go along. You know me, I can sneak through a ticket gate blindfolded. And I hate to leave a member of the opposite sex to you."

"What do you mean? A real operator has got to be smooth. He doesn't operate openly, out in public the way you do. You may have gotten some hanky-panky started with that widow downstairs, but from the way you were going at it, you'll have your hands full later on. If you're game, let me try to take her away from you. We'll see which way the wind blows."

"Boys, boys!" broke in their father impatiently. "Neither one of you has any experience, and listen to you! Why, I could tell you—"

"How filthy! There he goes!" The wife shook her head, crying, and the older girl cried, "Father!" The little boy and girl exchanged leers, and the old bag covered her toothless mouth with one hand, laughing scurrilously to herself.

The gentleman coughed, recovering his dignity. "All right, then, Taro, off you go, by yourself. We'll just have to trust you. If you'll be honest with us about the money, we'll promise never to lay a hand on Miss S——. Won't we, Jiro?"

"Yeah, sure," replied Jiro. "Young chicks aren't my thing, anyway."

"Don't be filthy," murmured his mother, coughing faintly.

"All right, I'm off," said Taro, grinning at me.

I felt as though my heart would peel away from my body and shatter in pieces at my feet, like worm-eaten, withered bark off a tree. Sensing the girl's eyes on me, I quickly looked away, not wanting her pity. A vagrant tear ran down the back of my nose and moistened the back of my tongue.

"Well, be quick about it, would you?" Jiro followed his brother to the door, turned, and said to no one in particular, "I'm going out for a minute, too. I haven't got a date with the widow downstairs or anything—well, even if I do, that doesn't mean I couldn't break it. Anyway I have a very wholesome reason for going: I've gotta get my hands on a smoke."

I was staring absently up at the darkening window, hands thrust into my pockets, when out from behind the neighbor's roof popped a terrifying moon, like the yolk of a soft-boiled dragon's egg. All at once my feet started for the door.

"Where do you think you're going!" the gentleman said indignantly.

I turned around and felt something soft and wet land with a splat on my forehead. The younger boy and girl were hiding in the old lady's shadow, laughing hysterically. It was a wad of chewing gum.

The gentleman approached slowly. "If I were you I wouldn't

just stand there," he said, "I'd get busy. Just because Taro and Jiro are gone, don't go getting any ideas, now. As I said before, I have a black belt, and I used to teach at a police academy. Come on now, get right at your chores and get them done so we can all enjoy living here."

"Father," said the girl, "I'll bet K— has no experience doing work like that. It's not his fault, it's the fault of the old society that brought him up. He probably can't escape from the old idea that washing dishes is woman's work. Just at first, let me show him what to do."

"You seem awfully eager to take his side," said the father, with a frown.

"That's not it at all," she replied quickly. "We don't want him breaking all our dishes, do we? Besides, democracy is based on humanism. Coercion isn't the answer."

I was handed the huge container full of dirty dishes and forced to march down the gray corridor toward the dark communal sink area, under the gaze of all the housewives. Their eyes sparkled with curiosity.

The work itself was exceedingly simple. "You're better at this than I thought," the girl said, and showed signs of wanting to say something more, but I preserved an unrelenting silence. I was finding my very existence increasingly hard to accept.

On the way back we heard peculiar, shuddering groans coming from Room 3. "Well, there's Jiro," I said maliciously. Then it was the girl's turn to fall silent.

Back in the room, the two little ones were wrestling on the floor, raising clouds of dust. Their mother had collapsed against the wall and was fast asleep, her enormous legs sticking straight out, her skirt pushed up. The old lady was leaning against the window, gazing up at the moon with a strange smile on her face. The baby was on her lap, crying like a house afire. The gentleman was seated at my desk, leisurely reading a book.

"All finished?" he said, taking an unlit cigarette butt from his lips. "Next make us some tea then, will you?"

"Haven't got any," I said rudely.

"I'm not asking if you do or not. I'm asking you to make us some. How are we going to get along if you don't do something about your attitude?"

"I can't make what I haven't got."

"Try to get it, then. Remember the New Testament: 'And let us not be weary in well doing: for in due season we shall reap, if we faint not.' You mustn't spare any efforts for the common welfare of all. Christ also said, 'It is more blessed to give than to receive.' So go, and let your neighbors experience the blessing of giving."

Wordlessly, I started for the door. All at once, the gentleman jumped up and grabbed me from behind. "Wait," he said. "You're sulking. Don't try to hide it—you mean to run away and never come back. Well, don't think you can get away with it. It's impossible, and that's that. You stay here and get the water boiling.

"Kikuko," he said, turning to his daughter, "you go out and borrow some tea from somewhere. If that doesn't work, we can always sell a few of these books."

4

After midnight, Taro staggered in, clearly drunk. Everyone stiffened, and Jiro in particular glared at his brother with such ferocity that he appeared ready to pounce on him. Taro was singing a line from a song, something about frogs under the eaves, birds in the sky. He hiccuped and opened his eyes wide in surprise. "Hey," he said disarmingly, "what're you staring at me like that for? Knock it off."

The gentleman took one step forward and said, "All right, where's the money?"

"Money?"

"You heard me, money. Don't tell me you spent it all on drink."

"Drink? Maybe I did have a little to drink. You can see that, can't you? What of it?"

"What do you mean, you had a little to drink? You'll have to do better than that, son."

"What do you want me to say, I had a little to eat, too? Bug off."

The argument grew more heated, Jiro joining in, until the room was electric with hostility. Who made the first move it was impossible to say, but in no time it had turned into a free-for-all.

Someone in the room below pounded on the ceiling with a broom handle, someone next door banged on the wall with his fist; just as the entire building had been shaken awake and abuzz with fury, like a hive of truculent wasps, the combatants finally tired, their arms falling limply at their sides. Whereupon, with a laugh, Taro tossed a white envelope on the floor.

"What!" yelled his father, snatching it up. Swiftly he counted the bills inside, something over eight thousand yen, then compared the total with the amount printed on the outside of the envelope. "Crazy kid. Why didn't you say so? If you'd told me sooner, we wouldn't have wasted all those calories fighting!"

Still laughing, Taro replied, "It was great exercise. A little scrap now and then is good for the soul. Besides, you should know me better than that. Did you really think I'd go out drinking on our money? I got the chick to pay. That S——, she's all right." He paused and cast a sidelong glance in my direction. "I fell for her. Made a date to take her to the movies tomorrow."

"Filthy, filthy," the wife said in a kind of sob. "No one pays any attention to me any more," she added petulantly.

Taro took a swig of cold tea and lay down, and everyone else returned to their previous spots with an air of weary relief, each breathing out a long sigh in his or her own way. The gentleman had a tight grip on my pay envelope, but something still seemed to be bothering him. Something was bothering me even more. Suddenly overcome by a violent paroxysm of rage, I rose fearlessly and challenged him. I need hardly record the result. A meeting was called, and the majority ruled that the money was theirs. Besides that, my eye swelled up, on contact with Jiro's fist.

"You fascist!" the gentleman hissed. "Training you is more trouble than teaching dogs to talk. K—, somehow you've got to adapt to our modern, civilized lifestyle. It's for your own good.

"I don't mind telling you that I'm engaged in research to teach language to dogs," he explained with pride. "When my work is completed, it will bring about a revolution in societal laws. I don't suppose you'd understand the technical aspects of my theory, but basically I'm building on Pavlov's groundbreaking work with the physiological origins of language; I alter the dog's brain through hypnosis, enabling it to acquire a language center a posteriori. I don't expect you to follow me. But I'm not the only one; everyone in the family is doing their own research. They've all designed fine, scholarly projects aimed at the betterment of society. Taro's field is experimental criminal psychology, and Jiro is doing research on the psychosexuality of menopausal women, with my wife a prime subject. My mother has now retired from the frontline, but at one time she was not only a keen student of male psychology, but an authority on the blind spots of female department store clerks. Young as they are, the smaller boy and girl are carrying on with her vital work. Kikuko here is rather unusual in that she writes poetry. She's planning to publish her collected works soon, under the title *Love for Humanity*. The littlest one can't even talk properly yet, but we've trained him to raise and lower his arm at meetings, besides which he is an invaluable source of data I can use in teaching language to dogs. This is how a modern, cultured family lives! Surprised? If you'd just co-operate with us, K——, not only would you make our work easier, you yourself would develop as a man of culture."

All of a sudden we realized that except for the girl, who was sobbing quietly to herself, everyone else in the room had fallen fast asleep.

"Why, Kikuko, what's the matter?" said her father, bending over her in surprise.

"Oh, I don't know, I just feel so depressed," she answered, sweeping her hair back off her forehead. Her face was pale and sad.

"Don't think about it. Don't have doubts," he said shortly. Then he surveyed the rest of his sleeping family and said, "Time for bed." He turned back to me. "K——, my friend, in line with democratic principles, I am certainly not going to force you into anything, but I do have a suggestion I'd like you to hear me out on. This is a small room. There isn't enough space, or oxygen, for ten people to sleep here all night. So this afternoon I looked around and discovered an attic space where no one lives. Now, if someone with a humble, unassuming spirit knew about that, what do you think he'd do?"

I spent the rest of the night in the cobwebby attic, fighting off rats, unable to sleep a wink, physically and mentally devastated by insomnia, humiliation, and terror. Vowing revenge, I made plans for the morrow:

First, slip out and see S—— before the eldest son left. (She was

in danger. I had to explain my position to her in full, and persuade her to join forces with me against them.)

Second, find a reliable lawyer.

Third, put up notices appealing to the other tenants. (Once
before, when the mariner in Room 2 had put up notices protest-
ing a rent hike, everyone had united in response.)

I heard the sound of the first train of the morning. Just as I
was preparing to leave, I heard someone enter the lavatory. The
ladder leading up to the attic was right next to the lavatory, so I
decided to wait until whoever it was had come out, but while
waiting I was overcome with fatigue and fell into a deep sleep.

5

I awoke to the sound of scratching on the trap door. Orange
light was streaming in from an unlikely place; the morning was
well along. "Hurry up, hurry up!" urged a voice. Wiping dribbles
of saliva from my mouth, I opened the door. It was Kikuko.

"I came to see you," she said, sitting down right next to me.
"You must be hungry," she added, handing me a buttered crust
of bread.

"What time is it?"

"Past noon."

"Oh no!" As I began struggling to my feet, she held me back
with a weak, shy smile.

"You're thinking about that girl S—, I suppose. It's too late."

"What are you people trying to do to me!"

"It's the law of human relationships. It's original sin."

"Thieves!"

"I feel sorry for you."

"Lunatics!"

"Who? The others? They're strange, but I don't think they're actually insane. Except for Mother. She's completely crazy. She's forgotten how to talk. All she can do is go around saying 'Filthy, filthy' and thinking filthy thoughts, or else repeating whatever Father says."

I stared at the girl in wonder. "Are you on my side?"

"Yes. I love you."

Immediately I revised step one of my plan as follows: Make an ally of Kikuko and sow internal dissension in the enemy camp.

"Then you'll help me?"

"Of course, that's why I'm here."

"I want to escape from all this. You do too, don't you?"

"Of course. We've got to make our getaway as soon as possible."

"Make our getaway . . . right. We've got to make a getaway. I can't go on living with this perverted reasoning."

"It's love that counts, not reason. Love is what we need. Only the power of love can make life worth living."

"Right, right. And where there's no reason, there can be no love, either."

"Oh, haven't you got that backwards? You mean reason can exist only where there is love."

"Yeah, my mistake," I said, assuming an air of frank humility. "Anyway, you and I see eye to eye on things, so we've got to stick together from now on. From the first time I saw you, I thought you were different from the rest of your family. I hear you write poetry. You know, now that I look at you, you're pretty as an angel. If only you'd distance yourself from your family, be more independent, I'd probably fall in love with you."

"In a democratic society, everyone is independent."

"All right, then, let's think of something. How are we going to get rid of them?"

"Get rid of them? You and I are going to escape," she protested.

"No, we don't have to do that. Why should we knuckle under to them? We can just get rid of them. That's my room, plain and simple. Besides, with this housing shortage, where could we possibly go?"

"That's not what I mean. Our escape is mental. We escape toward the path of love which bears all things."

"What! Then you mean you accept the way things are!"

"No, but I can't change it, either. It's rendering unto Caesar that which is Caesar's, that's all."

"Then you—" I got up, and wiped a cobweb from my face. "—you are my enemy, after all! You're a spy, someone I can't trust!"

"I knew you were going to say that." Kikuko stood up too. Her hair, softly fragrant, brushed my cheek. "I've loved so many people like you before, and not one of them has ever loved me back."

Her voice was melancholy, conveying a sincerity that seemed to resonate from the depths of her being. I wavered. But I was not completely won over.

"So many people . . . ," I repeated softly. The implication of her words hit me. Aghast, I couldn't help asking, "You mean other people have gotten the same treatment I'm getting from your family?"

Lowering her eyes, Kikuko nodded.

With greater intensity, I prodded, "What happened to them all?"

Like fish swimming in the shadow of a rock, her white hands reached out for me. Her voice was exquisitely sad. "They all got tired, and rested."

"You mean they died, don't you." Some magical power in the

attic room blinded my eyes. I drew the girl to me and kissed her gently. Tears ran down the crack between our faces.

6

That night, the intruders forced me to nail the trapdoor shut and saw a new opening through the roof in my closet. As a result, I had to go through my room to get in and out of the attic, putting me at all times under their strict supervision.

Days of humiliation followed one on another. I was a slave. On my way to and from work, the two little brats always accompanied me. Along the way they would take turns darting in and out to shoplift, going after anything from chewing gum and caramels to watches and necklaces—even things like screwdrivers and birth control pills, of no possible use to them. Sometimes they gave me their leftovers. I was starving, so I took whatever food they gave me.

At the office, S— no longer even nodded to me when we ran into each other. I tried to talk to her, but she always evaded me with a don't-think-you-can-pull-anything-over-on-*me* sort of look. After about two weeks, she quit her job. I still loved her.

When I returned home, someone was always there, watching me. The crazy wife never left the room at all. At first she displayed an odd coquetry (she seemed always to be flirting with no one in particular, as with some invisible partner), but when I showed no interest her attitude changed to one of profound hostility. Kikuko went on showing signs of goodwill toward me, but as we had no further chances to meet alone, our relationship stalled. Anyway, as our one secret meeting had demonstrated, there were definite limits to her goodwill.

I leave the rest to your imagination.

Why didn't I try to run away? Why didn't I seek to

escape—not the mental escape Kikuko had talked about, but real, physical escape? I hadn't given up the battle yet, nor had I lost all hope. I was waiting for a chance.

One day my chance came. On the way home from work, I spotted circus tents on a corner. I knew the two brats were dying to see a circus. Skillfully I conned them into going inside, reassuring them that I'd wait for them there until they came out. The show was ninety minutes long. I used the time to visit the office of a lawyer I'd had in mind.

Apparently the man had a ridiculously large family. The place was full of adults and children roaming in and out of my range of vision. Finally the most exhausted-looking, unprepossessing fellow of the lot appeared. This was the lawyer. When I kindly pointed out the cobwebs in his hair, he became flustered and clawed at his head. I grew uneasy.

I began to tell him why I had come. As the nature of my problem became clear, he put a finger to his lips and said hastily, "Lower your voice, lower your voice." The whole time we were talking, he kept looking around anxiously, and by the time I finished he was deathly pale. "Is that all?" he said hoarsely. Standing up, he gripped my arm and propelled me to the door. "If that's your problem, I'm sorry but there's nothing I can do for you," he said. "I have no power to protect you. As a matter of fact," he added, lowering his voice still further, "my place has been taken over by intruders also. You saw them, didn't you? A family of thirteen. For a single man like yourself it's one thing, but I had a wife, a family! It's a disaster. My wife took the children and left. No, I guess it would be truer to say they chased her out. Then they fired all my staff, so I have to be everything from secretary to errand boy. I lost 66 pounds in one month. Another month of this and I'll fade away to nothing."

Before leaving, I shook his hand. "Let's be friends," I said.

But he shook his head sadly. "No, please don't ever come back."

7

It was my last hope. Every time I came home I was forced to submit to a strict body check, so it wasn't easy, but somehow I managed to assemble scraps of paper from here and there, stealing time to write until I had thirty notices. "To residents of this apartment building," they read,

> and to all men and women of conscience and reason. This is a desperate appeal from one of your friends, a man who has fallen victim to a peculiar crime. A family of total strangers has suddenly and wrongfully deprived me of my room and taken control of my life. I have lost all freedom and am on the point of starvation. Not only that, I am forced to support them with my labor. They justify this by appeals to majority rule, using their greater numbers to push through their every demand. I ask you, can such goings-on be condoned? If so, we are on a one-way road to societal collapse! This is not an isolated problem. It is the fate awaiting each of you as well. We must band together to fight this abuse of democratic principles. Especially those of you who worked together once to resist the raise in rent—will you not join hands again to fight for basic freedoms? Your solidarity will protect me. And it will protect you at the same time.

Join with me to overcome this nonsensical "majority" with the real thing!

The problem was, how to bell the cat? I had no chance to put up the notices. But my next payday was approaching. Unless I did something drastic, I knew I'd have to endure another month of hopeless suffering. One day, in desperation, I pretended to be going to the lavatory and started putting up notices in the hall, one after another.

I had barely gotten three up when I heard someone clear his throat behind me. I spun around to face Taro and his father. "Well, lookee here," they said, regarding each other with little smiles on their faces. Not only did they not take down the notices, they made no attempt to stop me from putting up more. It was eerie. I became so flustered that I lost my nerve and quit after putting up only ten.

"Just when I thought he'd been acting quiet, now this. The fascist personality is frightening, isn't it?" said Taro.

His father nodded and grabbed my arm. "All right, come with us."

"Shall I take these down?" asked Taro.

"No, leave them there to teach him a lesson. We've got to make an example out of him."

The gentleman led me back to the room, twisting my arm more than was necessary. Grim-faced, he showed the remaining notices to the family and explained the situation in scandalized tones. Jiro, who was getting dressed to go out, stopped and stared at me, but then for no apparent reason he relaxed and grinned. Kikuko gazed at me as if heartbroken, a look of accusation in her eyes. The others, of course, paid no attention.

Speaking with deliberation, the gentleman said, "K—, you've got to take responsibility for this. In this building there are rules about putting things up on the walls: one hundred yen per sheet, to cover both the use of the walls and the fine for disfiguring them. You put up ten, so that comes to a thousand yen. Naturally, we wash our hands of all responsibility. Next, did you have permission to put those up? You didn't, did you? That means another five hundred yen. Naturally, we support the landlady's position. Which means that she is bound to support us. And you know, by the way, half of the occupants of these rooms are behind in their rent. Do you really expect them to stand up to the landlady? As for the other half, most of their wives have formed close, intimate relationships with my sons and me. Do you mean to tell me—"

"Filthy, filthy!" said the wife in a faint voice and began to sob, effectively cutting off her husband's remarks.

Beside her Kikuko sat wanly, with drooping head. The old lady patted the wife's back consolingly.

I went out without a word, pulled down the rest of the notices I'd gone to such trouble to put up, and kept walking.

Epilogue

On windy nights thereafter, fliers would drift out through the crack in the roof of K—'s apartment. Dozens, hundreds, thousands of them rode on the wind, scattering all about town. No one knew where they came from. But dozens, hundreds, thousands of victims read them.

One day the intruders filed a curious claim against the fliers: they said they were covered with dangerous bacteria. City health officials investigated the charge, and a certain type of harmful bacillus was in fact found. A reputable lawyer testified that any unsterilized surface was likely to be crawling with that very germ, but his opinion was ignored, and a law was enacted forbidding dispersion of fliers. A few days before that decision was announced, however, the flow of fliers from the attic had already stopped. Worn out from oppression and starvation, K— was "resting." Hanging by the neck from a low ceiling beam, his legs bent at the knees.

Noah's Ark

Old Noah was a great man. He always said so himself. Once when a friend of mine asked him just what a great man was, he answered that it was someone who held many offices at once. In that case, he really must have been great, because he held every office in the village, single-handedly. First off he was mayor. Secondly he was headmaster, third tax collector, and fourth chief of police. After that came chief justice, chief priest, hospital director, head of the vineyard, and assorted other titles, as the need arose.

His clothes and general appearance were such as to represent all of these offices at once. That black hat shaped like two halves of a broken eggshell placed side by side was the sign of the chief justice, and his face with its pendulous folds of flesh was the sign of the head of the vineyard. His long, salt-and-pepper eyebrows and stern beard marked him as the headmaster, and his fat, purplish lips like a pair of sea slugs were the emblem of the hospital director. The mark of the tax collector was that big leather pouch he wore slung from right to left across one shoulder, while his black boots and the pistol he wore slung from left to right across the other shoulder identified him as chief of police. Besides these, his breast was ablaze with medals and ribbons, each the insignia of some other office.

Appropriately enough for a great man with so many jobs to do, old Noah had a bicycle of twelve colors which he used to ride up and down the village, from house to house and job to job. That bicycle of his was so well greased that it might as well have been soaked in oil; it was so noiseless that he seemed to appear all of a sudden, as if he'd dropped down from the sky. People were terrified of those sudden appearances of his. Because when old Noah showed up at your house, he'd always start by collecting taxes, and then drink a bottle of wine. Anyone he caught muttering a word of complaint he'd haul off to court, fine, and sentence to death. Then he'd start the catechism. Any mistakes meant another trial. He ended by giving compulsory physical examinations, and always found something wrong, so that the patient would have to take some peculiar pills, and pay a fee.

Those peculiar pills of his were especially bad news. Minutes after taking them you'd break out in a general rash; then you'd start having trouble breathing and your pulse would slow to fifty beats a minute; finally things would get hazy, and you'd lie unable to move for three or four days. There was a one in ten chance of dying by the tenth day. But even if you managed to survive, you'd be a cripple till the end of your days. We pretty much knew that the pills were made from a powdered form of the deadly poison capitalan, but old Noah never went away until the rash came out, and if for some reason it didn't, then it was trial, fine, death sentence—so either way, there was no escape.

Well, there was one way. If you paid a bribe in the form of a special fee, then he'd give you some harmless kind of medicine made of what was apparently clay. But that special fee was so very special that hardly anyone could afford to pay it. From time to time there were even those for whom life was such a struggle that they'd ask for the pills, causing the doctor a good deal of emotion and pain.

Noah's answer to all this was as follows.

"A certain number of people have got to die, and that's that. You all know that maintaining a fixed number of deaths is what preserves the harmony of the universe. It's my job to regulate the death rate. Coming on top of all my other duties, it's a terrible burden. Do you understand?"

Anyone who said no immediately went on trial.

That explanation was persuasive enough as far as the villagers were concerned. To anyone who believed in Noah's doctrine, it made perfect sense.

In order for you to understand how that could be, and in order for you to accept the incident about the ark which I'm leading up to, I think I had better say something about that doctrine. It was the first thing we learned in school, and from then on, one hour a day, every day for the next three years, we heard it over and over again—and once more at graduation, in a final admonitory lecture. It was literally the one and only thing we were taught. Noah was so busy with all his jobs that he couldn't spare more than an hour a day for the school, so there was no time for other subjects. That's how central the doctrine was to the life of the village; you couldn't understand the one without the other.

Fortunately I have here the official pamphlet that he used for a textbook. It's short, so I'll quote it in full.

Greetings! Greetings to all villagers, students and nonstudents alike, all of you who are fortunate enough to be protected by me, the great Noah! You are all fortunate. I personally guarantee your happiness. Why then do you call me an old sot? What could be more unwarranted, more uncalled-for, more outrageous?

Listen, while I explain. I don't drink for the fun of it, you know. The stuff doesn't even taste very good. Really, when you drink as much as I do, you start to get sick of it. If you don't believe me, that just shows what low minds you have.

Anyway, my reasons are these. In the first place, is it or isn't it my responsibility to supervise and control the flavor of the wine, which is one of our village's main products? Certainly it is. As a medical doctor I am fully aware of the horrors of alcoholism, but I go right on doing my duty; does this or doesn't it demonstrate a noble spirit of self-sacrifice? Certainly it does.

Secondly, in youth I trained hard for the important offices I now hold, and once when I had evidently had a bit too much, all of a sudden Jehovah came before me. He said something, but I couldn't make out what it was. Later it seemed to me he'd said, "Drink! Drink!" And from then on he showed up every time I drank three bottles or more. The more I drank, the more clearly I could understand what he said. In appreciation, I did my best to drink even more. My faith led me on. That's why I made the rule that every time I visit one of you, I ask for a bottle of wine. Be grateful!

After I became acquainted with Jehovah, he told me the whole truth about everything from the creation of the universe to the law of the human race. Now listen, and I'll tell you. Death to anyone who refuses to believe!

In the beginning there was nothing. No up, no down, no right, no left. Then one time, along came two objects, floating in the midst of that nothing. One was Jehovah, and the other was his good friend and opposite, Satan.

As they both were solid objects they may have been moving along a fixed path for all I know, but this was extremely long ago, before measuring instruments, so I can't express it precisely.

After a while, they both began to yearn to be free from simple perpetual motion—to measure themselves against themselves, and confirm their dominion over themselves. They talked it over and thought about what to do.

Of course, in the beginning it wasn't clear which of them had which name. So first they had to decide who would be Jehovah, and who Satan. They settled it with a fistfight—and that's how our Jehovah got to be Jehovah, and Satan, Satan.

Next, in order to make space more manageable they decided to divide it into up and down. First Satan waved a finger randomly and said, "That's up, and this over here will be down. Okay?"

"Won't work," Jehovah protested. "Up and down can't be any old which way. They've got to express opposite directions, like head and feet, belly and back, mouth and anus."

"Now why would that be?"

"It's more useful."

"What's 'useful'?"

"Dividing up and down that way."

"Hmm," said Satan. "All right then, the way my head is pointing will be up, and the way my feet are pointing will be down."

"Hmm," said Jehovah. "Now that you mention it, you and I are pointing in opposite directions, aren't we? If we go by your rules, my head will be pointing down and my feet up. How awful."

"Everything's relative. Give it up."

"All right then. Shall we set a marker for reference?"

"Good idea. What can we use?"

"Well, to mark the upper regions we could cut off your head and set it there."

"And cut off your head to mark the lower regions?"

"No, no, as long as up is clearly marked, down will take care of itself."

"That's not fair!" Satan exploded. "Cut off my head, will you! You're not getting a fingernail!"

They began to quarrel. But being the distinguished gentlemen that they are, they quickly made up. Then Satan made the following suggestion.

"Jehovah, my friend, why don't we go to work? We're surrounded by unlimited energy: essential positive charges, stabilized by negatrons. All we have to do is break them down and create material energy. We can make all sorts of atoms and particles, and keep piling them up until we have matter."

Jehovah clapped his hands in agreement. "You know, I was just thinking the same thing myself!"

So saying, they each flew off in the respective directions their heads were pointing, at a speed of 11,811,726,000 inches per second, and, after approximately four minutes of flying, set to work.

In one year, Satan created a giant piece of fiery matter 6,000° C in temperature and 866,916 miles in diameter: the Sun. In the same amount of time, Jehovah did nothing but wander around tearing things up, and made nothing at all.

"What's the meaning of this!" Satan cried in consternation.

In perfect calmness (think, everyone, about the meaning of these calm words!), Jehovah replied, "I've got a plan. This work is so simple that I just don't feel like doing it any more. Besides, why should you and I do the same thing? It will just make it harder to tell which way is up. So I've decided to take some of this matter of yours, process it, and give it a special character."

"You shirker! Since when do you take the easy way out?"

"I've spent a lot of time going over this in my mind. There's nothing to get so hopped up about. I haven't got the slightest intention of taking advantage of you."

"But it might just end up that way anyway, eh?"

Jehovah made no reply. Instead, he reached out, laid a hand on Satan's sun, and shook it with all his might. Then, along with numberless tiny sparks, nine pieces of matter flew out. Jehovah studied them for a while, and then reached out and grabbed the second closest one to himself, rolling it around and blowing on it with pursed lips as if it were a hot potato he was cooling off. That became Earth.

Well, Satan was hopping mad, but he hated violence, so to work off his anger he flew around making a vast amount of fiery matter in every corner of the universe. This became the starry host.

Millions and billions of years went by. Then, as if just remembering something, Jehovah called out to Satan in a loud voice.

"Satan, I'm finished! Come down here and take a look."

"Where's here?" Satan's voice was still dark with anger. "Wasn't down supposed to be a direction? You talk about it if it were a place."

"That's another thing I want to talk about. You're partly responsible. You went and made so darn many heavenly objects that we've got to rethink the whole question of directions, in accordance with the principle of relativity. If you want to keep our original primitive concept, and give it substance, wouldn't it be a good idea to redo the concepts of up and down based on the Earth? In other words, divide the universe into the heavens and the Earth."

"You mean we don't need up any more? You mean all my work is wasted?"

"Oh, no. Where would the Earth be without the Sun? Just

come over here and look at the Earth which I made from your Sun. You'll be impressed. Never mind your up and down."

Following the direction indicated by Jehovah's finger, Satan spotted two tiny humans. Not having any idea what to do, they did nothing but yawn. That was Adam and Eve, our first ancestors.

"What are you going to do with those?" Satan said, controlling his intense interest.

"Carry out our original purpose," said Jehovah significantly. "I've made actors to play themselves, exploring themselves according to the inevitability of matter. They will act and change following their own inevitability, without any help from us. This is more complicated than any game, and we'll never tire of watching."

"But they're not changing at all."

"Just wait. They're not finished yet. One thing is missing. When I add that, then the real fun begins—although for them it will bring tragedy and tears. I don't want to take responsibility for that. To avoid being held responsible, I'm going to have them supply the missing part themselves, and take responsibility for their own downfall. I showed them an apple tree and commanded them not to eat from it. Of course that guarantees that they will. Once that happens, I can tell them it's not my fault, it's their own fault for not listening to me."

"You've thought it all out, haven't you?"

"The principle of dominance. But you know, Satan . . . ," Jehovah was suddenly cautious, though outwardly casual. "I have no intention of hogging the show. I mean for half of this to be yours. But you remember what happened before. To avoid trouble later, hadn't we better divide up the rights of ownership now? Which do you want, the heavens or the Earth?"

"The heavens or the Earth?"

"That's right. Surely you don't want the heavens. Nobody would. At least, I wouldn't. But I don't know, maybe you would . . ."

"No, thank you."

"That's what I thought. Well, how about if we include the surface of Earth in the realm of the heavens?"

"Then the rest would be meaningless. In that case, of course I'll take the heavens."

"What? Really? But no, wait, I haven't finished explaining everything yet, so I won't hold you to your word. That wouldn't be fair. Wait till I tell you what lies below the surface of the earth, in Hades, and then you can take your time, make your comparisons, and decide what you want to do. First, it's packed full of very dense matter. Then there are fish, and earthworms, and insect larvae. And powerful motive forces that control events above ground: underground minerals, fountainheads, terrestrial heat, ground pressure. And that's not all. Before long, after the way of humans, Adam and Eve will die and turn to souls. Souls are the real denizens of Hades. Human beings have power to reproduce and multiply, but in the end they all die. Souls, however, undergo no further changes, so they'll just keep on increasing forever. You could say people on the face of the Earth are just an interim form of life, on their way to becoming souls and living in Hades. Jostling forever, endless struggle—that will be something to see!"

"You're sure that people always die?"

"Absolutely. They're made of complex protein. See for yourself."

"All right. I'll take Hades."

What happened after that is pretty much the way our ancestors' legends have it. Jehovah set up the Kingdom of Jehovah, and controlled life on Earth. He enjoyed watching Adam and

Eve's consternation and sorrow over sin, he enjoyed watching them mate, and he enjoyed the thrill and suspense of fights between wild beasts. Meanwhile, Satan, under the ground, became impatient as Adam and Eve showed no sign of dying. His tantrums took the form of earthquakes.

Dozens of years went by, and then Cain and Abel were born. Earthquakes were becoming more frequent and more severe, so Jehovah started to worry. That's when he arranged to have Cain kill Abel.

But what do you think became of Abel's soul?

Listen! Students and nonstudents alike! All of you happy villagers under the protection of the great Noah! You know that when a man dies, he decomposes into carbon, calcium, phosphorous, and other elements. But do you know of any element called a soul? No. That's science.

"What's this!" Satan cried in a rage.

"What's what?" Jehovah replied innocently.

By the time Satan realized he'd been tricked, it was too late. Jehovah had firm control of the face of the Earth, so there was no way for him to escape. He roared and wailed in chagrin. He shed so many tears that the Euphrates started to overflow, and Jehovah became alarmed. So he turned to Satan and said, "You have to understand about souls. Otherwise it's just as if they weren't there. Satan, you've got to believe that Abel's soul came to you. There, how's that? Now can't you see that it exists?"

Satan decided that instead of spending more time lamenting in vain, he might as well try to do as Jehovah suggested. And when he did, he had a feeling he really might have found Abel's soul. Jehovah quickly spoke up.

"The trouble is, there are so few souls in your place that it's hard to make them out. In accordance with the dialectical principle that quantity converts to quality, as more souls arrive, they'll

become easier and easier to see. Not only that, but by my calculations, in less than five millennia a fellow called Dante is going
to pay you a visit, alive."

Hearing this, Satan was greatly comforted. The Euphrates
went down, and time went by. Human time, you know, passes
like a dream. Adam, Seth, Enos, Cainan, Mahaleel, Jared, Enoch,
Methuselah, Lamech: the generations passed.

And finally we come to this age of the great Noah.

Brothers, sisters, this is how it came about that even today, Jehovah watches our days with pleasure, and Satan keeps tally with
pleasure as day by day we die. Herein lies perfect balance, the
harmony of the universe. We all must take our turn to die. And
we all must know our share of suffering and confusion. As long
as Jehovah and Satan are at peace, the Euphrates stays within its
banks, and everyone is happy.

That, my friends, is the principle, the precept, the truth of the
universe. Listen to the words of the great Noah, and believe.
Let all who do not believe perish!

Signed,
Noah
Great man and mayor of the Kingdom of Jehovah,
and dignitary holding twelve offices

Once when Noah was fairly old, my father crossed in front of
him as he was riding his bicycle, surprising him so that he lost
control of the handlebars; in punishment, my father was sentenced to death. About the same time, my little sister was forced
to undergo one of Noah's physical examinations, swallowed the
poison pills, and eventually died. In despair, my mother then
went and asked for a dose of those same pills, and died, as she

had wished. My brother was so angry that instead of answering the catechism he spat, and was sentenced to death.

As a result I became an orphan, with nothing to fear from the dreadful law which said that anyone escaping from the village would be eternally banished, and his family exterminated. So one night I swam across the Euphrates and escaped.

The village was completely cut off from the outside world. It was surrounded by a high wall where Noah's sons, Shem, Ham, and Japheth, stood guard with their men. When there was a need for contact with the outside, say to trade, only they were allowed beyond the wall. So when I first set foot outside, everything was new and strange to me, and I set about learning all I could. What was worse than the village and what was better, what was more advanced and what was far behind—I chewed it all up in one mouthful, and swallowed it. And after a long, long time, in the course of walking around from place to place, little by little I learned how to think rationally.

Ten years went by.

One day I decided to return to the village. No sooner had the thought occurred to me than I was overwhelmed by a rush of the homesickness and hatred I had held in check all those years. I couldn't bear to stay away another moment. Besides, due to a chronic labor shortage, that village had a tradition of welcoming strangers. Those ten years had changed me within and without, so I had no fear that I would be recognized.

Getting in proved easy, just as I'd expected. Well, not exactly as I'd expected. I was able to enter easily enough, but not because of any village tradition of hospitality.

I could see at a glance that the village had changed. The outer wall was crumbling, and there was no sign of either Noah's sons or their men. The gates were wide open, and the entrance, which was choked with weeds, had an air of long neglect.

Everything within the walls had changed too. Those vast, once-splendid vineyards were nothing but a dense overgrowth of weeds, and the houses were dilapidated, full of holes that let in the elements, shelter only to wild birds and squirrels.

As I walked in a daze through the deserted village, along grassy roads, I came to an open space where there stood a queer building. It was at the foot of the small eminence with a broad slab of rock known as Meditation Stone, where Noah used to worship Jehovah, and people held feasts: a large building shaped something like a wooden shoe worn down at the heel. It had not been there in my day.

Going closer, I found to my astonishment that it was a type of boat. What in the name of heaven were they going to do with a boat this size, this far inland? It was nearly thirty yards high, and at least a hundred yards long, the size of a whaling ship. Was Noah really going to set it afloat here on the Euphrates? Why, that could only dam up the river!

As I drew closer, I could see that the boat had been abandoned in mid-construction, and left untouched for years. I felt sure there was some strong connection between this boat and the village's desolation.

Suddenly I noticed an old man squatting absently on Meditation Stone on the top of the hill. He noticed me too, and started to rise in a strange flurry, but then crouched down again and looked at me with fear in his eyes. I smiled and called out a greeting, which seemed to reassure him. "Traveling through, are you?" he said, and made room for me.

Of course, I had already figured out that this geezer was Noah. He was dressed now in a dirty peasant's smock, and the pistol, the boots, and the gold braid were nowhere to be seen, but the slack droop of his cheeks, the long beard, and the lurid hue of his heavy lower lip were unmistakable.

"Looks like this place has seen better days," I commented.

"Yes. It's all the doing of those foolish villagers. Fools, fools, fools!"

"What's that boat over there?" I asked, fighting off the desire to punch him.

"That's the famous Noah's Ark. Surely you've heard of it. Those fools . . . they went off and abandoned it before it was finished. But it's got to be completed. This can't be allowed to happen." All at once his neck retracted into his shoulders, in a strange, convulsive movement, and he clawed the air with stubby, gnarled fingers. Then he stared at me and said, "Traveler, you wouldn't have a drink on you, would you?"

I did, but of course I shook my head no.

He made a gurgling noise in the back of his throat and held his breath a moment, shaking as if in pain. Then suddenly he let his breath out as if his whole body had come undone, and spat out the following words without pausing for breath.

"Satan got suspicious. He decided there really wasn't any such thing as a soul. Decided Jehovah had pulled another fast one on him. So he made up his mind that no matter what Jehovah said to comfort him, he wouldn't stop crying. He decided he'd cry and cry and cry until the Euphrates overflowed its banks and flooded the whole world. So Jehovah says to him, 'Satan, it's a question of numbers. All you need is a few more souls.' Satan says, 'So much the better. I'll drown the whole world.' At that Jehovah gave up. He says, 'All right, Satan, then just wait a little. Give me time to save just one family. Time for the family of Noah, the most upright, the noblest, and the greatest man on earth, to build an ark to withstand your flood of tears.' That ark is still not ready. Satan will get tired of waiting. How can I explain it to Jehovah? Those fools! This will mean the end of the world."

"But even if you and your family were saved, it would still mean the end of the world for everybody else, wouldn't it?"

"No, no." My malicious question seemed not to bother him in the least. "That's what those fools all said, too. Said they were dead meat. But why should they complain about dying to save the harmony of the universe? I designed a special room in the ark to preserve a record of their lives. Why, that way I could preserve their memory for later generations better than they could themselves. Not only that, all the time they were working on the ark, I fed them. Even without the flood they were doomed anyhow. I just can't understand what they had to complain about."

"And you paid for their meals with village tax money?"

"Naturally. I was the head of the village, you know."

"Then in effect you forced them to pay for their own meals."

"Yes, all right. But that's life. And anyway, the flood was coming, they were all going to die sooner or later, so what difference did it make? But they didn't like it. The fools. The scum."

"The Euphrates doesn't show any signs of weeping to me."

"That's because of the promise. He promised Jehovah to wait until the ark was finished." He groaned. "What's Satan going to do when he finds out the ark's been abandoned?"

I decided to leave Noah and the ark, and turn my back on his village forever. All I can do now is hope that the legend of this foolish old alcoholic is transmitted faithfully.

The Special Envoy

Thirty-two special envoys
on a secret mission
and no way to speak of it—
taunted and hounded
to cold, mad graves

*W*aiting his turn in the ante-
room, where a faint stench from the nearby lavatory hung in the
air, Professor Jumpei Nara had been snoring lightly for some
time now as he sat straight up in the broken-springed sofa, his
hips sunk almost out of sight. He was of course not truly asleep.
He was merely demonstrating his spirit of modern pragmatism in
using this otherwise useless time for rest. Inwardly he felt far
from restful; he was enduring a teeth-gnashing attack of rampant
irritability.

Of all the damned luck. The movie scheduled before his talk
had started twenty minutes late, and then midway through it the
projector had broken down, delaying the proceedings by another
twenty-five minutes. Three quarters of an hour down the tubes.
Had he known this was going to happen, he'd never have insisted
on giving his talk after the movie. Judging from their name,
HOPE, the sponsoring group was a bunch of amateurs, and so in
order to teach them a little something, as well as to let them
know just how high his standards were, he had begun by

announcing his fee; then, while they were still recovering, he'd demanded to know which was the main event, the movie or his lecture? Naturally they answered that his lecture was, and so he'd given them a brisk talking-to, ordering them to reverse the order of the program because any fool knows the lesser attraction always comes first. Some people might contend it didn't matter one way or the other, but Nara knew that if you wanted to make a favorable impression, no detail was too small. Next he'd asked about the audience. On learning it would consist mostly of students, he had immediately offered to provide a short written introduction of himself geared to a student audience. "After all, no one knows me better than I do. I'll mail it in ahead of time. If you have any questions, just give me a call. No, don't bother to thank me. I have five different versions printed up, each for a different type of audience."

But all the civic spirit in the world was wasted on people as un-civic-minded as these. By rights, they ought to offer to pay him for these extra forty-five minutes. If only they would, he could of course turn the offer down, saying courteously that the thought was all that mattered and thus establishing a pleasant bond of mutual sympathy. Instead, they did nothing but flutter and fret, like infernal fools. He resolved never again to be taken in by sentimental blather about sponsors' sincerity.

But the waste of three quarters of an hour would have other consequences as well. It would have a direct effect on the contents of that introduction, for one thing. He didn't much like students to begin with. Students nowadays had no respect for intellect; everything had to have a political bent. They clung to the ground like so many bullfrogs and refused to allow for leaps in thought. The only way to handle them was to season the talk with keen humor, he knew, and with that in mind he'd gone over the text of the introduction fairly carefully. "Our lecturer for today is Professor Jumpei Nara, regular columnist for S— Newspaper and one of our nation's foremost critics of contemporary civilization. Professor Nara is familiar to seventy percent of the student body, exclusive of the department of athletics." That sort of thing.

Actually, this introduction was not nearly so well received as the one he had worked out for women's and business groups, and there were times when he thought of redoing it completely, but something kept him from going to so much trouble for mere students. He never got around to it. For today's lecture he had simply supplied a new opening line, as follows: "Allow me to introduce our speaker for today, Professor Jumpei Nara, whose impassioned and incisive views on the topic 'Outlook for the Space Age' have been widely reported in the press, arousing the admiration of the experts." He had sent it off without further changes. Students always seemed embarrassed by such statements, but there was something foul about their sense of superiority, he wanted to tell them. If he left it up to the organizers, no doubt they'd give him a bare-bones, perfunctory introduction, short-changing him and the audience. Just because it had no relation to the contents was no reason to sell a product with an inferior label.

What he despised more than anything else was the spirit of compromise, of talking things over. All judgments of right and wrong were relative, and in the end you had to stick by your values and allow the other guy to do the same, or democracy was a joke. In that sense it didn't really matter what people thought—but the extreme disorganization of the young men sponsoring this event gave him pause. The text of Nara's introduction could have the proper effect only if read with a certain liveliness and wit. And now, with an edgy audience that had had to endure a forty-five-minute delay as well as a documentary film little better than a cartoon, the reading would require more élan than usual. The way things were going, though, the master of ceremonies would make some stupid blunder as soon as he got to the podium, driving people away, and then, in front of a crowd half as large and twice as mean as before, read the damn thing in a nervous, supplicating singsong. It was inevitable. The very thought was chilling. He could see it now—every lip in the audience starting to curl in a sneer.

Unable to contain himself any longer, the professor had decided to use the extra time to give those young men a thorough grounding in the spirit of his introduction. Exceedingly thorough. With the patient concentration of someone stripping shelled peanuts of their skins, he had made an exhaustive study of every particular, pouring an unearthly ardor into each word. The young men, who had at first attended him diligently out of a sense of obligation, gradually had become terrified; singly and in pairs they had found pretexts to leave the room. In ten minutes nobody was left.

It seemed as if a long time had gone by, but when he checked his watch he found it was only a few minutes. He heard the sound of footsteps returning, and someone paused outside the door. There was no further sound. Just as Nara was starting to wonder, the handle slowly turned and a man came in. He was an angular fellow, thirtyish, in a nondescript gray suit. He seemed a trifle older than the kids running the show, but Nara assumed he was one of them and paid him no great attention.

Holding his hands behind him, the man shut the door, took a few steps forward, placed his feet neatly together and bowed formally. Then, in a strangely clipped voice, he said "May I disturb you for a few moments?"

From his manner, Nara realized that this man was not one of the organizers. Whenever he made a public appearance there were always one or two pushy people wanting to get a word with him in private. "No, you may not," he said flatly. "I'm trying to order my thoughts."

The man lowered his eyes apologetically. He leaned forward slightly, rubbing his left thumb on his right palm, and said, "I'm very sorry. But this seemed like such a good opportunity. I've had other chances to speak with you in the past, but somehow I always lost my nerve at the last moment. Learning that a man of your eminence was going to appear at a paltry gathering like this completely altered my image of you; I realized how easygoing and approachable you must be. Of course, I never doubted your earnestness about our problems, but I did have some fear that you might simply be taking advantage of the renewed interest in the subject of space exploration."

"I haven't got the faintest idea what you're talking about. I've never given a moment's thought to you or your problems, whatever they may be. Now will you go away and leave me alone?"

"But really, professor, now that the interest in space is starting to cool off, for you to have to speak in places like this where the toilets smell—"

"You have your nerve. Whether I do or not is my business!"

"Forgive me, I didn't mean it that way. What I actually meant to say is that since you seem to take such a deep interest in us—"

"Look, you—." Nara began wheezing, bellowslike, as though he were having a severe asthmatic attack. "—I don't know who the hell you are, but do you have any idea how rude and impertinent it is to think you can just barge in here and monopolize me like this? Everybody has paid the same money to hear me talk. What makes you think you deserve special treatment? You're no better than a thief!"

This bellows-style breathing of Nara's was well known and caused most people to capitulate on the spot, but the man showed no particular concern. With an abject look, he only said, "You're quite right, of course. Perhaps I should have introduced myself from the beginning. But as you will, I think, realize if you hear me out, that isn't as easy as it sounds. If I came right out and told you who I was, it might be difficult for you to believe . . . perhaps impossible . . . and yet, if I explain things thoroughly perhaps you will understand, more than anyone else would . . . not completely, I know, but because of your special interest in outer space you might somehow come to see how it is. No, you must see how it is. You are my only hope."

Nara stole an uneasy glance at the door. Damn those idiot students, where were they now? A fine mess he was in. This guy was definitely not normal. Must be slightly schizophrenic. He was a little pale, come to think of it, and had a funny look in his eyes. He had an unbelievably long neck, round shoulders, and yet overall an angular, rawboned look. Classic schizoid type. If he'd realized that, he'd never have spoken to the guy in the first place. Anything he might say would egg him on. The only thing to do was silently show him the door, or just ignore him and walk on out. This was what he got for letting himself be roped into appearing at places like this. One misfortune led to another.

After a brief silence, the man dropped his voice and said, "I'm sorry. You don't trust me. All right then, I may as well come out with it. You see, I'm a Martian."

Nara stared at the man, aghast. He was of two minds: he wanted to laugh, yet at the same time he felt an inexplicable fear crawling up his spine. Most unsettling. For this fellow with features so unmistakably human, for all their irregularities, to be convinced he was a Martian was hilarious; and then, to have a fellow so absurd place all his confidence in him, Nara, was less funny than it was offensive.

He longed for those brash young student organizers to come

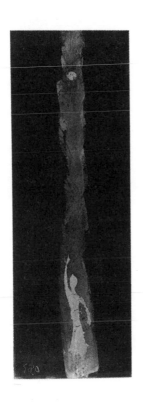

back; until they did, it would be best to sit tight here, biding his time. Eventually, however, the peculiar pride of a professional writer got the best of him. He wasn't the type to fall for a child-ish stunt like this. He'd teach this imposter just who he was up against. Eyes focused on the table legs, Nara wrinkled the tip of his nose in scorn as he spat out the following words.

"Mars? Mars, you say? Don't be ridiculous! It's been scien-tifically established that there is no intelligent life on Mars. You do consider yourself intelligent life, don't you? Then how could you possibly be a Martian? Come now, surely you don't expect me to fall for an old trick like that! This isn't the age of Orson Welles, you know. Mars has a horribly cold environment, lacking both water and oxygen; it's a wasteland 20,000 meters above sea level. Nothing could grow there but moss or mold."

"That's absolutely correct, technically. You *are* well informed."

"How dare you!"

"And I must admit that I am not a Martian in the sense you speak of. But in the sense that European immigrants become Americans, I am indeed a Martian."

"I know. You bought a plot of land there through the Mars Association. But that—"

"Nothing of the kind. That is only a cute gimmick, so there's no point in getting worked up about it. Our government would never recognize those deeds. And if the government fails to recognize them, then they're worthless."

"Aha. Then you belong to the Martian government?"

"No. I'm a special envoy, with plenipotentiary power to do business with people on Earth."

"Now I get it. So you propose to set up a new company to start selling off Martian property legally, under your supervision? In that case, you've come to the wrong place."

"You don't understand, Professor Nara," the man said in a sorrowful voice. "I really am a Martian. I belong to a race of people who moved there long ago from another planet."

"You expect me to believe that! Look at you! You're an ordinary human being!"

"Yes, Professor Nara, and that's exactly the source of the problem!" The man relaxed for the first time, spreading out his long, narrow fingers on the surface of the table. "We Martians have been seriously troubled by that very resemblance. When we realized it would be possible to visit Earth, it seemed at first that this physical resemblance would help us to make friends, but the more we thought about it, the more we realized that the resemblance would actually prove to be a fatal obstacle. After all, once we're here on Earth, how can we prove we're really Martians? Look at me! As long as I can't prove I'm not an Earthling, I can't expect anyone to understand that I'm a Martian, either."

Somewhere in the recesses of his mind, Nara felt a flicker of interest. Of course this was nothing but sophistry, like the punchline of a joke. But the idea was potentially useful: there was easily enough material here to use in his next three manuscripts—or his next nine lectures, for that matter.

"That's an interesting idea. But if you're really a Martian, then you ought to be able to come up with some sort of proof: the vehicle you came in, for example, or something else unique, not found on Earth. . . ."

"Yes, we've given a lot of thought to that. Because there are many unique features of Martian life. Just as our landscape is distinctive, so is our style of clothing, for example. But the uniqueness of our vehicles is particularly . . . well, as a matter of fact, it's so distinctive that it wouldn't work. The trouble is that our vehicles are not actually matter, but rather pure function. Nothing but a form of energy. You see . . . how can I explain it? I'm not a scientist so I can't put it very well. You know it's possible to transform matter into energy, right? That much could be done even with very old technology. But changing energy into matter is a lot harder. You people on Earth have succeeded in a very rough way, but you're still far from being able to produce complex structures on the spot. Whereas we've been able to do that for a long time now. We call it 'phase physics.' After that discovery, it was just a matter of time until we developed the technology to convert matter to energy, transport it to another place, and then reconvert it. That technology could be used as a powerful weapon. Just think what would happen if you transported one piece of matter inside another for even a moment. Why, if we took one of our moons, Deimos or Phobos, and implanted it inside Earth, this whole planet would explode in a matter of seconds! We wouldn't be foolish enough to do anything like that, of course, but it is possible. Fortunately, Mars no longer has any nation-states—"

"You have a world government?"

"Well yes, you could call it that. Of course our history goes back a lot further than yours."

Aha! One of those loonies from the early fifties, Nara thought, but again curiosity got the better of him. Never mind. "You were saying?"

"So with that new technology, rapid changes were made in the field of transportation. At first, it was used only for inanimate objects. Strictly freight. Then in a short time it became possible to transport animate objects as well. But there turned out to be a slight difference in the time it takes to transport inanimate and animate objects, so they had to have separate stations, which were set up all across the globe. Travel became virtually instantaneous, regardless of the distance involved. Passenger stations are full of rows and rows of capsules that look kind of like the phone booths you have here. You request your destination, go to the designated booth, push a button, and the next instant, you're there. As research went on, travel to other worlds became possible. The only trouble is, you can't build stations ahead of time to prevent collisions. It's possible for us to pinpoint a specific position on the Earth's surface accurately enough that there's little fear of landing buried in mud up to your knees, for example, which would have the same effect as stepping on a landmine. But suppose a dog happened to be walking in the targeted area: instant nuclear fusion. Our calculations can't allow for everything, you see. We tried to be as careful as we could in coming here, aiming for deserted schoolyards in the dead of night and that sort of thing, but we knew we were risking our lives. It was terrifying. Even after I realized I'd made it here safely, I couldn't stop shaking."

"I see. Well, that explains why you can't show anyone how you came. What a handy invention! But tell me, can you get back the same way?"

"Naturally. Every four hundred days, they come for me in the same place where I landed."

"Every four hundred days?"

"That's right. That's the way it works out, based on our respective rates of rotation and orbital motion."

"But you don't have a station. There's no button to push, or anything."

"I know this may sound strange, but animate objects can make return trips even without a station. Inanimate objects are far simpler, so you'd think it would be even easier, but in fact it's just the opposite. Not only is it impossible for inanimate objects to make return trips at all, but on ordinary trips the point of arrival varies in direct proportion to the square of the distance traveled. I don't really understand all the details, but animate objects seem to contain an internal energy that functions just like train tracks."

"So that's why you didn't bring any inanimate objects from Mars with you?"

"That's right. I couldn't take the chance of causing a terrible accident."

"Yes, but tell me this," said Nara, curling his lips in a sardonic sneer that would have tied the nerves of any ordinary person in knots, "why not bring an animate object, then? A Martian dog, for example, or a chicken."

The man lowered his eyes with a start and gave a slight nod. "Oh dear," he said. "I knew this was going to happen. It sounds like I'm making it up, but I can't help it, because it's true. The fact is, there aren't any. No dogs or birds on Mars. When our forefathers moved, they didn't take any animals with them at all. Only people. They already knew how to manufacture synthetic protein, you see."

"Well, what about a photograph? You could have brought a snapshot or two, couldn't you? Something to show the natural features, buildings, lifestyle. . . ."

"Yes, of course. Our paper is all made of mineral fiber, so it is inanimate, but as long as it's sent somewhere high in the air and allowed to fall naturally to earth, there's no particular danger. Dozens of photographs have actually been sent from time to time, but they all got caught in the wind or one thing and another, and landed in the hands of Earthlings. Exactly what became of them I have no way of knowing, but apparently they now form the basis of the popular image of Mars—everything from the natural features to the domed cities. It would do no good to trot them out now. People would just laugh them off and assume they were stills from some Disney film."

Nara stared at the other man with irritation, but when he

spoke there was surprising gentleness in his voice. "But you do plan to leave sometime, don't you? When? How long before your current four hundred days are up?"

"Actually, there's very little time left." The man raised his eyes again, with what seemed to be a look of imploring.

Nara smiled. "Well, then," he said, "your problems are solved! Invite some newspaper reporters, and whoever else you like, to witness your departure. I'll be happy to come along too. When the moment comes, suddenly you vanish from the middle of the schoolyard, while up in the sky, a red star gleams. . . . Why, if that happened, there isn't a person alive who'd doubt that you were a Martian."

"No." The man leaned forward and spoke bluntly. "I can't go back until I've completed my mission. It's extremely dangerous to land on Earth, so I can't go back and forth lightly. Those of us here have no choice but to carry out our mission."

"Mission? What mission?"

"I must find one Earthling who will acknowledge that I am a Martian."

"What then?"

"For the sake of interplanetary trade, that person will help me promote the construction of landing stations on Earth. If I could get that person to go back with me to Mars on a fact-finding tour, and then submit a report to the proper authorities here on Earth, the project would proceed much more smoothly."

"How much is it going to cost to build one station?"

"I'm not sure exactly. In your currency, perhaps around five billion yen."

Nara cocked his head. This might not be a lunatic after all, he was thinking. He might be deliberately taking me for a ride. Of all the dirty, malicious tricks. If the guy's going to all this trouble just to make a fool out of me, he must really hate me. But what

163

have I ever done to deserve such hate? Maybe he is a lunatic.

If he's a lunatic, he's a smart one. But wait—if he's really crazy, then he won't mind if I use his story. If I can do that, then this day won't have been a total waste after all. Why not go ahead and work it into today's lecture? It's got a nice touch of satire . . . yes, not bad at all. I'll call it "The Would-Be Martian." Too commonplace? How about "Logic in a Box"? No, too highbrow. Better make it something in between.

The man spoke in an intense whisper. "Professor, will you come with me?"

"Listen. Tell me the truth. Who are you?"

"I told you. I'm a Martian. Please, you've got to believe me. I'm staking everything on you. You do believe in the existence of life in outer space, don't you? Well, here I am! Please come with me."

"What do you mean?"

"It's almost time. There's only half an hour till my next chance to return to Mars. I'm tired. Earth's gravity is very strong, you know. Just standing up exhausts me. Please, I beg you, come back with me!"

As the man grabbed his sleeve, Nara brushed him off and hastily stood up. "Get your hands off me!"

"I apologize. I don't want to use force, believe me. But look at it from my point of view. Being a Martian, without being able to prove that I am, is indescribable torture. Coercion—yes, if you won't believe me, I have no choice. . . ."

"Out of my way! Don't talk nonsense!"

"Please!"

"I said get out of the way!"

"I'm fully aware of how dangerous the use of force is. Thirty-eight other Martians have visited Earth in all. Seven of them blew up on landing. Look it up; you'll find records of unexplained explosions and fires. The other thirty-one all tired of the struggle and tried to force someone into going back with them. Every one of them was turned over to the police and hauled off to an insane asylum. I'm the thirty-second envoy to land safely. Everyone told me not to give up, to be patient, never to get desperate and try to force someone into coming with me—but I can't take any more. I've had it. But you, Professor Nara—you have such a fertile imagination. I know you won't let me down!"

"You've got to let go of me!"

"No, I know you wouldn't do that. You believe in alien life. Please come along. Or do I have to drag you off by force? Have I got to knock you out? You wouldn't send me to an insane asylum, would you? No, not you. Only scum would do a thing like that. The other thirty-one Martians were no judges of character; they all staked themselves on scum. Not me. I was lucky to meet a man like you, professor. Wasn't I?"

As if Earth's gravity, double that of his native planet, were really too much for him, the man staggered forward holding his arms out clumsily in the air. Nara shoved him away as hard as he could and ran out into the corridor.

"Professor, wait!"

Listening to the man's cry and the sound of his unsteady footsteps in close pursuit, Nara ran for all he was worth down the dim corridor toward the backstage stairs. The student organizers were standing in the wings leaning against a wall, peering in at the movie. Not guessing that the professor's bellows were actually cries for help, they scattered like baby spiders, so swiftly and lightly that he had no idea where they'd gone. In a daze he ran on up the stairs until he found himself standing before the movie screen, just as a rocket ship was shown taking off for Mars. The rocket ship came crawling out of its space station, spinning like a top, and was swallowed in Nara's shadow.

"Get out of the way!" yelled voices from the audience, while the voice of the Martian pleaded from the wings: "Please, professor, please!"

Nara leaped down into the audience. Someone yelled in the half-dark and jumped up, heading at full tilt for the exit in the back of the room. Apparently one of the organizers was under the illusion that Nara was after him. That set up a general pandemonium all over the auditorium as others of the group, under the same misapprehension, began to jump up and race out; but the hubbub was drowned in the soaring music of the finale as the Mars-bound rocket slid off silently into the darkness of outer space.

Flinging open the exit door, Nara rushed out and tore straight into the office, picked up the phone without a word, and called the police. "You've got to come right away, there's a lunatic on the loose and he's violent!"

In ten minutes the police were there. When they found the self-styled Martian, who had continued to search for Nara, unable to reconcile himself to failure, they lifted him up and carried him off lightly, holding him up on either side like a small child and then throwing him in a white cage with an engine attached.

Professor Nara, who had been secretly watching all this from the office window, thought suddenly, "What if he's a real Martian after all?" He suddenly felt very ill, as if the space between his eyes had widened and his head had grown out three meters in either direction.

That evening his lecture was so garbled that no one could understand a word of it. But as he finished speaking, a beatific look came over his face. It had come to him—the perfect title: "Outer Space Madness." That more than made up for everything.

Beguiled

*T*he two benches in the waiting room were occupied by a pair of women waiting for the first early-morning train on the branch line. The last train on the main line had departed for the night. Belatedly, a tall, thin man came into the room. He had thick eyebrows and closely-cropped hair and was wearing a snug sport shirt.

Glancing around, he turned to the station attendant who was closing up the ticket gate, and inquired in a tired, apologetic voice, "There's five hours till the next train. Would it be okay if I slept here?"

The station worker nodded, not pausing in his task of fitting the heavy sliding door onto its rails.

Of the women on the benches, one was old, the other only slightly less so; now, as if by agreement, each pushed her bamboo basket to the far edge of her bench, leaned against it, stretched out full length, and pretended to be asleep. Their baskets were filled with fresh produce that they would take to market on the next train. Each wore a soiled dark blue apron and had wrapped around her head a thin towel decorated with the logo of some country inn. The younger of the two, who wore a red train pass around her neck, lay on the grimy black bench in front of the ticket counter. The other woman's bench, over beside the concession stand, still bore a few traces of faded, peeling paint as well as an ad for caramels.

The man glanced from one reclining figure to the other as he paced slowly around the room. On his third circuit, he stopped in front of the older woman and said politely, rubbing his hands together, "Excuse me, but would you mind sl-sliding over?"

The old woman stared up at him expressionlessly through half-closed eyes, showing no sign of hearing.

Suddenly the man leaned forward and fastened his glance on her legs, which hung out over the end of the bench. Startled, she quickly drew them in, whereupon the man spat noisily into a dirty spitoon.

"Slide over, would you?" he said again.

"I was here first. It's mine," she retorted. She pointed a short, battered finger at the other woman's bench and said, "Go over there and sit with her, why don't you. Go on." She paused, then added petulantly, "All summer long, we've had this place to ourselves."

"That's right," the other woman chimed in, giving up any pretense of sleep. "Ask anybody. What gives you the right to come along and talk that way, anyway?"

"Yes, but I-I'm tired. I just want to lie down, and sleep."

"Everybody's tired," said the older woman irritably, and pulled the towel down over her face.

The man spat again. The younger woman clucked her tongue and shifted her position. Her bamboo basket creaked. For a moment the man stood there motionless with his head bowed, waiting. The light went out in the station office. A slight wind came up, diffidently rattling the windowpanes. He hunched his shoulders as if cold; his thin sport shirt was apparently inadequate for the time of year.

Suddenly the man rubbed his hands together briskly, stroked his stubbly beard, and boldly yanked the old woman's towel off her face. She looked up with a frown, seemingly blinded by the light, and he made placating motions with his open hands.

"P-please, get out of the way, would you?" he said. "I've got . . . an important job ahead and I'm tired as hell. Go on over there yourself, for Christsake."

The old woman started to say something, but all at once her eyes filled with fear. She sensed a strange frenzy lurking in the stubby fingers of the man's hands as they waved in the air; it seemed to her his hands were closing in on her throat.

"Go!"

Was it her imagination, or had a change come over him? As he spoke, his right hand slipped into his trouser pocket.

"Is he still here?" the other woman called out in exasperation.

But by now the first woman was so intimidated that her companion's outburst sounded impertinent. She pulled herself upright and stood, taking her basket with her.

The man sank down into the place vacated by the old woman, as if drawn there by a magnet. Watching her totter off, carrying her basket before her, he spat again into the spitoon.

The other woman raised herself to a half-sitting position, on her face a look of mingled annoyance and suspicion—a look aimed not only at the man but also, clearly, at the old woman, for capitulating without a fight. The old woman turned and gestured back toward the man to vindicate herself, only to feel deflated at the sight of him sitting harmlessly rubbing his hands together, a dark languor on his face. What had she been so afraid of?

"Some people!" she muttered to herself, as she heaved her

basket atop the other woman's, shoved them both toward the center of the bench, and plopped down in the empty space.

"This is ridiculous," said the other woman. She took out a hard-boiled egg from her basket and began to peel it. The first old woman sullenly lit a cigarette.

The tall man, hunched over now as if unsure quite what to do with his gangling frame, sat with his legs wide apart, elbows on his knees, and continued rubbing his hands as he kept a weather eye on the old women. They kept their eyes downturned, unable to meet his gaze. Finally they turned back to back, leaned up against the baskets, and tried to doze. The man pulled his collar closed and sighed, then folded his arms across his knees and bent forward until his forehead rested on his arms.

For a while there was perfect silence. Even the wind died down. Sounds of mice nibbling a newspaper behind the concession stand, and of the man spitting at ten-minute intervals, served only to intensify the quiet.

After many minutes had passed, through the silence there came the crunch of solitary footsteps across the plaza. The footsteps were slow, but with each step they dug into the plaza gravel, persistent and cautious. Surely a patrolman on his rounds would walk with a lighter, more businesslike step—and too much time had gone by for this to be a disembarked passenger back from an unfruitful search for lodging. Moreover, it was still too early to be a morning commuter. Had the trio in the waiting room not already been asleep, they would certainly have pricked up their ears suspiciously.

The footsteps paused outside the glass doors. Then the doors were pulled boldly open and someone slipped into the room, looked back, and carefully shut the doors again, waking the three sleepers as he did so. The new arrival crossed in front of the old women with a preoccupied air, not glancing in their direction, and stood in front of the wicket, gazing up at the timetable. He was a small fellow with the look of a clerk, standing with his hands pushing out the pockets of his cheap, gray summer suit. Drawing out a large, soiled handkerchief, he wiped off the back of his neck and nodded several times to himself.

The first man blinked at the sight of the other man's back. Every muscle in his body went taut. When the man in the summer suit spun around lightly on his right heel and faced him, the larger man emitted a faint cry and stood up.

But the agitation of the small man was still greater. Panic-stricken, his eyes darted around, swiftly measuring off the distances between the doors, the other man, and himself. Seeing escape to be impossible, he stepped backward and took a defensive stance, drawing his elbows in. His lips curled in an ironic smile. "Aha!" he cried sharply. The effect was somewhat theatrical.

"So you found me," he continued. "What, have you been laying in ambush? How the hell did you know I'd come here?"

The tall man shrugged noncommittally, sticking the fingers of his left hand down the front of his shirt and scratching his chest while his right hand instinctively covered the right pocket of his trousers. He cast a sidelong, searching glance at the door. The women held their breaths, feeling their spines tingle.

"Don't worry, I won't try to escape," the small man said. "I know you're too much for me. I surrender."

"I . . ."

"No, I'm not going to try. Jeez, I never expected you to catch up with me. Looks like I walked straight into your trap. You win. Mind if I sit down?"

"Stay away from me!" bellowed the tall man, holding up a fist.

The small man looked down and smiled weakly. "Okay, I hear you. That's a knife in your pocket, isn't it."

The tall man started to say something, stuttered, let his lower lip fall slack, and sighed. Doubt and confusion were registered plainly on his face.

The small man relaxed and shifted his weight from one foot to the other. "I won't be causing you any more trouble," he said. "You beat me in a battle of wits, and I might as well admit it. My hat's off to you." Then, catching sight of the women, he laughed awkwardly and said, "Well, ladies, have a look. This gentleman has recaptured me. I never thought I'd see the day."

The tall man swallowed hard and started to speak. The small man quickly cut him off.

"I'll go ahead and sit down here, shall I? If you want me to put my hands in the air or anything, just say so. You can search me, do whatever you want. You know me—when I'm out-smarted I admit it. I give in without a struggle. Why, it's almost an honor to lose to a brilliant opponent like yourself." As he spoke, he approached the bench and perched casually at the far end, keeping a careful eye on the other man. "Cigarette?"

The tall man bridled, and held up an arm, but then after a moment's hesitation he lowered it resignedly and took the cigarette. "You can't put anything over on me," he growled.

"Oh, of course not. I know that. I'm perfectly aware I'm no match for you. I'm certainly not going to try anything stupid. You know, you've got a mind like a steel trap. Imagine anticipating my moves like this. How'd you do it? How did I give myself away? I can't figure it out." He paused. "Damn, my molar's been killing me all day."

"Wha . . . so has mine."

"Really? Now that's a strange coincidence. Very strange."

"But I . . . you . . . I mean, I figured you probably . . ."

"Oh, yes, I thought I'd given you the slip once and for all. I was sure of it."

"But—what's going on!"

"What do you mean?" The small man ran the dark tip of his tongue over the corners of his mouth, and an amused chuckle emerged from the back of his throat.

His companion clenched his laced fingers until they were white, and suddenly yelled, "What the hell is going on! You tell me! You bastard, what did you come here for! Out with it!"

The small man scrunched down and nodded quickly. "I'll tell, I'll tell. You don't have to get so excited. After all, we've got all night and I'd like to get to the bottom of this, too. As long as things have come to this, let me try to work it all out in my mind. After all, you've succeeded in capturing me—which means, of course, that you anticipated my every move. I guess you want me to verify the details. That's fine with me. I'm interested myself in knowing how you were able to figure out so exactly where I was heading. Life is a contest of wits, I say. Win or lose, it's fun playing the game. Brains are the name of the game; and if someone outsmarts you, the least you can do is admit it with good grace. Isn't that so, ladies?" he added, turning suddenly and addressing the two women, who were listening with suspicion.

"No fair whining and making excuses," he went on, still speaking to them. "If you know you're going to lose, you'd better stay out of the game. The key to winning lies in how well you can read the other guy. If you can't do that, he'll take you by surprise. Supposing you ladies and I were to match wits—I try to get your wallets, you try to get mine, and anything goes. We're allowed to coax, trick, even kill. I'd be a cinch to win. Not just because I'm a man and have superior strength, but because your baskets and clothes tell me everything there is to know about your work, your lifestyle, your way of thinking. Whereas what do you know about me? Zilch. That gives me a powerful advantage. For example . . ."

As if testing the effect of his words, he fell silent for a moment and moistened his lips. The women shifted uneasily, and the other man's eyes, beneath his shaggy black eyebrows, stared vaguely into the distance as if he were deep in thought.

"Suppose I make a sudden dash for it," he began again. "This gentleman here would be sure to catch me. But then suppose I hit him where it hurts, hard. He's lying there on the floor groaning in pain. I strangle him. Then I drag the body off to the john, come back, and find you two still here, shaking in your boots. I say, 'Sorry, ladies, you saw me do it, didn't you? I can't just let you walk away. You'll have to spend the night in the john with the stiff. You can hold a wake for him for all I care. But the place stinks to high heaven, so I'll do you a favor and bump you off first so you won't notice. You don't look too happy about that. If you want, you could each fork over a little something, as a sign you promise to keep your mouths shut.'

"And that's how I help myself to the contents of both your wallets, ladies, with your blessing. Or I might just haul the two of you off to some secluded woods, gag you, and tie you to a tree. Then you're found, and on the strength of your word the authorities rush over and check out the john, but it's clean—no stiff. Small wonder. Turns out the murder you thought you saw was a fake. We aren't an escaped convict and his pursuer at all, but partners, a team. When your story doesn't check out, they decide you probably staged the whole thing yourselves, to cover up the disappearance of money you were entrusted with." The small man chewed on his lower lip thoughtfully, lit another cigarette, took a deep drag, and went on.

"But you can relax, ladies, because this gentleman beside me is my pursuer and he's caught me, fair and square. If I tried to get away, he'd kill me before I could kill him, no doubt about it. And pardon me, but you ladies don't look as if you have enough money between you to be worth bothering about."

The younger woman snorted and started to say something, but the tall man groaned, and interrupted with a cry of exasperation. "Cut the crap and tell me who you are, you bastard," he growled. "Who the hell are you?"

"Me? You want to know who I am?"

"Yeah, you. Let's hear it."

"Aha . . . I've got it! I thought so all along. So that's the secret of your victory over me! Wouldn't you know it. You, the pursuer, tried to become me, the escapee. Once you did that, and learned to think like me, then finding me was child's play. Of course, that's a well-known method. But you did it so thoroughly, got so deeply into your role, that you lost sight of your real self—and now you no longer even know who I am. Must be like coming across your reflection in a full-length mirror and not knowing who it is. What a detective!"

The tall man grimaced, and pressed the balls of his thumbs firmly into his temples.

"That explains another thing," the small man continued, lowering his voice. "It's bothered me ever since I saw you—why would he be wearing a sport shirt, I say to myself, in weather like this? Now I get it. You decided to dress like I was dressed the day I escaped. Why, you identified with me right down to the toothache, for crying out loud! You were so determined to hunt me down that you went and got the very same pain in your molar as me. Whew. What determination! Don't tell me—I suppose you feel as if you're on the lam by now. Right?" He gave a sardonic laugh. "While you're at it, why not dump me here and make tracks? Just joking, of course. I've surrendered." He paused briefly, and went on.

"Still, whoever thought I'd end up like this? Makes me sick to think of it. I wonder where I slipped up? I knew all along that with a man of your caliber after me, no ordinary plan would work. I knew you'd make yourself over into me, so I allowed for that. Any plan that's too logical is vulnerable—if one part falls apart, the rest falls apart with it. I decided to try something completely haphazard, hit-or-miss. But it's harder than you think to behave in a totally random manner. A person may think he's being unpredictable, but if you look closely there's usually a pattern of one kind or another. Even in the behavior of madmen, for example . . ."

The tall man made a choking sound, and spat. The small man started to get up, instinctively poised to flee. But the tall man was laughing. Rocking slowly back and forth, he laughed quietly on and on, through clenched teeth.

The small man grinned. "You know," he confided, "I thought I had taken a course as random as the wanderings of a madman. When I got off the train here I had no idea why, or where I'd be heading next. So how did you figure it out? No, don't tell me, let me think. It galls me to think I could have been so careless. There has to have been some rational explanation for my actions, after all. What was it about this place that drew me to it? That's holding me here now? Something dark and fearful . . . something vaguely cruel, and desperate . . . something that could suddenly slice through the bonds holding me. . . . Yes, it has some connection to death. Money? A woman? But if it were money, it would have to be carefully planned, so it can't be that. A woman, then, was that it? Wait . . . a woman who escaped with another man . . . a station where I changed trains once long ago with a woman. Damn it, I don't like this. Then you . . ."

The tall man sat motionless, eyes fixed on his hands, which were cupped together as if he were going to scoop up a drink of water.

The small man nodded deeply to himself and shot a glance at the old women. "It's true," he murmured. "If everything in life means more pain, then instead of waiting for them to come to you it's better to get up, go out, and kill them first. For your own preservation, it's best to kill women in way stations. It's just kind of smoothing the way, that's all."

The tall man grunted and nodded his head. The old women had closed their eyes, pretending to sleep, and lay with their heads back against the back of the bench, but now they began to squirm in apparent discomfort.

The small man reminisced. "After I killed that other woman at a way station once—was it here?—the way became so clear."

"That's right, it did," muttered the tall man, rubbing his knees.

"You remembered that. You knew that the more random and reckless I tried to be, the more drawn I'd be to this station—this room—and so you set your sights on it. Or I guess I should say that because you had entered so completely into my mind, you yourself were inevitably drawn here."

"Yeah . . . yeah, maybe so."

"But I can't get over it. Imagine, another person knowing me better than I do myself."

"I—"

"But listen. I'll admit I'm beaten this time, but what do you say to another round? Now, I'm not suggesting that we start all over. That wouldn't be fair. I'm talking purely mental combat. I'll wait with you here for the first train and I'll go back with you when it comes. But between now and the time we get there, I'll try to fool you. All you have to do is say 'Gotcha' and I'll stop. You won't have to slug me or tie me up—I won't cause you any further trouble. That's the way I am; I'm man enough to know when I'm beaten. I have some pride. But just once, if I could slip away right from under your eyes, maybe do in those ladies over there who are just asking to be murdered. I say this only because of the deep respect I have for you: just say 'Gotcha,' and I'll stop whatever I'm doing. I know I haven't got a prayer, but the challenge is irresistible—sort of a mutual mental reconnaissance. Once long ago, I heard about a man who loved *go*. It became an obsession. Finally he couldn't stop playing even when he wanted to. All night long, on top of the bedcovers, he would go on playing by himself, and weeping. That more or less sums up my type."

"Yes, I suppose it does at that." Suddenly the tall man let out a laugh. It burst forth like a popping cork.

"Am I right?" The small man chuckled too. "All right, fair enough? The bet's on, okay? It's now three a.m. The first train leaves at 5:40. Either I kill those women before then, without your catching me, or else I escape on the way back with you. There's plenty of time. What do you say, you want to catch a little shut-eye now while you've got the chance? Those women probably aren't looking to be killed, so you can be sure they'll sit up and keep a sharp eye on me. The minute they see me start to try anything, they're bound to scream and wake you up. Then all you have to do is open your eyes and say, 'Gotcha.' Right, ladies?"

The old women regarded the short man stonily through narrowed eyes. The younger one cautiously mopped perspiration off her forehead with her sleeve. The small man stuck out his lower lip and smiled craftily, at which the tall man rubbed his unshaven chin and gave a cavernous yawn. "Maybe I will catch a little sleep," he said.

"Be my guest."

The tall man slowly laid an arm across the back of the bench, rested his head on it, and closed his eyes, all as if hypnotized.

After about a minute, he began to snore softly. The small man smiled and nodded in the direction of the women, then turned his back to them, likewise buried his head in his arms, and went to sleep. The old women listened with disbelief to the quiet, even breathing of the pair. They sighed, exchanging anxious looks, and stayed awake without ever taking their eyes off the sleeping men.

Eventually lights came on in the office, and there was the murmur of voices. The old women looked at each other in relief. Their eyes debated whether or not to seek help, but for some reason they hesitated, afraid of ending up the butt of ridicule. Had it all been a ludicrous practical joke? The older woman spat, the younger one snorted and scowled.

Before long, an old man whom the women knew entered the waiting room, carrying a basket similar to theirs. After returning his greeting, the women pointed to the men on the bench, and silently drew circles in the air beside their heads.

"What's that you say?" said the old man, who was hard of hearing, in a loud voice.

At that the small man sprang awake, stood up, and stretched. At the same time, the tall man uttered a cry and assumed a defensive posture with such speed and force that he nearly upset the bench.

The small man laughed. "I fell asleep, too," he said. "It's all right. Well, ladies, glad to see you're both in good health."

The old women turned away angrily. The small man sat down again, still smiling, and began whispering in the ear of his companion, who was sitting listlessly, as if wrapped in fog. "The real gamble starts now," he said. "Everything's more fair and aboveboard with us both wide awake. Unfortunately I missed my chance to do in the ladies, but I'll find a way to escape, never fear. You'd better keep your eye on me. When the ticket window opens, you've got to exchange your ticket, don't you. Let this one be on me."

The tall man was staring at an area just behind the small man's ear. His small, black pupils grew smaller and smaller, shrinking in distrust. He spat and cleared his nose. The two men agreed to go take a leak together. When they returned, the number of people waiting for the first train had increased to five. The women had evidently been talking about them; everyone turned to look at the two men. But time passed without incident until the wicket opened.

The train pulled in, and the two men climbed safely aboard. There was only one vacant seat. The small man grinned.

"Which of us should sit down?" he said. "By rights you, the pursuer, should be the one to sit. But standing would make it child's play for me to get away. It would also be easier for you to watch over me while standing. I guess I'd better take the seat."

The tall man looked at his companion closely and drew his head back noncommittally.

The small man nodded and sat down. "Better keep your eyes peeled," he warned.

The train crawled slowly forward. The two men each downed coffee and a jam-filled bun. The ride was uneventful.

Arriving at their destination, the small man said with resignation, avoiding the probing stare of his companion, "Damn. I never stood a chance. You never took your eyes off me for a minute. I've never known anyone with such strong will. But you won't give up, will you? How do we go from here? Train, bus, taxi? Taxi might be the safest. On the other hand, it might be better to stay where there are a lot of people. Maybe bus is the best bet."

"Bus it is," ordered the tall man in a voice tight with anxiety.

The small man led the way aboard the bus, which grew more

crowded at every stop. Jostled, he looked back at his companion and called out good-naturedly, "Hang on tight."

The tall man sucked on his molar, which had clearly started to hurt again, and scowled, breathing heavily. They arrived at their stop without incident.

It was a quiet suburb. In front of them lay a small river, with vegetable patches beyond. A gravel road led through the rows of vegetables to a small hill of red clay, and in the shadow of the hill were rows and rows of sparkling, blue-tiled rooftops.

"Another five minutes on foot. Looks like you win. But don't be too sure yet. There are gullies and huge tree roots along the way. The last seconds of a game can be the most intense."

Instead of answering, the tall man put his hands to his throat and gave an anguished groan. His eyes were hollow and ringed with dark circles.

"What is it?"

"You can't pull anything over on me," he muttered, flecks of saliva showing from between his clenched teeth.

Watching each other warily, they walked so close together that their elbows touched occasionally. Once again, they arrived without incident.

As they walked through the gate side by side, the small man muttered, "Son of a gun. You did it, didn't you. Got me back here. Guess I'd better throw in the sponge."

The tall man made a sound midway between a laugh and a howl, and slapped his own ribs hard. At the same moment, a group of stalwart men in white coats jumped out from behind a hedge. They worked swiftly and professionally. The tall man, struggling in their grip, screamed, "You've got the wrong man! It's him! It's him!"

But shrieks and all, he was soon firmly encased in a strait-jacket. Robbed of his liberty, the man turned wild eyes on his erstwhile companion, who nodded to himself a number of times.

"Yes, the safest way to go is to convince them they're doing everything of their own free will."

The Bet

Seated at my drawing board, I looked across at the director of general affairs at AB Company. I held myself perfectly straight, my spine a full two inches from the back of the chair, unable to relax until I heard the man's reply. He showed no sign of answering.

In the strong light from the draftsman's lamp over my desk, a thick bundle of blueprints gleamed brightly where the pages had been freshly cut. The director's face was in shadow, partially obscured by the lampshade. I looked at my watch. It was 6:15. Everyone had gone home but my assistant. Fluorescent lights flickered with a noise like the beating of insect wings.

"Well? Is there some problem with my proposal?" I asked.

The man shifted, his chair squeaking as he did so, and probed his jaw with the balls of his fingers as if pushing stray whiskers back into the flesh. At last he spoke. "Not in the least. We are perfectly content to leave everything in your hands. It's just that this time, the alteration we want done is rather substantial, you might even say drastic."

"I realize that. It's a great change. This wall, right here, the wall of Room 17 adjacent to Room 18—you want this juxtaposed to the president's office."

"Yes, yes." Chuckling, the man took the unlit cigarette he'd been fingering and rubbed its tip over the plans.

"But the president's office, you see, is on the third floor. And Room 17 is on the second floor."

"Ah, yes. I suppose the technical aspects involved in putting two rooms on different floors next to each other would be quite difficult."

"That's putting it mildly."

"But you've solved any number of equally difficult problems before."

"Well, all I want to know is, is this change really worth the trouble?"

"Well, of course, if we didn't think it necessary then we'd never—"

"Wait. Let's not worry about that now." I slid forward, leaning back in my chair. The man's beige tie was reflected in the shiny blade of my letter-opener. But then I had to sit up again quickly to begin an explanation of the blueprints. "As you know, this makes the thirty-sixth time I've had to revise the blueprints."

"I apologize for all the trouble we've caused you."

"The number of times doesn't bother me. This is my job, after all. It's only fair that I redo the work as often as necessary, until you're satisfied. All I'm concerned about is . . . well . . . the results. What do you say? Will you look these blueprints over and tell me exactly what you think?"

"But I'm not sure what I—"

"Let me be specific. Here, on this page, will you take a look at this?"

"Uh huh."

"You see?"

"I'm afraid maps and drawings are not my forte."

"This is a lateral cross-section."

"So . . . This would be a stairway. . . . This line is an extension of this line, and . . . wait a minute. There's something peculiar going on. How does this line? . . ."

"It connects here."

"Then what's this? There seems to be another stairway, right behind the other one."

"There most certainly is. That was the only way I could connect the first mezzanine with the second, without going through the second floor."

"Why on earth would you want to do that?"

"There, you see? Even you think it's strange. But that's the sort of thing that happens when I have to put in changes haphazardly, one after another."

"There's nothing haphazard about any of this." For the first time, his expression revealed a hint of strain. "All of the changes we have requested are the result of laborious surveys and meticulous planning."

"If that's the case, fine. Then I assume you are satisfied with these results?"

"Yes, very interesting. I must say I'm intrigued."

"Good. You've set my mind at ease. Then you're willing to sign this provisional consent form?"

"I beg your pardon?"

"You see, I need evidence that you agree, in principle, that the blueprints are finished as they are."

"But what about the new alteration?"

"Yes, yes, I know. But apart from that, in order to wind up the work I've done so far—"

"I fail to see what you're driving at."

"Surely you realize that this design is totally lacking in common sense."

"Maybe."

"Yes, and so I'd like to make it perfectly clear that you're entrusting this work to me in full awareness of these anomalies. Otherwise you might come along later and say, 'Well, if you knew it was going to turn out strangely, you didn't have to stick so slavishly to our requests. It's your job to listen to our requests, and make sense out of them.' If that happened, all my hard work would go right down the drain."

"Naturally, you are expected to follow all instructions to the letter."

"But just because you had a hundred people, you wouldn't need a hundred hallways! However many hundreds of staff you had, one or two hallways would be enough! Just because you might need a detailed street map, there'd be no reason to record the number of branches in every tree along the road! Architectural design is more than numbers."

"Somehow you seem to have gotten the wrong impression. Every one of our requests is the product of careful study. There's nothing hit-or-miss, and any apparent duplication is deliberate."

"Then you'll sign?"

"No, I'm afraid I couldn't."

"Why not?"

"As long as everything has been left to you, I've got to have some sign of assurance from you. Otherwise that puts me in a very awkward position. Don't you see that? But in fact, the more I listen to you, the more it seems to me you have no self-confidence at all and are just trying to escape responsibility."

"Wait—now you're getting the wrong idea."

"Then you do have confidence that you know what you're about? Well, in that case—"

"Wait, wait. This job is something everyone in the business has his eye on. I mean after all, the chance to design the new annex for the showcase AB Building—it can't help attracting attention. And I'm as ambitious as the next guy. If this succeeds, it will be great publicity. But if it doesn't . . ."

"Leave the publicity angle to us. That's our specialty."

"Yes—yes, of course."

"Or do you expect to fail?"

"No, of course not. But frankly, I am a bit worried. What we've got here goes completely against conventional theories of modern building design."

"But theory and function are surely not the same."

"Of course not. But you can't equate architectural function with mechanical function, either. Especially in a large-scale project like this, rather than analyzing every last little detail, a better way to improve function is to maximize the efficient use of space overall. For that reason it works best to begin by dividing the whole into large, simple blocks—"

"Look, who cares about modern theories of design?"

"This happens to be my theory."

"Then you regret having taken on the project?"

"No, no. Well, there may have been times I felt that way. Sometimes I'd think, I can't show these plans to anybody, my client has made some kind of horrible mistake. And then I'd wonder whatever possessed me to take all your specifications at face value. I spent a lot of time worrying. But I never could get you to see it my way."

"So you gave up trying?"

"There definitely were times when I felt like it. But as time went by, I don't know, gradually I became intrigued."

"Intrigued?"

"Yes. These plans definitely fly in the face of all previous architectural theory, especially theories of space utility. But the more I toy with them, the more I sense new, unforeseen possibilities. This just might be the wave of the future. And yet, unable to back it up with any known theory, I wind up confused, at a total loss. I guess you could say I'm starting to lose my bearings."

"Ah."

"So you see, in order to shore up my confusion from some outside source, I'd like very much to have you sign here."

"Good, now I think I understand your position."

"Then you'll do it?"

"But listening to your account has convinced me more than ever that such a step is totally unnecessary."

"It has?"

"All you have to do is build up your confidence. That's the only way. Don't you see? It would be easy for me to sign the paper, but that would only underscore your lack of confidence. For your own sake, I have to refuse."

"But do you people have any idea just how extraordinary these plans are?"

"Don't worry. Look, I have an idea. Why don't you stop by our office some day and see how we operate?"

"I've been by before. . . ."

"Yes, but looking in from the outside doesn't give you the real picture. The advertising business is as complicated as a living organism. Once you understand how it operates, I'm sure your doubts will evaporate."

"Really?"

"Absolutely. Your lack of confidence just goes to show how much you don't understand. So you'll come? When?"

"Any time, as far as I'm concerned."

"The sooner the better. Tomorrow morning?"

"Fine with me."

"Good. Then I'll see you tomorrow, say at 8:30."

"That's just when everyone gets to work, isn't it?"

"Right. I'd like to have you spend the day with us. As a sort of temporary employee, if you don't mind."

"Fine."

He nodded, smiling with satisfaction, and started to get up. "Well, I managed to get by without smoking a single cigarette the whole time I was here," he said, brushing bits of crushed cigarette from his hands into the ashtray. "Whenever I feel like a smoke, I crush one in my hands this way. I recommend the technique. Somehow, feeling the tobacco between your fingers drives home what poison it is, and before you know it you've lost all desire to light up."

"Yeah . . . well . . . thanks for everything." I stood up to see him out, switching off the desk light.

2

The following morning, at 8:30 sharp, I arrived in front of the AB Building. The taxi driver wiped the windshield with his glove, waiting for me to count out the exact change. A utility pole stood among the trees by the side of the street.

Three young women came along, walking in step, and entered the building with a sidelong glance at me. One of them removed her earrings and stuffed them quickly into an overcoat pocket. I followed them up the stone steps.

A cleaning woman by the entrance plunged a rag into a bucket and sloshed it around with red hands as she called out to the young women. "Welcome home!"

I couldn't believe my ears. But then the trio responded in unison, "Hi, we're back!" Evidently I had heard correctly.

Did they live here? Maybe they had only gone out for breakfast. This might be one sign of what that fellow last night had spoken of—the hidden complexity of the advertising business.

"Welcome home," called out another female voice. Certain she couldn't mean me, I went by without replying. "Yoo-hoo," she called again, so I turned to find it was the receptionist. Apparently she did mean me.

"Pardon me, are you a visitor?" She was a young thing with a timid, artless expression. "Could you sign in, please?"

"I guess you almost mistook me for an employee, didn't you?" I said, smiling cheerfully as I accepted a freshly sharpened pencil. Suddenly my glasses fogged up on the inside, and the receptionist disappeared. There was a vague smell of cosmetics and singed paper.

"No, sir."

"But you said 'Welcome home.'" Swiftly rubbing the insides of my lenses with the balls of my thumbs, I added, "You must have a lot of live-in employees in this building."

"No, it's our custom to greet each other that way."

"Strange." I finished filling out the form and said, "Is this okay?"

"Wait a moment." Without the slightest hint of a smile, she dialed a number and after a short consultation announced "You can go on in," as if letting down her guard for the first time. "Take the elevator in front to the reception room on the second floor, and wait there."

The hall was dark, the color of used cooking oil. A group of employees passed swiftly by me, filling up the elevator. The doors closed. Looking around, I caught sight of a stairway on my left. Next to it was a green light. There seemed no point in waiting for the elevator, so I decided to take the stairs.

Wisps of steam rose toward the walls from the radiator in the hallway. Across from the stairway was a door with a wooden sign marked "Supplies Department," silhouetted with white light from within. As I set foot on the stairs, I spotted a sign beneath the green light on the wall.

DON'T DEFEND—ATTACK

Halfway up, I passed a man who stuck his index finger through his black bow tie and scratched his chin as if performing some rite. Then he paused and said, "Say, on that card, was there a fire engine siren?"

"Card? What card?" I said.

"Right. Well, you've got me there," he said, and hurried on by. This time, apparently, I really had been taken for an employee. On the landing I came to another sign.

GIVE FORM TO DESIRE

I kept going up, and came to another landing. Judging from the height of the ceiling on the first floor, there couldn't possibly be two landings on the way up. This had to be the second floor. A wall must be blocking the way. That explained why the receptionist had gone out of her way to tell me to take the elevator. It looked as if I had no choice but to go back down and start over.

Unless by chance there was a secret door somewhere in the wall. I went over to the wall and examined it carefully. Sure enough, I found a small, half-size door. After making sure no one was around, I pulled the latch.

Suddenly, from the other side of the door I heard a low moaning, followed by shrieks that sounded like cries for help. The voice was lifeless, hoarse, and male. Hastily I closed the door and stood stock still. I wanted nothing to do with this.

Just as I was turning to head back down the stairs, footsteps came clattering toward me from above.

"Goodness, did you have a red light?!"

In front of me stood a thin woman, her hair chocolate-brown in the dim light, her kneecaps livid, like peeled hard-boiled eggs. Rather than try to make sense of her words, I hesitated, unable to decide whether I should pretend I was on my way up or down. Which would arouse less suspicion? Unless I knew the meaning of this secret door, there was no way of telling. I ended up standing there, waiting for her.

"It was a red light, wasn't it? Wasn't it?"

"Gee I—I really don't know what you mean—"

"But you just came out of there, didn't you?"

"Out of there?"

"Yes, of course!"

"No, I—"

"Don't be mean."

"I'm telling you I didn't!"

"Hmm . . . then you're just on your way up?"

Apparently, if you had no business here, it was assumed you were heading up, not down.

"Yeah . . . I guess so."

And so I had no choice but to continue on up the stairs. The woman sniffed, lowered her eyelashes tantalizingly, and passed on by, leaving in her wake a fragrance of lemon drops.

Oh well. Might as well take a peek at the third floor, and then pretend I'd just caught on to my error. On the way down I'd be sure to take the elevator. A pebble was embedded in the sole of my right shoe. I tried to scrape it off on the edge of a step, but I seemed only to have driven it in deeper. Leaning against the banister, I bent over and examined the underside of my heel. It turned out to be an old-fashioned anti-abrasion metal guard.

Must have fallen off someone else's shoe and worked its way into mine. I tried prying it off with a fingernail, but it wouldn't budge. I gave up and walked on up the stairs, my right and left shoes making different noises as I went, distracting me.

Third floor.

Once again, my expectations were betrayed. This time there was no wall blocking the way, as on the second floor, but again no corridor. Instead, a room opened up in front of me.

The entrance was open, with no doors. Coughing, sounds of typing, pages being turned—typical office sounds came floating out in a shapeless mélange. Posted over the entranceway was another sign:

KEEP YOUR MIND ALWAYS IN FULL GEAR

As long as there was no hallway, I had no business here. If I couldn't get to the elevator, there was nothing to do but retrace my steps. Just as I was turning, pivoting on that irksome piece of metal stuck in my shoe, a man stepped out from the shadow behind the entrance and beckoned to me, leaning forward with a friendly smile. If he hadn't had such a reassuring, trustworthy sort of expression, I probably would have ignored him and continued on my way downstairs.

3

"Somehow I got turned around. Which way would the elevator be?" I asked.

The man nodded, put a finger to his lips, and threw a meaningful look over his shoulder. Apparently it was forbidden to talk in a loud voice here. Then, in a low, disarming voice, he said, "There's nothing to be afraid of. You're new, aren't you?"

"No, you see I was told to take the elevator up, and then I managed to get totally lost, and somehow—"

"Don't worry about a thing," he said soothingly, shaking his head back and forth. "It's hard on everybody in the beginning. You feel as if you're being pulled apart, right? Just relax. Tensing up is the worst thing you can do. Just leave everything to us and go ahead and let yourself go, freeing yourself from the bonds of consciousness . . . then, spontaneously—" As he spoke, he grabbed my hand and began slowly to massage my palm with his fingertips.

Taken by surprise, I flung him off and cried, "You don't understand! You've got the wrong idea!"

"Do I?" he said, his affable smile never fading. "With that attitude, you're only going to cause yourself greater distress. Think carefully. What is it you're afraid of?"

"I'm not afraid of anything!"

"That's the spirit! You haven't got a thing to fear. Why should a publicity man, supervisor of the fourth estate of democracy, be afraid of any fixed ideas?"

"Huh?"

"What is it, you're worried about the poverty of your subconscious, is that it? Well, relax. The subconscious is an inexhaustible vein. The deeper you dig, the more jewels you find. Or tell me, could it be—" He broke off, gave me a searching look, and said, "Have you by any chance got an Oedipus complex?"

In an effort to recover my poise, I forced myself to smile. "No, you see, I wandered in here purely by chance, and—"

"You did? Good. You seem to have relaxed, finally." With an air of relief he nodded, stepped aside, and motioned me inside.

"No, you still don't understand, I'm here by mistake."

"Mistake?"

"Yeah, the girl told me to take the elevator, but it was full, so here I am." Having at last found a chance to defend myself, I raced along, scarcely pausing for breath. "You see, I'm just a visitor. I came here to see the director of the general affairs department. I signed in at the receptionist's desk, and she told me to wait on the second floor, and then I missed the elevator, so I took the stairs on the spur of the moment, not knowing where they went."

"On the spur of the moment . . . not knowing?"

"I'm terribly sorry."

"Now I get it." The man moaned, paused, and then mumbled again, "Now I get it."

"This building seems to have a very unusual design."

"I've made a terrible mistake!" Suddenly his face lit up. "But you know, you've discovered a new rule. I didn't realize it at first. 'Just empty your head, and enter into a realm of detachment.' This is the first time you've tried it this way, isn't it? You know, it just might work. I can't wait to see your results."

"No, no, everything I'm saying is the truth. I'm just telling you what happened."

"Even the way you talk is precious. It's a shame to let it all go to waste out here. Come on in and let's get it down on tape."

He grabbed my shoulder in absolute faith and pushed me in the direction of the room. How could I relieve him of his misunderstanding? Either I should go along with him and do whatever he asked, or I should run back the way I had come. There were no other options. A young man walked toward us, hands thrust into his pockets, and passed in front of me, mumbling to himself. I caught fragments: "Dragonfly, peppermint, autumn sky." The young man's shoulders were broad. Looking at them, I sensed the futility of running. First Smiley would cry out and then this young fellow would catch me, which would only make things worse. It might be smarter just to play along for awhile.

The room was a long rectangle, extending off to my left. What met my eyes was quite different from the usual office setup. Down the middle of the room stretched a long aisle, and on either side of it were rows of cubicles lined up like stalls at a festival. The cubicles were partitioned off from one another, as in a visiting room in a prison, and each faced a counter beyond which everything appeared normal. A dozen or so female employees were absorbed in their work. On closer inspection, I saw they were each dextrously shuffling a pile of cards about as thick as three decks of playing cards. Cards . . . cards . . . hadn't the man on the stairs said something about cards? And about a siren?

On the counter in front of each booth were paper, pens, and a typewriter. A full set of ordinary office implements. There were also a few things whose use I couldn't guess. A black cylindrical tube hung over every cubicle and was evidently a small microphone. Virtually every booth was occupied. Some people were typing, others writing, others muttering into their microphone. What surprised me, however, were the people who would reach out to select a certain number of cards held out in a fan by a girl across the counter, then turn them over eagerly, and study them with a mixture of expectation and uncertainty, as if playing some sort of game. They couldn't really be playing games, and yet it certainly did look that way.

"All right, this will do." The man's soft hand took hold of my elbow and guided me to a booth, well back on the right side. There was a mat on the floor, and an old-fashioned, high-backed chair. I was afraid I was about to make a total fool of myself. Why hadn't I run away when I had the chance? The man leaned over the counter and motioned to the young women. One of them noticed, nodded, and walked over, fingering the cards with such skill that they danced between her slender fingers like living things.

4

Before my eyes was an array of cards spread out in a large half circle.

None of this had anything to do with me. It was insulting.

"Go ahead, take three cards, any three."

Failure to state your intentions meant resigning yourself to this sort of misunderstanding.

"Don't think about anything. . . . Just relax."

Cards . . . games . . . games with no rules . . . Slowly I reached out my hand. . . . The tips of my fingers felt feverish.

"Well, so this is where you were!"

All at once I heard a familiar voice. It was like a spot of color suddenly appearing in a strip of black and white film. For a moment, time stopped, and then my blood began to flow again. Hastily I withdrew my hand and turned around, already rising from my chair. It was the director, my negotiating partner over the plans for the new building. A man like a well-bound antique book, angular and musty.

"Hello! I've been looking all over for you."

"I got lost. The elevator—"

But suddenly I was too embarrassed to say more. The man who had hauled me in here looked back and forth at us in amazement.

"Well, if the professor's been showing you around, that's fine. He's in charge of this room; he's a great authority on psychology."

"Well, actually it wasn't quite like that." The professor inclined his head until it seemed about to settle permanently on his shoulder, and stared at something in the vicinity of my ear.

"I was going to show you this room eventually, anyway," said the director. "But it might not be a bad idea to start here. This, you see, is what you might call the heart of our company's operations. Well, what do you think?"

"I haven't actually heard the explanation yet."

"How far did you get, professor?"

"How far?" Coming back to himself, he rubbed his temples with the fingers of both hands. "I hadn't actually begun. So you really are a visitor?" he said, looking directly at me. "Ah, what a surprise. Inexplicable truth. What a rare experience I've had. I might just be able to discover some new law because of it." His genial smile returned. "Well, you must have been rather startled yourself!"

"I'll tell you, I didn't have the faintest notion what to do."

"I can well imagine. But this experience will have wide application. I've got to make a note of it." No sooner were the words out of his mouth than he spun around and returned to his own desk, at the end of the row of booths.

"Interesting fellow." The director looked fondly after the retreating figure, adding "He's really quite the scholar, you know. We're very lucky to have him."

"Yes. Sorry for all the trouble I caused."

—This room has no particular designation. We usually just call it the System. All of our employees are required to come here for testing once each morning. A sort of psychoanalytical test. Those cards are printed with all sorts of pictures and symbols. Each person has to choose three cards, immediately derive some connection between them, and come up with a meaningful statement based on that connection. The typewriter is used in much the same way. Without thinking, you type out a random assortment of three letters, and then free associate with whatever you come up with. Here, listen for a moment to the sounds coming from this booth.

—Nails . . . clock . . . penguin. Nails . . . dirt under finger-nails . . . boil . . . penguin medicine . . . clock. Medicine for a clock is winding it up. Nails . . . light fire under nails . . . fire clock . . . thermometer . . . thermometer and penguin. A penguin has a thermometer under its wing. An ad for cold medicine . . .

—And next door here, we have free association using the typewriter.

—A, C, M. A is for America, C is for commercial, M is for . . . M . . . is for *manju*, bean-jam buns. America, commercial, manju. Manju with America as commerical base. X-brand manju, exported to America with great success . . .

—That's roughly the way it goes. Everything these people say is recorded by the overhead microphones. The tapes are sent to the consolidation department, where they are screened, and anything that sounds promising is picked up. The ideas are then sorted by division—design, draft, radio, TV, outdoor advertising—and preserved. This system also works as an aptitude test for employees. We strive scientifically to increase productivity by transferring people to new sections according to the nature and trend of their associations. Besides, this is excellent mental training aimed at strengthening the power of association. Three birds with one stone. Shall we move along?

"It seems kind of like milking cows," I commented.

"Yes. You see, advertising that works on the subconscious has the most powerful effect of all. But the ideas must be arrived at unconsciously, or they lack conviction."

"Then this staircase also has a sort of psychological function?"

"Yes, yes, it does. Well, it sounds as if you've started to catch on."

199

"Yes, I think I have. Now that I see how it works, it all makes perfect sense. I think I did the right thing by coming."

"I'll show you around the rest of the place and then you can attend to that new alteration I proposed yesterday."

"No, I think I've seen enough. After all, even the greeting 'Welcome home' which surprised me so much at first now seems perfectly natural."

"Oh? How so?"

"Well, I'm still kind of excited by everything I've seen, so this may be somewhat of an exaggeration, but it seems to me that the employees have all already entrusted their souls to the System. The System is them, even more than their physical selves. That's why the greeting is—has to be— 'Welcome home,' and the only response can be 'I'm back.' "

"It looks as if we should have hired you as one of our regular employees, not just our architect. A terrible oversight. Why, you're one of us!"

And so, for a little while, I was able to forget the metal guard wedged in the sole of my shoe.

5

Just then, we came to the second-floor landing, with the secret door.

"By the way," I said, "what does the red light mean?"

"Red light?" He turned around and came to a stop. "You mean the green light, at the foot of the stairs. That's a sign that there are still empty booths in the System room."

"No, the red light." I wasn't sure why I was so insistent, but I remembered shining kneecaps . . . a thin woman . . . "Oh, but you just came out of there, didn't you?" . . . "Out of there?" . . . the secret door and its handle . . . yes, and then a scream for help . . . Suddenly, I became conscious of the metal guard in my shoe.

"Are you sure it's a red light you mean?"

"Positive."

"Well, well. You've got sharp eyes. It's a little dark here and hard to make out, but I suspect what you are referring to is that light just overhead."

As if waiting for something to happen, we looked up together at a dark corner of the ceiling where nothing could be seen. Naturally, nothing happened.

"I just happened to notice it."

"Ah. Hmm. Let me think. All right, I suppose it wouldn't be a bad idea to stop in here next. Yes, why don't we do that?" The director of general affairs bent over, grabbed the handle on the secret door, and pulled.

"What is that?" I asked sharply.

"Surprised? A passageway."

"Leading where?"

"It's a shortcut to the president's office."

The explanation was so simple that I blurted out, "What, that's all?"

"What do you mean by that?" There was something stiff in his manner, as if he was offended by my response. I was forced to go on.

"As a matter of fact, I opened that door before. I had a feeling it might lead onto the second-floor corridor."

"And what happened?"

"It was probably my imagination, but I could have sworn I heard a strange voice."

"A voice?"

"Yes. It sounded like the screams of an old man."

"Are you sure?"

"Yes. At least, that's how it sounded to me."

The director opened the door quietly, looking tense, reached around behind the wall and pushed a switch. A light came on, revealing a narrow passageway barely wide enough for one. It was painted bright white, making it impossible to judge how far back it went.

"I don't hear anything."

"Neither do I."

"Are you sure it couldn't have been a radio or a tape recording?"

"Well, maybe. Yeah, I suppose it could have been."

"Don't scare me like that. Well, let's go have a look."

"Has this all got some connection with the red light?"

"Oh, yes. Very much so. You'll see."

The director led the way. I followed close behind. The click of metal embedded in my shoe echoed down the narrow, high-ceilinged passageway. It was shorter than I had thought. At the end it curved left and we came to a heavy-looking white door. He rapped on it three times, twice in succession, and we waited until a shrill, lifeless, asthmatic voice replied, "Who is it?"

"It's me, sir." The director stepped back and whispered in my ear, "The president of AB."

A bell rang and the door opened. There stood a little man covered with wrinkles, as if someone had scribbled all over him. Behind him, an incongruously large room. A flood of colorful posters plastered on the walls.

"Sir, may we have a few moments of your time?"

"What?"

"I brought the architect."

Behind the director's back, I bowed my head respectfully.

"Ah. But I can only give you five minutes."

"Thank you very much."

"What is it, the red light?"

"Yes, sir."

"Come this way."

Over in a corner of the room was something like a telephone switchboard. The president, whose gestures were as angular as his appearance, stood in front of the device and looked around with an air of triumph, for all the world like a ship's captain at the helm.

"Tell me," he said to me, "do you know who the real politicians are, the ones moving our age? No, you don't. Everyone still thinks that the elected representatives and the ministers of state are the politicians. Well, nothing could be further from the truth. We advertising men are the ones holding the reins. We're the only ones who know how to get the stallion of public opinion and the stallion of capitalism to run in tandem."

"That's right!" chimed in the director.

"Shall I tell you how? First we plant a seed of desire in the belly of public opinion. A seed so tiny it seems insignificant—the product of our best brains. Once that seed takes hold, it never lets go. It grows like a weed, crying out for fertilizer. We bide our time and just at the right juncture we let people know where to get premium manure. Then they set happily off to buy it, ready to turn their pockets inside out if need be."

"And the 'manure'-producing companies are happy, too," added the director.

"True."

"And you, Mr. President, are the overseer of production of those secret seeds."

"It's a heavy responsibility, believe me. I have to oversee the whole process from the word go. Look at this."

With a solemn, ritualistic air, he pulled a lever toward him. At once a low murmur emerged from the bowels of the machine.

"This is coming from one of the System booths," he explained. "The System is set up so I can listen in directly from here. Let's see, this is number B-8."

B-8 was mumbling:

—Robinson Crusoe and bet. Robinson Crusoe and bet. Robinson Crusoe is naked, he's got nothing to bet with.

"I listen in like this, as necessary. And as necessary, I can summon people straight here."

"He waits for the person to approach," added the director, "then switches on the red light. So the red light is a handy way of sending a private signal to anyone he wants to see."

"Whoever sees the light goes through the small door and comes in here. I then announce that he or she is being transferred, or getting a raise or cut in pay. Sometimes I encourage them to dig deeper, if they've come up with a promising idea."

"Keep your mind always in full gear!" cried the director.

"Don't defend, attack!" returned the president.

"Yes, I think now I have a pretty good idea," I said, at last managing to get a word in. "So the average construction of space utilization—"

But the president was no longer listening to me. The very wrinkles on his face seemed to be intent on B-8's mutterings.

—Robinson Crusoe and bet. Robinson Crusoe made a bet. He bet that he could go to an uninhabited island and come back within one year wearing modern, civilized clothes. Three million yen prize. He lost. Stupid Robinson."

"Director, the red light!"

"This Robinson Crusoe thing?" said the director. He immediately picked up the wall receiver and relayed the message to the switchboard.

"Get me through to System. I want B-8, and hurry!"

"What happens if two people come down the stairs together?" I asked the president.

"Of course, we try to arrange it so that won't happen. The present System is still flawed. That's why we want the new annex to be perfect."

Before I knew it the muttering had stopped. The director was calling into the receiver. "B-8 left, did he? Anyone else? Is he alone? Good. Over."

"This button turns on the red light."

Was it my imagination or was the president's finger shaking with anticipation as he placed it on the white, round protuberance in the center of the machine? "Light's on."

"Does it stay on indefinitely?" I asked.

"It goes off the moment he turns that handle."

"You're calling that man in here to demonstrate to our guest exactly how the System operates, is that it, sir?"

"Don't be an idiot!" bellowed the company president, his chest stuck out, arms akimbo. "Didn't you realize the genius of that idea we just heard? My calling B-8 in here has nothing to do with either of you! Robinson Crusoe's bet—what an idea! Pure genius. If you can't see that, then there's not much hope for you."

"Yes, but—"

"But what?"

"The idea's impossible, isn't it?"

"You are an idiot!"

There was the sound of a knock. The president bounded over and opened the door. There stood B-8, stoop-shouldered, looking rather dazed. He wore a blue suit sagging at the shoulders, the pants too short. Small jaw; high, balding forehead.

"Come in, come in! I'm going to use your idea!"

There was a short, compressed silence, about the space of two heartbeats.

"Well, come on in! Your idea is dynamite!"

B-8 did nothing but scrape his feet nervously on the floor.

"Aren't you going to thank me?" cried the president. "I'm going to use your Robinson Crusoe idea!"

"My Robinson Crusoe idea?"

"Yes—that bet about going naked to an uninhabited island and coming back fully dressed, in civilized clothes!"

"Oh, but that was just a game. Free association. It would never work in real life."

"We'll offer a grand prize for succeeding in less than a month—ten million yen!"

"It won't work. However much you offer, you won't find any takers."

"Why not?"

"Because it's impossible."

"What makes you so sure?"

"Take this shabby old suit of mine. To make it, you'd need special machinery. To make the machinery, you'd need copper and steel. To make that, you'd need ore and coal and a blast furnace."

"What else?"

"Workers to supply all that, food to feed them, farmers to grow the food."

"Excellent! You've got the makings of a great slogan there—'To make this shabby suit takes the sweat of the nation.' Well, maybe that's a little weak. But the idea is great: countless people you don't even know are working together for your benefit." He turned to the director. "I want you to get on this right away!"

"Yes, sir."

"But, sir," B-8 put in defensively, "it's a foregone conclusion that it couldn't be done, so there's really no bet."

"Of course! That's exactly why it's such a brilliant idea! Everybody's going to think it's impossible. But then a daring challenger comes along and captures the nation's imagination!"

"Is there any such person?"

"Certainly!"

"I can't really imagine anybody—"

"Why, he's standing right here in front of me!"

"Who?"

"You!"

"But—"

"Don't defend, attack! Why, what greater honor could there be than for you, the originator of the idea, to become the challenger!"

"But I—"

"Believe! Believe you can do it! Whether you actually can or not isn't the issue. You've simply got to believe that you can. Now, where shall we promote this?" He turned to the director. "Where do you think?"

"Well, let me see. Uh, what sort of place did you have in mind?"

"You numbskull! You still haven't begun to grasp the beauty of this plan, have you? The possibilities are infinite. The pitiful figure of Robinson Crusoe, struggling all alone on his uninhabited island, will make a vivid impression on everybody's mind. And they'll start to think 'Gee, it's pretty wonderful to be able to go to the store and buy things with money; I don't just throw away my money, I'm able to exchange it for things I need.' Then that slogan we were talking about before will come home to them. For example, while they're washing their hands with soap, they'll think, 'Through this one little bar of soap, thousands upon thousands of people are waiting on me.' Watching the lather, they'll start to feel like royalty. Imagine—thanks to Robinson

Crusoe, people's purse strings will loosen like worn-out elastic bands!"

"And the soap companies who didn't take us up on the bet will disappear without a bubble," added the director of general affairs.

"Well, finally you're starting to catch on."

"But what if this modern-day Crusoe should win, by some fluke?" the director queried. "Wouldn't it have exactly the opposite effect? People would start to feel like fools for spending money."

"He doesn't have a prayer," said the president flatly.

"Right! That's exactly what I—" began B-8, but the president swiftly cut him off, waving his hand in the air like a fan.

"You keep out of this! I told you before, you've got to be sure of winning! Who's going to give a damn about a fixed deal, a bet they know you're going to lose? I'm convinced you'll lose, you insist you're determined to win. Only then does the outcome become interesting."

"But however much I personally might subjectively feel I was going to win—"

"Don't throw in the towel! Get out there and try to win! Of course, we'll do what we can to make it easier for you. For example, at regular intervals we'll lower the prize money and lengthen the time span. Ten million if you succeed within a month, nine million for two months, and so on, down to one million yen for the tenth month. That will build up the excitement. We can have people guess what month they think you'll succeed in and heighten the suspense. Don't worry, as long as you project confidence and authority you'll attract your share of believers."

He shifted his attention back to the director of general affairs, and began issuing orders. "I want you to round up some big-name sponsors, doesn't matter who. Raise all the money you can. Tell them if they pass this up, it's suicide. Oh, and you'll have to scout around for some uninhabited Pacific island, and charter a boat."

"Are you really serious?" B-8's face suddenly shriveled, as if it had dehydrated.

"Good Lord, how many times do you have to be told? You mean you still won't believe it? All right, we happen to have a third party here, so let's have him serve as witness."

The third party he referred to was of course me. Needless to say, I was unable to refuse. To B-8 this little man was his boss—someone not to trifle with—and to me he was someone just as important: a valuable client.

And so the Robinson Crusoe bet between the company president in AB Building and his employee, B-8, was officially on. (But that same day, B-8 was dismissed. This was of course owing to the president's determination to eliminate any conflict of interest, and thus any concern that the outcome might be fixed.)

6

Now, it surely goes without saying that this peculiar experience was extremely fruitful in terms of helping me to understand my client's wishes. As a result, I no longer minded in the slightest if a room on the third floor shared a wall with one on the sixth floor, or you came down a flight of stairs to find yourself on the next floor up. Even if I had been ordered to put in all the ceilings and floors upside down, I probably would have done so without giving it a second thought. It was as if I understood even better than my client just what was wanted in this building.

So in the end I was able to complete the job without any

further qualms, and if I do say so myself it came out gratifyingly well. The president apparently liked it too, because at the ceremony he personally handed me a special gift, in a very moving scene.

So it's about time to draw these notes to an end—although of course the Robinson Crusoe bet is left hanging in the air. Since by now it's become famous, I probably should say a word or two more about it, even if it does have little relevancy to my main topic.

But don't expect too much. Frankly, I haven't got anything of any great interest or importance to share. Still, compared to more ignorant third parties, I may be slightly better informed, so for what it's worth, I'll go ahead and set down what I know.

Officially, of course, B-8 is supposed to be on some uninhabited island surrounded by a coral reef, working away at his challenge. Maybe he is. According to the report of the First Interim Investigating Team, the helicopter which took them from the mother ship was able to touch down on the island only briefly, due to an approaching typhoon, so they had to leave before establishing contact; but just before lifting off, they apparently heard a loud screeching that sounded like a gigantic bird in its death throes. Later they decided that it must have been the sound of a seabird known as the wajiwaji caught in a trap, which they declared proof that "Robinson" is alive and well. Certainly it's not impossible. I half think they may be right.

But there's another plausible theory making the rounds. Some people say the moment reporters stopped following the chartered boat, it swung around and headed in the opposite direction. And another theory claims that while the boat did indeed reach the island, instead of B-8, what went ashore was a skeleton once used for experiments at some university hospital. Of course, I don't think we need pretend surprise at such shenanigans in this day and age; in fact anyone who believed in the legitimacy of the bet might well risk being labeled not only naive but a dunce.

The next rumor, however, strikes me as a little too dramatic to be real. According to this, B-8 was so stricken by the magnitude of the problems he faced that he committed suicide shortly after setting sail and arrived on the island a dead man. This, it seems to me, involves an entirely too romantic view of the monstrosity we call modern life. Of course, if I hadn't accepted the job of designing that new building and subsequently encountered the inner workings of the System, I might very well have been taken in. But fortunately, having gained the opportunity to design certain aspects of the System with my own hands, I know better. The monstrosity of modern life is far more prosaic, consisting simply in the fact that the wires connecting all the separate elements have gotten hopelessly entangled. That's why I can't help suspecting that there is more truth in the rumor that B-8, disguised in sunglasses, was spotted one day timidly waiting in line in a department store supermarket for economy-size packages of meat.

Then what was it that the investigating team heard? I haven't the slightest assurance that this is true, but as I heard that story I recalled the shrieks I heard through the wall outside the president's office when I visited the old building. Had someone told me those despairing, agonized cries were made by a bird, I probably would have believed it.

Besides, there was one other disturbing coincidence. I have no solid proof and it's probably no more meaningful than, say, the similarity in shape between a starfish and a star, but the fact is that after the opening ceremony, the company president dropped out of sight. Of course, no one ever said so in so many words, but there must have been good reason for him to do so. He was a figure of such commanding authority that his employees, unaccustomed to doubting him, could well have overlooked the significance of his absence. But I, for one, being thoroughly acquainted with the structure of his new office, couldn't help experiencing an ominous twinge of presentiment.

From the time I first set to work on the plans for the president's office, I was given one supreme order: it had to be located at all times squarely in the center of the System. But the System itself was by no means stable, so the only solution was to design a building as fluid and fluctuating as an amoeba. Inhabitants of such a building would suffer from a kind of motion sickness many times worse than seasickness, and no work would get done at all. Well, I wracked my brains and finally hit on a solution: I worked out the path of the president's office as a mathematical function of the System and constructed a maze of twisting tunnels winding through the building, leaving it to an electronic brain to determine the location and direction of the office based on current conditions. I have a certain amount of confidence in the mechanism and am justifiably proud of it, so I hold myself fully accountable for how it functions. But, of course, I can bear no responsibility for how it may have been used. If someone altered the conditions—conditions that in themselves, taken separately, would have meant nothing—to overlap in such a way that the set path of the office was diverted, by however little, then even if the door of the president's office should have opened one day on something totally beyond the scope of my design, I could hardly be blamed. Not even if the president himself ended up smack in the middle of an uninhabited desert island.

The Dream Soldier

On a day so cold dreams froze,
I had a frightening dream
In the early afternoon
My dream put on its hat and went out—
I locked the door

*I*t happened nearly fifty years ago. They say truth is timeless, but this story has a time. It was a time of no truth.

Since the night before, the little village tucked away in the mountains along the prefectural border had been engulfed in a fierce snowstorm, winds howling as if in agony. Early in the morning, a company of soldiers out on a cold-weather endurance exercise staggered into the village from the town over the ridge. Dragging their large straw shoes through heavy snowdrifts in time to a martial song, they crossed unsteadily through the village, only to disappear back into the blizzard like so many shadows.

Evening came and the wind died down. In the police substation on the way into the village sat a solitary old police officer, absently peeling potatoes as he warmed the soles of his feet at a red-hot stove. The radio was droning on about something, but he paid no attention. He was lost in a pleasant reverie.

"Not much gets past me," he mused. "I know very well that

the village headman and his assistant are busy selling rationed goods illegally, and that the head priest of the temple is in on it too, and hides the goods under the temple floorboards. But I keep my mouth shut—and everybody in the village knows I do. The gifts they bring me aren't meant to keep me quiet, but to demonstrate their good will. When I retire, I won't have to run away like the other resident officers. I'll be able to stay put, settle down, maybe even marry me a widow with a little property, and enjoy my old age in peace. As long as you haven't got expensive tastes, there's no better life than the life of a farmer. I'll be needing a house to welcome my boy home in after he gets out of the army, too. And thanks to the war, now there are three widows in the village who own property. Of course, as things stand, they each have a son, but you never know—any one of those sons could die for his country, any time now. I'll come out ahead, I know I will. I've never done a single thing to turn the villagers against me, and the number of widows is bound to rise. There's no hurry. I'll just sit back, take my time, and give it plenty of thought. Size of paddies plus family, divided by two . . ."

Suddenly the phone rang. The potato he was peeling slipped from his grasp and fell into the ashes. He picked it up, wiped it off on the hem of his undershirt, and stood up, stretching as if in pain before stepping down to the entryway. He picked up the receiver in the peculiarly offhand manner of his profession and answered in a languid voice, but then his expression grew tense and the fingers clutching the potato began to tremble.

Once past the village, the soldiers had marched straight into the mountains. Along the way they passed hills and valleys and woods, holding maneuvers as they went, so that by the time they reached the last ridge, it was already well past three. The wind raged with ever-mounting intensity, whipping the snow up around them until they could hardly breathe; in all this time, they had not eaten and they were forced to march double-time on the return. Severe punishment was known to await anyone caught lagging, yet six men fell behind. Because this was a special exercise designed to test the combined effects of hunger, exhaustion, and cold, the possibility of stragglers had been anticipated, and a medical corps was following behind. But when the medics rejoined the company, they turned out to have only five stragglers in custody. One soldier, it seems, had disappeared.

The missing soldier would be famished. He would be certain to head for the village. Given the slightest encouragement, he might even try to seize clothing, or whatever else he had a mind to, by force.

The old officer replaced the receiver, hunched his shoulders, and slowly returned to his place by the stove. He sniffed, and scratched the top of his bald head for a while. He looked up at the clock. Seven-thirty. He didn't want to move; it was too cold outside. Besides, this wasn't a clear case of desertion yet. What a blizzard that had been, after all! The fellow might easily have gotten separated from his buddies and lost his way in the snow. Who'd be fool enough to desert in weather like this? Footprints in the snow would be a dead giveaway. He must have gotten lost. By now he must be frozen stiff. On the other hand, as long as the wind kept up, the snow might be safer. A strong wind would erase any footprints. Maybe he'd even planned it that way; it could have been a premeditated crime. But now the wind's died down. He may have fallen into his own trap. After all, crime doesn't pay.

Well, I've received a briefing, but no orders. This is a job for the MPs, of course. Besides, unlike an escaped prisoner, a deserter's nothing but a well-meaning coward. Let it alone, let it alone, nothing to be gained by sticking your nose into other people's troubles. Besides, no deserter I ever heard of got away.

He thought he heard a faint scratching at the front door, and spun around. He listened carefully, but there was no further noise. Must have been his imagination. But for some reason he was beset by a strange uncertainty. It was more than that—it was a feeling akin to terror, an intricate tangle of fears he could not explain, even to himself. Not fear of the deserter, mind you. This time, there had been none of the surge of hatred he generally felt for run-of-the-mill criminals. His failure to feel that hatred awoke him, for the first time, to the existence of people and forces ordering him to hate, and allowed him a glimpse of the abyss separating the pursuer and the pursued—an abyss that his own position, secure among the pursuers, had prevented him from ever seeing before.

Stricken with pangs of guilt, he sprang to his feet and shouted hoarsely, "He can't get away with it!" But this bluster had no discernible effect on his uncertainty. It was still only a small, inner uncertainty, wrapped in a larger fear. Deep inside, he worried over the possibility of ending up an accomplice—a worry surely shared by every villager. His inability to escape that worry was the source of his larger fear. I've gotten old, he thought. Then he felt a burst of anger. When the time comes, there'll be an accounting and it will all be settled, he thought. It's not as if I'm the only one responsible. The back of his throat felt strangely wet. He closed the damper on the stove, fastened on his sword, turned up the collar on his overcoat, and went out.

The snow was light and fine and crunched pleasantly beneath his feet. Footprints showed in it, but not clearly. Just around the corner from the fishmonger's was the village headman's house, boasting the only Western-style window in the village. Light shone brightly there and the muffled sound of hearty laughter carried all the way to the street. That would be the head priest. Instead of going around to the back as he usually did, the officer suddenly flung open the front door.

The air inside went taut with surprise. Overlaid on the noise of chinaware being hastily put away came the headman's tremulous drawl. "Who's that, at this hour?"

Wait till you see, thought the officer, clearing his throat and deliberately not answering. The inner *shoji* door slid partway open, and the headman's assistant poked his head through the opening.

"Well, look who's here! If it isn't the officer!"

"Come in, come in," joined in the head priest, opening the door wide.

Clearly, all three had been drinking.

"There's been a bit of trouble, I'm afraid," said the officer.

"Trouble? What is it?"

"Oh, he'll tell us in good time—come on in, anyway, close the door, and have a drink!"

"It seems an army deserter is on the loose," the officer continued, "heading toward the northern mountains."

"A deserter?" The priest looked over the tops of his spectacles. "If he's going that way, he's got to come through here, whichever way he takes."

"Yes. I'm told he's aiming straight at us."

"Aiming?" The village headman rubbed a finger along the high bridge of his nose, in seeming annoyance.

"They say he's devilishly hungry, too," the officer added.

"Oh-oh. Sounds like trouble, all right."

"What are you talking about!" exclaimed the assistant heatedly. "Deserters are traitors to their country. The worst kind of low-down cowards. Why don't we go right out and hunt him down?"

"Yes, but he's got a gun," the officer pointed out. "Besides that, the man's so hungry he's liable to do anything."

"In China," said the headman with a sigh, "every village and community has got a castle wall around it."

"Not a castle wall," retorted the assistant.

"All right, not a castle wall."

"Just an ordinary mud wall."

"All right, a mud wall."

Surprised at a sound like the creaking of chains, they all swung around in time to see the wall clock start to chime eight. The priest coughed and turned back. "So, what are we going to do?" he asked.

"I say go catch him ourselves and pound him to a pulp!" It was hardly surprising that the assistant should speak so boldly. In the entire village, he was the only male in his thirties who had yet to join the army. Even so, his voice had lost a little of its earlier conviction.

As if to encourage him, the officer nodded and said, "Good idea. The man's nothing but a traitorous dog, after all. Still," he cautioned in a low voice, tilting his head to one side, "don't forget he's armed. Put a gun in the hands of a hungry, cornered desperado, and who knows what he might do?"

"That's true," agreed the priest. "It'd be like giving a sword to a maniac." He waved a hand at the assistant, vetoing his suggestion, then looked at the officer and said, "What shall we do?"

"Do?" said the headman, pinching his nose. "Well, we'll just—" and then as an afterthought he blurted out, "You don't suppose the deserter's someone from our village! Is he?"

"Impossible!" said the assistant loudly and forcefully, sticking out his chin. "A coward like that could only be from a warm climate."

"Then why did he run away here, of all places, in this cold?"

"Who knows! He can't escape. Think of his poor parents."

"But don't you remember—wasn't there a story about a widow in some village around here sheltering a deserter for over two months?"

"That was a long time ago. Nowadays nobody would do such a traitorous thing."

"True, true."

Look at them, thought the officer, they're all scared to death. I'm not the only one. They're all afraid of being tainted somehow. Yet just knowing about him means they can't avoid dirtying their hands. If they stop their ears, their very hands will hear his cries for help. And the act of stopping the ears is in itself a sign of complicity.

"Well, if you ask me," he said in a deliberate tone, sniffing, his face expressionless, "we've got to alert the villagers right away, with an emergency notice to be passed door to door. They've got to be told there's a deserter headed this way, so they'll know to lock their doors securely and stay inside. They should take the same precautions as during an air raid, make sure no light escapes through a crack. And not answer even if called to. Once they talk to him, he'll play on their sympathies. He'll start out by asking for water, say, and they'll think, Well, what harm could a glass of water do? So they give it to him, and next he wants food. Once they give him that, next he asks for a change of clothes. After clothes, it's money . . . and then what do you think happens? Thanks for everything, he says, but you've seen my face now, so that makes things a bit difficult. And right before he goes, oh, one more thing, he says, and he lets them have it, BANG."

The three men waited breathlessly for the officer's next words. But as none seemed forthcoming, the village headman timidly asked, "Is that all?"

"The rest is up to the MPs."

The priest got up, saying awkwardly, and with evident distaste, "Well, my place is a ways from here, so I'd better be going."

As the village headman hurriedly began dialing the guardhouse of the civil defense unit, his assistant got up, following the priest's example, and said, "He may be roaming around the village right now, for all we know."

In less than an hour, word spread throughout the village. As if a typhoon warning had been issued, at every house storm shutters were latched into place, and boards nailed across them for extra fortification. Some people even went to sleep with bamboo spears and hatchets at the ready. By a little after ten, the entire village, except for the police substation, was sunk in a profound and silent darkness. An animallike uneasiness prevailed.

Most of the households fell asleep, cowering in the dark. Only the old police officer stayed awake, ears alert for the slightest noise outside, as if waiting for something. Though, of course, the villagers barricaded in their houses had no way of knowing this.

The next morning, just as dawn was breaking, from beyond the ridge to the south there sounded the shrill whistle of a train, in a long succession of rapid blasts. Low-hanging clouds funneled the eerie scream relentlessly into the village, waking most of the villagers. Several of them, recognizing what it meant, tore open their shutters.

The old officer, eyes bloodshot from lack of sleep, turned toward the southern window and gazed out at the hills. He could plainly see a faint gray line in the snow, leading straight over the ridge. The train whistle fell silent, and soon thereafter the assistant headman came along with two other men, a pair of skis under his arm.

"Looks like somebody's gone and thrown himself under the train," he said. "Might have been the traitor. We're going down to have a look. You want to come along?"

"No, I'll stay here. In case there's word from town."

The three skiers quickly found the gray trail leading over the ridge, nodded to one another with satisfaction, and began to follow it. The old officer left the window and crouched down in front of the stove, hugging his knees.

When the assistant headman came back, the officer was still there in the same position, dozing. The assistant waited silently for him to wake up, but he gave no sign of doing so. Just when the assistant had given up and was starting to leave, the officer opened his eyes and whispered, "Well? Did you see him?"

"Yes, I did."

"Ah . . . ," said the officer, sighing.

"You knew it all along, didn't you?"

"Yes, I knew."

"And it was you who made him do it?"

"Yes . . . but I . . . oh, the shame of it. Why did he have to choose here? He did it just to spite me. He's no son of mine." A pause. "You won't tell the rest of the village, though, will you?"

"But the other two already know."

"Oh. Yes, so they do. I'll have to take responsibility for this somehow. . . ."

"He died well. His gun was hung up on a tree branch, out of the way."

"Was it?"

"One more thing—don't you think you'd better do something about those footprints under your window?"

"Yes, I suppose I had."

Ten days later the old police officer left the village, dragging a cart behind him.

> On a day so hot dreams melted
> I had a strange dream
> In the early afternoon
> Only my hat came back

Beyond the Curve

$\int$lowly I came to a halt, as if springs in the air were holding me back. My weight, which had started shifting from my left toes to my right heel, came flowing backwards again, settling heavily in the region of my left knee. The incline was good and steep.

The road was surfaced not in asphalt but in rough concrete, with narrow grooves at four-inch intervals to prevent cars from skidding. But that did pedestrians little good. Besides, the rough texture of the concrete was effectively smoothed out by deposits of dust and tire scraps. On a rainy day, in old, rubber-soled shoes, the going would be slippery. Still, those grooves could make a significant difference if you were driving. They could be just the thing in the winter, draining off excess water from melting snow and ice.

Despite these provisions for vehicles, there were almost none on the road now. And there were no sidewalks. Four or five women with shopping baskets hooked over their arms came along, chattering animatedly, filling the whole width of the road.

A boy with roller skates fastened to his bottom came racing down the center of the slope, making honking noises. I jumped out of his way at the last moment—for I, too, had been standing in the middle of the road.

I walked on. Then slowly I came to a halt, as if springs in the air were holding me back. My weight, which had started shifting from my left toes to my right heel, came flowing backwards again, settling in the region of my left knee. The boy with the skates ran off and the women moved on. I was alone. Just as everyone disappeared, my surroundings appeared to fall still. But that was because I had come to a halt; it couldn't possibly be why I had come to a halt.

To my left there was a high retaining wall of quarried stone, built on a slight incline. To the right, across a small ditch, was a sheer cliff, nearly perpendicular. Ahead, the way was blocked by another wall, but from there the road veered left, leading straight to the top of the hill. Another five or six steps and the view would open up to reveal the little town there. Of that I had no doubt. This section of road was so familiar to me that ordinarily I paid it no attention, oblivious to its existence. Why, I must have gone up and down this section of hill hundreds of times; I knew it like the back of my hand. At this very moment I was about to traverse it as usual, on my way home.

But unexpectedly, I had come to a halt. As if springs in the air were holding me back. As if recoiling from my oddly vivid impression of this hillside scene—a scene I'd never paid the slightest attention to before. Of course I had some notion of why I had stopped, but it was hard to believe: For the life of me, I couldn't visualize what lay beyond the curve—scenery that I surely knew as well as that now confronting me.

Not that I felt uneasy. I knew I had experienced similar memory lapses any number of times before. I decided to wait a moment or two. These things happen. Staring at a wall of tiny square tiles can play tricks with your vision and throw off your sense of perspective. And it's not at all unusual to have the name of an acquaintance suddenly slip your mind. I set my left heel on the ground, stabilizing my balance, and decided to wait until things came back into focus. It wouldn't be long. I knew perfectly well that beyond the curve was the town on the hilltop where I lived. My temporary lapse of memory in no way altered the fact of its existence.

The sky was obscured by a light, homogenous blue-gray cloud, appropriate to the season, making the time of day— 4:28 by my watch—virtually indistinguishable from dusk. There was just enough light for me to make out the grooves in the road but not enough for shadows to form. The retaining wall on my left, no doubt made of some dark rock to begin with, was covered with damp, mottled moss that seemed to absorb the darkness, transforming the entire structure into one large, looming shadow. As my eyes traveled upward along the wall, I found that a vague, weathered line cut obliquely across my vision, clearly marking off the blue-gray sky from the dark wall. I could not penetrate beyond that wall, of course, but I seemed to recall that behind it lay three wooden houses and a tree-fenced dormitory or inn. These buildings were serviced by a separate road that began at the foot of the hill, so I'd hardly ever been there, and my memory was a trifle vague on that point.

Still, it was encouraging that the remnants of this distant memory did remain, however hazily. Somewhere in the scene before me must lie a passageway connecting the present moment with the past. If I were somehow deluded into thinking I recognized a strange place, then everything outside my immediate line of vision ought to have disappeared from memory—but, in fact, all that was missing was that town beyond the curve.

The low-lying area to the north (There! I knew my directions, even without reference to the position of the sun), below the cliff, posed no problem. At this height, all I could see was clusters of houses roofed in tile or sheets of galvanized iron, a maze of vegetable gardens, a forest of antennas greedy for airwave signals, and the chimney of a public bathhouse, the top of which rose almost to the level of the stone wall in front of me. But I was confident that I could mentally trace every path leading through that maze to the bathhouse: the way always taken by old men who like to sit on the doorstep until opening time, smoking cigarettes, each hoping to be first in line; the way taken by women hurrying along after three o'clock, soap and towel in hand; the long way around under the cliff, taken by small delivery trucks. Once, I remembered, there'd been a pile of broken placard frames and props by the side of the road. I even remembered when the bathhouse owners had replaced the old-fashioned bamboo baskets that customers put their clothes in with blue plastic ones. I had wanted them to change the dismal mat in front of the old sliding glass doors, which were always hard to open and clouded with steam.

I shifted my balance and held my breath, feeling anxiety mount. Or was it the other way around? Did I start holding my breath after I grew anxious? In any case, my clarity of mind was not returning. Far from it: every image I held of what lay beyond the curve was fast disappearing, as if it were being wiped clean with a very efficient eraser. First colors, then silhouettes, and then forms, until it seemed the town's very existence would fade away and then vanish.

From behind, near the bottom of the hill, footsteps approached. A businessman passed me by, attaché case under his left arm, umbrella in his right hand. He was walking bent forward to combat the steep incline, toes touching first, shaking the handle of his umbrella with every step. The clasp was apparently broken, so that the spokes opened and closed as if the umbrella were breathing. I lacked the courage to call out, but I was tempted to follow after him, striding confidently forward in the same way. That was probably the best course. Another five or six steps and whatever lay beyond the curve would spring into view. Once I'd taken in the view with my own eyes I was sure the problem would settle itself, like a pill dislodged from the throat by a drink of water. The man rounded the bend and disappeared from sight. There was no subsequent scream, so the town on the hilltop was undoubtedly still there. Anything he could do, I could do. It was only a matter of five or six steps, barely ten seconds at the most. Certainly worth a try.

Or was it? I suddenly had the uneasy feeling that if I took such hasty action without waiting for my memory to return, I would be inviting disaster. Just supposing I did come on unfamiliar territory—what then? For all I knew, even this scene before me, seemingly so familiar, might also be transformed on the spot to something alien. Those houses along the way might turn out to be the contrivance of my imagination, and my "memories" of the labyrinthine network of roads below could easily have been suggested somehow by the prominent bathhouse chimney. Even my observation that this was the north side of the hill might turn out not to be a memory so much as a deduction from the presence of dingy moss spreading like a stain from the wall onto the pavement.

In fact, my sense of familiarity with this place might not be based on true memory but on a deceptive sense of déjà vu. In like manner, my assumption that I was on my way home might, logically, be a mere extension of the feeling. In which case, taking the thought to its logical conclusion, I myself was no longer me, but some mysterious other.

No longer able to hold my breath, I let it all out. After the man with the umbrella came a girl in a long green jacket, the coin-purse in her hand jingling as she came running down the hill in great bounding strides. And from then on there was no letup. Like magic, someone was always disappearing into the hidden town, or materializing out of it. As an excuse to loiter here, mid-way up the hill, I took out a cigarette, stuck it between my lips, and took my time about lighting it, deliberately letting the matches burn out one after another. It would have been nice if someone I knew had come along. But then what if people I thought I knew had been transformed with one flourish of the magician's handkerchief into total strangers, as remote from me as the town beyond the curve?

I felt a wave of nausea. Probably from straining too hard to see the impossible. Then out of nowhere, the word "fire" popped into my mind to use should someone stop to speak to me. "I hear there's been a fire up ahead. Would you happen to know where?" Was it an association from the activity of striking one match after another? Along with the nausea, the word "fire" bobbed in my mind like a skiff. Why? There had to be some reason why the doors of my mind, usually wide open, were now so tightly shut. I remembered reading somewhere that amnesia is often an instinctive form of self-defense, brought on to escape an unpleasant memory. This word "fire" might be the key to un-locking that door, and I might be toying with it carelessly, not re-alizing its gravity. Had I lost family or property in a fire, for example? Or wait—what about the theory that a criminal returns to the scene of the crime? I might not be the innocent victim I thought I was; for all I knew, I could be a dangerous arsonist. Appalled, I threw down my cigarette and stamped it out. I sniffed the air. It did seem vaguely as if a suspicious odor lingered on the breeze. Sweet, smoky, damp; the smell of ashes in an old brazier. Of course, there was that chimney from the bathhouse just below; low-quality fuel plus a blockage of some sort could well cause an odor like that.

Now I was dizzy, as well as queasy. I'd hesitated too long. It might be too late. If I were a criminal returning to the scene of the crime, surely by now some eyewitness would have reported my presence to the police. Even if I weren't an arsonist, there were plenty of other possibilities. If I didn't have the courage to go beyond the curve, I'd just have to change my approach. As I turned around, a funny little horn sounded from below, and a battered three-wheeled scooter loaded with vegetables zoomed by spouting a white cloud of smoke. Mentally, I tagged along. I heard the sound of the engine even after the vehicle had disappeared from view around the bend, but it did seem to me that the sound of the engine clearly changed, as if the driver had shifted gears. Yet what did I know of such things? Overwhelmed by a sudden sense of desolation, as if I'd been splashed with liquid eraser from the head down, I turned and started dejectedly back the way I had come.

Going down a steep hill is much harder than coming up. It was hard to get a footing on the worn surface of the road, and the skidproof grooves were of no use. I had to keep my balance solely by tensing my knees. The retaining wall, which was now on my right, got higher as I descended, seeming, as it did so, to drag me deeper into the night. Just as I reached the bottom of the hill, the streetlights came on. On one of them was a blue metal plate printed with the name of the town, in white lettering. I sensed that it was the very name that lingered somewhere in the back of my mind, but my old confidence was gone.

2

I was encamped in the recesses of a coffee shop, by the window.

Holding the wallet in my left breast pocket between two fingers of my right hand, I kept an eye on the woman at her perch over by the door, where she was sitting with her legs crossed. She'd gotten up twice already; the next time, I would swing into action.

There was only one line of seats, all along the windows, and just five tables, each with seating for four. The only employee visible was the young woman doubling as waitress and cashier—the one I was keeping my eye on. Behind the counter was a little window about the size of the door to a pigeon coop, where orders were passed through as soon as they were ready. I could see the hands of the person inside but never the face. The hands were white and pudgy, giving no indication of their owner's age or sex. If a man, he must have been excessively effeminate, and if a woman, excessively masculine. But the way I saw it, the owner of those hands had to be a man—the woman's husband, or something like it. He must have confined himself behind the wall out of sheer jealousy. There, I thought, he writhed in agony, imagining customers' eyes crawling over his wife's body. Maybe there was a secret peephole from which he kept a furtive eye on the house. Otherwise why should she remain perched, birdlike, on that extraordinarily high, round stool in front of the counter, legs crossed and one knee drawn up? After she had languidly attended to a customer's order, she would return to her seat and shake out her shoulder-length, glossy black hair, her bangs falling slantwise across her forehead. Then she would recross her legs as if posing for a pantyhose ad, motionless in that strangely precarious perch, exuding an air of utter vulnerability. How could the man help himself? Even I, a total stranger, couldn't help feeling a trifle jealous.

Of course, the situation could have been defused by knocking down the wall. I've heard that in coffee shops, customers like being able to see into the kitchen, anyway. Then the woman's manner would seem contrived, and depending on how the man came on, even ridiculous. The risk would be considerable, of course. Her value—if deserving jealousy can be considered a kind of value—would be halved, at least. A painful loss. No, whatever the outcome of her performance on that perch, the man behind the wall would surely never give up his wall. However bitter the resolve that had led him to confine his jealousy there, he must be receiving adequate compensation. No doubt so was I—that must be why I couldn't keep from coming here. Assuming my hunch was right that I was a regular patron.

At the table by the door, two people had been gesticulating at one another, having an animated discussion about some sort of business affairs; now they stood up, apparently ready to leave. At the same time the woman uncrossed her legs, smoothed her skirt, and got down from her perch. Her shins seemed outlined in a bright haze, as if a fine down were reflecting the light, but surely she wasn't bare-legged? Her long hair was strangely at odds with her short skirt.

In any case, that was the third time she'd gotten up, the signal I'd been waiting for. I promptly took out my wallet and set it on the table. It was a square, black leather wallet, the corners rounded and worn. I wanted to empty out all my pockets and line everything up on the table at once, but it would be too conspicuous—especially on this pink tabletop. I decided it would be better to examine everything in turn, one item at a time, starting with the contents of this wallet. The clasp was worn and came apart with barely a sound. On the back of the top flap was a key holder with two keys, one large and one small. One was for a proper cylinder lock; the other was of a very simple design. Each bore a number but no other distinguishing marks. Unfortunately, I had no recollection of what they were for. One thing nagged at me—a feeling, like the feeling I'd had earlier when I heard the engine shifting gears, that knowledge of a technical term like "cylinder lock" didn't jibe with my mental impression of myself. Who was I?

The central compartment of the wallet had space for a commuter's pass, defined by transparent plastic on both sides. It was empty, but then it only made sense to keep your pass separate from your wallet. I moved on. Next I unzipped the back, and counted up the bills. Three crisp ten-thousand-yen bills, two thousand-yen bills, plus 640 yen in change. That made 32,640 yen in all. Even if I couldn't find my way home right away, that would hold me for a while. But the amount seemed to call for some sort of explanation. It struck me as rather more than the average working man would walk around with. I must have had a particular use in mind for it. What could I have meant to buy with 30,000 yen in cash? It was too much money to have slipped my mind. Of course, it didn't have to be shopping money. Maybe I'd been put in charge of a collection taken up at the office for the family of a deceased colleague. But that wasn't much better; there'd be little chance of forgetting something like that. Enough of these forced explanations. Actually, when you got right down to it, what grounds did I have for thinking that I was an office worker in the first place? My very image of myself was suspect, a hit-or-miss montage of bits and scraps of evidence. I might be able to fool myself, but facts were facts. And anyway, I reminded myself with mounting irritation, I had yet to find any clues to one vital thing—my name!

A numbing pain shot up from my neck toward my forehead, and the nausea, which had temporarily eased, came welling back from deep inside. It was true; I had forgotten my name. But as long as I remained convinced that I was myself, finding out what my name was should be easy once I set my mind to it. The elusive town at the top of the hill represented the contents of my life, but a name, however much you made of it, was no more than a registered mark. Why, right in my pockets there were bound to be all the clues to my name I could want—a dozen or more. Knowing this full well, I did nothing to that end. Just as earlier I had turned back, not wanting to go beyond the curve until my memory returned. Grinding my teeth, I focused my attention on the woman's legs. This seemed to be the best way to suppress my nausea.

Back on the slope when I was lighting my cigarette, the label on the book of matches in my hand had instantly suggested to me the location of this coffee shop. At the bottom of the hill you turned left, went under elevated train tracks, and past a cigarette stand, a plumber's, and a dry cleaner's, in that order; then across a little street there was a gas station and just beyond it an intersection with a traffic light. If you crossed there and continued on to the right a little way, at the second streetlight you came to a bus stop. For me, that bus stop had been—was now—the jump-off point for the rest of the world.

Impressions of standing there and waiting for the bus were interwoven with sensory impressions from every season of the year. This coffee shop, I remembered, was right across the street. And here, in fact, I now was—unarguable proof that the memory had been no mere déjà vu. If necessary, I could produce physical evidence—the matchbook with the establishment's name—but that was only the shadow of reality. What would be the use in setting aside reality and concerning myself with shadows? By the same token, what I needed now was not my own name, but the names of other people.

All of a sudden the cup and saucer on the table jumped with a clatter. Luckily the cup was empty and nothing broke. I could only suppose that I myself had somehow jerked and bumped the table with my knee. I had no difficulty ignoring the woman's accusing stare, but psychologically I was in turmoil. Whatever excuses and pretexts I tried to come up with, I was making no progress. In fact things were getting worse by the minute. How could I help getting jumpy? The more I thought about it, the more it seemed that my memory did nothing but swing back and forth like a pendulum between the slope and this coffee shop. So what if my memories of waiting for the bus were mixed with seasonal impressions? That in itself didn't prove that I was ever a commuter. I leaned an elbow on the table and it wobbled noisily, jerking me upright. In fact proof was impossible. I had lost all memory of my place of work. Of course, where I worked could be dismissed as of no more importance than my name; but if I had not been on my way home from work when all this began, then the significance of what lay beyond the curve changed completely. The notion that I was a criminal returning to the scene of the crime gained further credence. I would have to alter my approach; I needed desperately to learn my own name, not those of other people. Never mind the town, either; my first priority had to be finding an escape from this narrow oscillation of memory.

I started searching busily through all my pockets. If only I could find a commuter's pass! I still felt a trifle reluctant to learn my own name and address first. But despite all my efforts, nothing turned up. Someone looked through the window and apparently noted my odd behavior. I couldn't afford to worry about what people might think. I began emptying my pockets onto the tabletop.

Handkerchief . . . matches . . . cigarettes . . . button . . . sunglasses . . . somebody's old business card, folded in half . . . a small, triangular pin, of the sort businessmen wear on their lapels . . . a scrap of paper, with some sort of diagram written on it . . .

The windowpane breathed fire. Lights from a passing bus

grazed the glass pane, highlighting the web of branches formed by slender trees along the street, a fine-meshed net that was starting to unravel. I stared straight at the bus with intense concentration, recalling the feel of the worn step, the location and coolness of the stainless steel rail, the view of the interior, the tense, determined search for an empty seat, the advertisements hanging behind the driver's seat, that peculiar odor of humanity and gasoline fumes, and the hum of the engine, which varied according to the make and year—all of this came back to me vividly, like a physical extension of myself. I imagined the route the bus would take, mentally setting off. The main bus stops, natural features of the landscape, and well-known buildings along the way all rose before my eyes as a single, firmly intertwined structure. Could there be any doubt that I was a regular passenger? The matter of the missing bus pass could be accounted for in a hundred ways. I might have dropped it, or had it stolen . . . or, even likelier, it might just have expired. Maybe I was in the process of applying for a new one. Maybe that's what the money was for, at least in part.

No, I told myself, stop making up these scenarios based on mere circumstantial evidence. However plausible, that sort of reasoning could lead only deeper into the labyrinth. Besides, there was one other thing. In my mind the bus went here, there, and everywhere, but never reached its destination.

The driver of the bus stepped on the accelerator and drove off. The windowpane once more reverted to darkness, reflecting the interior of the coffee shop. Where the bus taillights had been, now the image of the woman was reflected. Part of a streetlamp beyond the web of branches was superimposed on her face, so I couldn't be sure, but she appeared to be watching me. That was hardly surprising. Look at me, a clumsy scatterbrain who'd mislaid something and was dumping everything he possessed onto the table. Of course, there was no way of judging her awareness of the severity of my predicament. I had mislaid something, but she would hardly suspect that what I had mislaid was myself.

Was I the self that had done the mislaying, or, perhaps, the self that was mislaid? In fact, when that bus left, I had felt a sharp pain, as if I'd been pushed off. Then the me sitting here was the me that had been deliberately lost, not the one that had done the losing. And it wasn't just the town beyond the curve that had vanished; the rest of the world had disappeared, with only the area between the hill and this coffee shop intact, and me in it. Now I saw that I hadn't lost my memory halfway up that slope; rather, my memories all seemed to begin there. Perhaps the lost town was not the issue so much as this part which had failed to disappear. Could this coffee shop have some other, unimaginable meaning?

I returned the woman's stare, lifting my eyes to hers in the reflection. Maybe she was behind a plot to enclose me within invisible walls of forgetfulness. I studied her on her perch. The window-mirror was dark, and headlights cutting across it formed a perpetual distraction, so I turned and looked straight at her. Naturally, she noticed. But she only kept looking at me through the reflection in the window, apparently unperturbed, a trifle smug. This woman might be the key to the whole thing. She herself might be a far more important clue than anything in my pockets.

A young man and woman came in. The man looked like a clerk in one of the neighborhood stores, the woman like his girlfriend or younger sister or possibly a country cousin. They sat down two tables away and the man ordered coffee in a loud voice, holding up two fingers. Then they began an excited, whispered exchange, trading dramatic looks, like siblings discussing the medical expenses of a dying parent. While the woman was up, I ordered another cup of coffee. It had been forty or fifty minutes now since I came in and I was starting to worry about the man on the other side of the wall. To be sure, he was only someone I had imagined. But the imaginary predicament of that imaginary person seemed to have a great deal in common with my own dilemma. Just because I had imagined him, that was no grounds for dismissing his importance. The fifth bus stop from here was a major train terminal, with five movie theaters and three department stores—this too was sheer conjecture on my part, but I had no doubt of the accuracy of that conjecture. So why shouldn't I believe in the man behind the wall in the same way? If amnesia goes by any rules or logic, I thought, then imaginary or not, he must be of key importance, no less so than the woman.

I looked back at her. I willed her to look at me through the hair spilling down the front of her face. I matched my breathing carefully to the movement of the tendons in the hollow at the back of her knee as she swung one leg sleekly back and forth beneath her short skirt. At the same time I listened expectantly for sounds beyond the wall, where I was certain the man would soon drop a boiling kettle in a frenzy of jealousy. But however long I waited, there wasn't so much as the sound of a tongue clucking, let alone the crash of broken crockery. Instead, those same pale hands stole through the window, quite as usual. Not even the cups on the tray seemed to shake. What was shaking was me, myself. With my thumbs on the edge of the table, my wrists were shaking like those of a drummer striving to muffle the drumbeat so that it would trail away with pathos. But I refused to believe it. Explosive power is in proportion to compressive power. Very well, I would make an all-out effort to seduce her. Once I left here, my world would only come to an abrupt stop at that hill. For now, the only place I could sit and relax was here. This coffee shop had taken on extraordinary significance. The hidden meaning of this ordeal might very well be (it now struck me) that I was supposed to seduce her. Now it was up to her to realize the purpose of my gaze and awaken to the role she had to play.

Gazing at my reflection in the windowpane, I smoothed down the hair over my ears, raised my chin, and straightened my tie. It wasn't a very expensive one, but the pattern was in the latest style. Of course I wasn't so vain as to suppose I possessed the true qualifications of a seducer. And yet my position was clearly advantageous. Since I was to take a woman who knew nothing but love away from a man who knew nothing but jealousy, it was all as simple as a chemical equation. As long as I was the seducer, that was enough. In time the woman would begin to show the proper reaction. At the proper moment I would hand her some money and ask her to close up early and put me up for the night. Her response would quicken according to formula, finally reaching its inevitable conclusion. The man would explode, tearing down the wall in proof of the correctness of the equation. I would be freed suddenly of my role—not without a sad wrench—and find, instead, that the world beyond the curve was restored to me.

Again the pale hands slipped through the small window, this time with my coffee. The woman started toward me through the narrow space between tables and wall, tray in one hand, straightening chairs as she came. Hurriedly I cleared off the tabletop, slipping back into my pockets whatever seemed clearly useless.

Handkerchief (no monogram) . . . matches (from this shop) . . . cigarettes (four left in the pack) . . . button . . . sunglasses . . .

Sunglasses? Did I have weak eyes? From what I could see of my reflection, there seemed nothing terribly at odds with my image of myself as a businessman. The suit I had on was of a sober, intermediate grade, not at all the type of thing to go with sunglasses. Of course, I might have a job that involved lots of outside work, sales, say, or public relations. Then there would be nothing strange about habitually wearing sunglasses, as long as I didn't wear them while visiting clients. And if I were a salesman with an office in my own home, working on commission for some company far away, that would explain the lack of a commuter's pass. But in that case, weren't my possessions a bit too scanty? It also nagged at me that I had no business cards in my wallet. Or did I have a habit of keeping them in my briefcase and depositing that in some station checkroom?

By the time the woman reached my table, just three items were left out: the scrap of paper, the folded business card, and the metal pin. They seemed to offer the most promising leads and they left plenty of room for her to set down the cup of coffee. Also, I wanted to see the woman's reaction. It was just possible that she might recognize one of them and provide a way for me to grasp a thread of memory. As she set the coffee down, placed the cream pitcher and sugar bowl side by side, and refilled my water glass, she glanced over the three items at least twice. No reaction. Probably it would have been no different with the cigarettes, matches, and button.

Disappointed, and taken aback at the deepness of the crow's-feet etched at the corners of her eyes, foolishly I let slip the chance to ask her the few questions—mere small talk—that I had prepared. What day was today, for one. The question itself had no particular meaning. But how she answered would have given me some clue as to how I appeared in her eyes, and how I might proceed to ask more pertinent questions. After all, this was now the sole person I knew by sight. If she helped me, it would be a godsend. If possible, I wanted her to tell me everything she knew about me. All the more reason why I had to exercise caution so as to arouse no misunderstanding. Judging from outward appearances, anyway, she didn't seem likely to be interested in listening to anyone's problems. Which might have something to do with why the man with the pale hands had had to shut himself behind a wall.

The woman went back to her perch and crossed her legs. The shoe on the upper foot dangled provocatively, emphasizing the curve of her ankle. I suppressed my shaking and lowered my eyes. Resolutely, I decided once and for all to see what I could make of the three clues. If I failed, my only hope was the woman. There would be nothing for me to do then but hole up here behind my own wall until she took some notice of me.

First the pin, which was triangular, the corners blunt, the surface rounded. It bore a design of seven blue jewels with a silver border; in the center was the letter *S*, in relief. It was embossed in a stylized pattern of straight lines, like a zigzag bolt of lightning. Something to do with electricity? It meant nothing to me. I couldn't very well go to the phone book and start calling up all the companies listed under *S*, so I just sat there, not knowing what to do. It was well made, clearly no bauble. It had to mean something. The more I stared at it, the more I began to suspect that it was the badge of some dangerous, clandestine group. It was only a gut feeling, though, with nothing to base it on. I had to admit I was stumped.

My luck was no better with the scrap of paper, despite its suggestive diagram—which, depending on how I looked at it, might equally have been a map, a blueprint of gas or water pipes, or a cross-section of a pump. I had no memory either of having drawn it or of having receiving it from someone else. It was an insoluble problem, one I could do nothing but gnash my teeth over.

The business card, however, seemed more promising. It was folded in two, face out, and bore a name and business address, neither of which meant anything to me. A telephone number was scribbled on the back. I had no way of knowing the connection between the owner of this card and the telephone number, but for now that mattered little. What did matter was that this phone number bore a definite connection with my past. If only I could track down that connection, the door to my past would swing open. This was the single slip-up my turncoat memory had allowed. Nothing is ever one hundred percent foolproof.

There was a phone right next to the counter, just behind the woman's perch. When I crossed in front of her, she barely changed position—even when my elbow seemed about to graze her knee, she made no move to get out of the way. She pursed her lips and then suddenly released them, making a sound like a soft kiss. It might have been a kind of greeting, but if so it was certainly dangerous. If not, I couldn't imagine what it was. I had a vague feeling she was warning me it would be useless to place the call, but that might only have been due to my psychological submission to her. I wanted to escape and was in the process of trying to—and yet, I could not deny that somewhere inside I wished the rest of the world would vanish once and for all, leaving her and me alone forever.

As I lifted the receiver, I felt a surge of anxiety like that of someone dismantling a shell without knowing how. Perhaps I was rushing into a trap. I dialed the number, slowly and carefully. What should I say when someone came on the line? It depended on who it was, but the main thing was to avoid rousing suspicion. Somehow I would have to draw the other person out, find out who and where he or she was. Damn, a busy signal. I tried again, and again it was busy. I lit a cigarette and tried again, seven times in all over a period of about twenty minutes, but all I ever heard was that same insistent beeping sound.

Feeling rather foolish, I went back to my seat, raised my cold coffee to my lips, and drained the cup. I sensed someone watching me and looked up to find her reflection peering at me in the window. The moment our eyes met, the lower half of her face twisted strangely. Of course the windowpane itself could have been warped, so I can't really say for sure, but it did seem as if she had penetrated my feelings—or, more accurately, misunderstood them—and was smiling derisively.

It suddenly occurred to me that I'd made a gross error. I'd been making too much of the fellow I imagined to be on the other side of the wall—and that had almost caused me to overlook a possible way out of my dilemma. He might well have the same claim to reality as that train station at the end of the line, but there was one crucial difference.

My knowledge of the train station (like that of the bus route) was completely lacking any element of time. Without any experience of the place in time, I could only conclude it was indeed a fantasy. The man behind the wall had spatial reality, a point I had consistently overlooked. If his walls were spatial, mine were temporal. There was no reason whatsoever for me to shut myself up here like him, a living fossil.

Pouring off half the water in my glass into my mouth, I stood up and swallowed as I left the table. The woman recrossed her legs, giving no sign of leaving her perch. Perhaps she assumed I was heading for the telephone again. Silently I laid my check on the counter, and for the first time she looked straight at me, in seeming surprise. Her eyes were innocent enough, but I no longer trusted her. It was not true that all the world had disappeared except for this one spot. All that had vanished was the town beyond that curve, I decided. In order to close off that road, every corridor of memory leading there had been sealed off, creating a wall of time. Until I found that town beyond the curve, there could be no resolution.

Silently I handed her a thousand-yen note and silently she handed me my change. Or not quite silently, either; again that noise with her lips, three times. It might have meant something, or nothing at all. I couldn't tell. Maybe there was yet another wall of time, one I had no inkling of, between her and me. Even if there were, there wasn't anything I could do about it, since a wall of time is beyond awareness.

Still, anticipating some comment from her, I waited a moment. Then, one last time, I tried dialing that number. Again, busy. That was one hell of a long conversation. Surely it wasn't deliberate interference from someone anticipating my every action. . . .

3

I hailed a taxi. It was dark blue with a yellow top. The automatic door closed behind me, rattling as if it were about to fall apart. In the open ashtray lay a cigarette left by the previous passenger, still burning. As I hesitated, unable to come up with the name of my destination, the young driver grew irritated, took off his cap, and flung it down on the seat next to him. I handed him five hundred yen and explained that I wasn't going far, so all he had to do was follow my directions. That reassured him, but he left the cap where it was.

"What the heck is the name of that place on the top of the hill?"

"Hilltown, you mean?"

"Right . . . top of the hill . . . that makes sense."

As we spoke, we were already heading up the crucial slope. Suddenly the sound of the engine changed and I blanched. With me as a passenger, would the car, too, come to a halt as if held back by some invisible wall? Impossible. He'd only changed gears. The car zoomed around the curve. I braced myself, pressing back against the seat, holding my breath in anticipation.

We hadn't hurtled into a vacuum. Far from it—beyond the curve was a huge, sprawling place with clusters of four-story residential buildings wedged against the dark sky, forming an endless lattice of lights.

I'd never dreamed the town was this big. That in itself was a problem. Spatially, the town had a solid physical existence, but temporally, it was a vacuum. It existed—yet horribly, it had no existence whatever. The wheels of the taxi turned steadily over the ground, setting up waves of vibrations that penetrated to the bone. And yet the town I knew was gone. Clearly, I should not have gone beyond that curve, after all. Now it was eternally impossible for me ever to reach the other side.

I began shouting frantic orders at the driver who had slowed to a crawl, as if inviting directions. The main thing was to get away. I had to escape, to find freedom of space. If I stayed here, I would end up losing space as well as time and find myself trapped like the owner of those pale hands behind solid walls.

Fortunately, the outer world was still safe. Good thing I'd chosen to come by taxi. We pulled onto a main street and I got out at the first public telephone. I had little hope, but that telephone number was my sole lead. Of course, I felt trepidation— I might be letting myself in for another nightmarish experience. More likely, the line would still be busy. I lifted the receiver and deposited a coin, which fell with a cold clatter that only increased my sense of hopelessness.

But this time it was ringing. I was so little prepared for this to happen that I almost hung up. Given my mental state, I doubted my ability to cope if someone did pick up the phone. I began counting cracks in the phone booth window. If the number of cracks was even I'd wait, and if odd, hang up. But before I could finish counting, someone came on the line.

It was a woman. Fortunately for me, she identified herself straight off—not with her personal name but with the name of a shop. I felt weak. Good Lord. It was the coffee shop I'd been sitting in all that time. I'd been calling the very number I was dialing from—no wonder it was always busy! Now what? On the telephone, even three seconds of silence seems long. Five is unnatural. Any longer and you start to suspect the phone is out of order. Yet she waited patiently, without prodding, making that familiar smacking sound with her lips. Then it had no particular meaning, after all. It was just a habit she had.

Finally, I remembered the name on the card. I decided to try asking for that man, whoever he was. It was the woman's turn to be silent. She didn't say she didn't know who it was, so probably she did know. Then why not speak up? She'd stopped making that noise with her lips and seemed extraordinarily tense. I must have come close to the heart of the matter. Just as I'd suspected. . . .

A sigh came pouring out of the receiver. No, not a sigh—a muffled laugh, then a cheerful voice.

"He's my husband. You knew that, of course."

"Your husband . . . him?" Imagining the eyes beyond the wall pricking up their ears, I felt a sudden disgust. But the woman gave another low laugh.

"Of course, him."

"I just spent nearly an hour sitting in your place—do you remember me?"

"What's going on? This is a strange sort of game you're playing. Naturally, I remember perfectly."

"Does he know me, too?"

"I would hope so. He always talks about you as if you were his best friend."

"His best friend?"

"Well, aren't you?"

"Oh . . . yes . . . of course . . ."

"All right, then, see you at ten."

"At ten?"

"Is that inconvenient?"

"Where, at ten?"

"At the coffee shop, of course, the same as always."

"But what about him?"

"Him? Look, what are the rules of this crazy game? I can't play if I don't know the rules. Either you or him, it doesn't matter which, but will one of you please take the money I gave you this morning and pay the landlord?"

"The landlord? But I—"

"I gave you a map, didn't I?"

"I don't feel at all well. You tell me, is this a game?"

"I have to go. Someone just came in."

I squatted down inside the phone booth. In the corner was a rolled-up newspaper, and sticking out from beneath it, a dry, black turd.

Beyond the curve which has no existence, I go plunging to the ground, shoulder to shoulder with her. Prisoner at last. Now space itself would be stripped from me. And in the end, I would become a living fossil.

"Somehow I get the feeling I'm being duped," I murmured.

"Everybody feels that way sometimes," she replied.

Number 18, B3 . . . stepping over a KEEP OFF THE GRASS sign, we went from stairs to landing, landing to stairs. . . . However stealthily I tried to walk, my footsteps rang out to the heavens, walking over gravestones. . . .

"If you don't believe me, just try opening it with your own key."

The key in my wallet. No need to bother testing it. I knew very well it would fit. Everything was just as she said it would be, and I alone was lost, uncomprehending.

"Then, can you explain this, too?" I held out the triangular pin.

"What is that?" she said

"You don't know?"

"Something you picked up along the way?"

"You can't explain it to me, then."

"No, but is it worth getting upset over?"

"No, but—"

"You can't try to understand everything, you know."

Maybe so. Maybe it was enough to understand this much. Maybe the sense of continuity I had had in front of that curve—the sense that everything up to then was normal—had itself been a strange dream. I held the corner of the mysterious pin between my fingers, turning it around. It terrified me. First thing in the morning, I'd have to take it somewhere far away and get rid of it.